W9-AXG-019

THE LIFE WORK OF
HENRI RENÉ GUY
DE MAUPASSANT

Embracing
ROMANCE. TRAVEL. COMEDY & VERSE.
For the first time Complete in
English.
With a Critical Preface by
PAUL BOURGET
of the French Academy
and an Introduction by
Robert Arnot, M.A.

ILLUSTRATED FROM ORIGINAL DRAWINGS
BY EMINENT
FRENCH AND AMERICAN ARTISTS.

Printed for Subscribers only by
M. WALTER DUNNE, Publisher
London and New York.

AFTER THE ORIGINAL DRAWING BY FERDINAND BAC.

"Duroy saw his wife seated by Laroche-Mathieu, both of them almost hidden behind a group of palms."

(See page 179)

BEL AMI

OR

THE HISTORY OF A SCOUNDREL

A NOVEL

BY

GUY DE MAUPASSANT

VOL. VII

M. WALTER DUNNE, PUBLISHER
NEW YORK AND LONDON

5323

TABLE OF CONTENTS

YVETTE

ILLUSTRATIONS

BEL-AMI

CHAPTER I.

POVERTY

AFTER changing his five-franc piece Georges Duroy left the restaurant. He twisted his mustache in military style and cast a rapid, sweeping glance upon the diners, among whom were three saleswomen, an untidy music-teacher of uncertain age, and two women with their husbands.

When he reached the sidewalk, he paused to consider what route he should take. It was the twenty-eighth of June and he had only three francs in his pocket to last him the remainder of the month. That meant two dinners and no lunches, or two lunches and no dinners, according to choice. As he pondered upon this unpleasant state of affairs, he sauntered down Rue Nôtre Dame de Lorette, preserving his military air and carriage, and rudely jostled the people upon the streets in order to clear a path for himself. He appeared to be hostile to the passers-by, and even to the houses, the entire city.

Tall, well-built, fair, with blue eyes, a curled mustache, hair naturally wavy and parted in the middle, he recalled the hero of the popular romances.

It was one of those sultry, Parisian evenings when not a breath of air is stirring; the sewers exhaled poisonous gases and the restaurants the disagreeable odors of cooking and of kindred smells. Porters in their shirt-sleeves, astride their chairs, smoked their pipes at the carriage gates, and pedestrians strolled leisurely along, hats in hand.

When Georges Duroy reached the boulevard he halted again, undecided as to which road to choose. Finally he turned toward the Madeleine and followed the tide of people.

The large, well-patronized *cafés* tempted Duroy, but were he to drink only two glasses of beer in an evening, farewell to the meager supper the following night! Yet he said to himself: "I will take a glass at the Americain. By Jove, I am thirsty."

He glanced at men seated at the tables, men who could afford to slake their thirst, and he scowled at them. "Rascals!" he muttered. If he could have caught one of them at a corner in the dark he would have choked him without a scruple! He recalled the two years spent in Africa, and the manner in which he had extorted money from the Arabs. A smile hovered about his lips at the recollection of an escapade which had cost three men their lives, a foray which had given his two comrades and himself seventy fowls, two sheep, money, and something to laugh about for six months. The culprits were never found; indeed, they were not sought for, the Arab being looked upon as the soldier's prey.

But in Paris it was different; there one could not commit such deeds with impunity. He regretted that he had not remained where he was; but he had hoped to improve his condition — and for that reason he was in Paris!

He passed the Vaudeville and stopped at the Café Americain, debating as to whether he should take that "glass." Before deciding, he glanced at a clock; it was a quarter past nine. He knew that when the beer was placed in front of him, he would drink it; and then what would he do at eleven o'clock? So he walked on, intending to go as far as the Madeleine and return.

When he reached the Place de l'Opera, a tall, young man passed him, whose face he fancied was familiar. He followed him, repeating: "Where the deuce have I seen that fellow?"

For a time he racked his brain in vain; then suddenly he saw the same man, but not so corpulent and more youthful, attired in the uniform of a Hussar. He exclaimed: "Wait, Forestier!" and hastening up to him, laid his hand upon the man's shoulder. The latter turned, looked at him, and said: "What do you want, sir?"

Duroy began to laugh: "Don't you remember me?"

"No."

"Not remember Georges Duroy of the Sixth Hussars."

Forestier extended both hands.

"Ah, my dear fellow, how are you?"

"Very well. And how are you?"

"Oh, I am not very well. I cough six months out of the twelve as a result of bronchitis contracted at Bougival, about the time of my return to Paris four years ago."

"But you look well."

Forestier, taking his former comrade's arm, told him of his malady, of the consultations, the opinions and the advice of the doctors and of the difficulty of following their advice in his position. They ordered him to spend the winter in the south, but how could he? He was married and was a journalist in a responsible editorial position.

"I manage the political department on 'La Vie Française'; I report the doings of the Senate for 'Le Salut,' and from time to time I write for 'La Planète.' That is what I am doing."

Duroy, in surprise, glanced at him. He was very much changed. Formerly Forestier had been thin, giddy, noisy, and always in good spirits. But three years of life in Paris had made another man of him; now he was stout and serious, and his hair was gray on his temples although he could not number more than twenty-seven years.

Forestier asked: "Where are you going?"

Duroy replied: "Nowhere in particular."

"Very well, will you accompany me to the 'Vie Française' where I have some proofs to correct; and afterward take a drink with me?"

"Yes, gladly."

They walked along arm-in-arm with that familiarity which exists between schoolmates and brother-officers.

"What are you doing in Paris?" asked Forestier.

Duroy shrugged his shoulders.

"Dying of hunger, simply. When my time was up, I came hither to make my fortune, or rather to live in Paris—and for six months I have been employed in a railroad office at fifteen hundred francs a year."

Forestier murmured: "That is not very much."

"But what can I do?" answered Duroy. "I am alone, I know no one, I have no recommendations. The spirit is not lacking, but the means are."

His companion looked at him from head to foot like a practical man who is examining a subject; then he said, in a tone of conviction: "You see, my dear fellow, all depends on assurance, here. A shrewd, observing man can sometimes become a minister. You must obtrude yourself and yet not ask anything. But how is it you have not found anything better than a clerkship at the station?"

Duroy replied: "I hunted everywhere and found nothing else. But I know where I can get three thousand francs at least—as riding-master at the Pellerin school."

Forestier stopped him: "Don't do it, for you can earn ten thousand francs. You will ruin your prospects at once. In your office at least no one knows you; you can leave it if you wish to at any time. But when you are once a riding-master all will be over. You might as well be a butler in a house to which all Paris comes to dine. When you have given riding lessons to men of the world or to their sons, they will no longer consider you their equal."

He paused, reflected several seconds and then asked:

"Are you a bachelor?"

"Yes, though I have been smitten several times."

"That makes no difference. If Cicero and Tiberius were mentioned would you know who they were?"

"Yes."

"Good, no one knows any more except about a score of fools. It is not difficult to pass for being learned. The secret is not to betray your ignorance. Just maneuver, avoid the quicksands and obstacles, and the rest can be found in a dictionary."

He spoke like one who understood human nature, and he smiled as the crowd passed them by. Suddenly he began to cough and stopped to allow the paroxysm to spend itself; then he said in a discouraged tone:

"Isn't it tiresome not to be able to get rid of this bronchitis? And here is midsummer! This winter I shall go to Mentone. Health before everything."

They reached the Boulevarde Poissonière; behind a large glass door an open paper was affixed; three people were reading it. Above the door was printed the legend, "La Vie Française."

Forestier pushed open the door and said: "Come in." Duroy entered; they ascended the stairs, passed through an antechamber in which two clerks greeted their comrade, and then entered a kind of waiting-room.

"Sit down," said Forestier, "I shall be back in five minutes," and he disappeared.

Duroy remained where he was; from time to time men passed him by, entering by one door and going out by another before he had time to glance at them.

Now they were young men, very young, with a busy air, holding sheets of paper in their hands; now compositors, their shirts spotted with ink — carefully carrying what were evidently fresh proofs. Occasionally a gentleman entered, fashionably dressed, some reporter bringing news.

Forestier reappeared arm-in-arm with a tall, thin man of thirty or forty, dressed in a black coat, with a white cravat, a dark complexion, and an insolent, self-satisfied air. Forestier said to him: "Adieu, my dear sir," and the other pressed his hand with: "Au revoir, my friend." Then he descended the stairs whistling, his cane under his arm.

Duroy asked his name.

"That is Jacques Rival, the celebrated writer and duelist. He came to correct his proofs. Garin, Montel and he are the best witty and realistic writers we have in Paris. He earns thirty thousand francs a year for two articles a week."

As they went downstairs, they met a stout, little man with long hair, who was ascending the stairs whistling. Forestier bowed low.

"Norbert de Varenne," said he, "the poet, the author of 'Les Soleils Morts,'—a very expensive man. Every poem he gives us costs three hundred francs and the longest has not two hundred lines. But let us go into the Napolitain, I am getting thirsty."

When they were seated at a table, Forestier ordered two glasses of beer. He emptied his at a single draught, while Duroy sipped his beer slowly as if it were something rare and precious. Suddenly his companion asked, "Why don't you try journalism?"

Duroy looked at him in surprise and said: "Because I have never written anything."

"Bah, we all have to make a beginning. I could employ you myself by sending you to obtain information. At first you would only get two hundred and fifty francs a month but your cab fare would be paid. Shall I speak to the manager?"

"If you will."

"Well, then come and dine with me to-morrow; I will only ask five or six to meet you; the manager, M. Walter, his wife, with Jacques Rival, and Norbert de Varenne whom you have just seen, and also a friend of Mme. Forestier. Will you come?"

Duroy hesitated, blushing and perplexed. Finally he murmured: "I have no suitable clothes."

Forestier was amazed. "You have no dress suit? Egad, that is indispensable. In Paris, it is better to have no bed than no clothes." Then, fumbling in his vest-pocket, he drew from it two louis, placed them before his companion, and said kindly: "You can repay me when it is convenient. Buy yourself what you need and pay an installment on it. And come and dine with us at half past seven, at 17 Rue Fontaine."

In confusion Duroy picked up the money and stammered: "You are very kind — I am much obliged — be sure I shall not forget."

Forestier interrupted him: "That's all right, take another glass of beer. Waiter, two more glasses!" When he had paid the score, the journalist asked: "Would you like a stroll for an hour?"

"Certainly."

They turned toward the Madeleine. "What shall we do?" asked Forestier. "They say that in Paris an idler can always find amusement, but it is not true. A turn in the Bois is only enjoyable if you have a lady with you, and that is a rare occurrence. The *café* concerts may divert my tailor and his wife, but they do not interest me. So what can we do? Nothing! There ought to be a summer garden here, open at night, where a man could listen to good music while drinking beneath the trees. It would be a pleasant lounging place. You could walk in alleys bright with electric light and seat yourself where you pleased to hear the music. It would be charming. Where would you like to go?"

Duroy did not know what to reply; finally he said: "I have never been to the Folies Bergères. I should like to go there."

His companion exclaimed: "The Folies Bergères! Very well!"

They turned and walked toward the Faubourg Montmartre. The brilliantly illuminated building loomed up before them. Forestier entered, Duroy stopped him. "We forgot to pass through the gate."

The other replied in a consequential tone: "I never pay," and approached the box-office.

"Have you a good box?"

"Certainly, M. Forestier."

He took the ticket handed him, pushed open the door, and they were within the hall. A cloud of tobacco smoke almost hid the stage and the opposite side of the theater. In the spacious *foyer* which led to the circular promenade, brilliantly dressed women mingled with black-coated men.

Forestier forced his way rapidly through the throng and accosted an usher.

"Box 17?"

"This way, sir."

The friends were shown into a tiny box, hung and carpeted in red, with four chairs upholstered in the same color. They seated themselves. To their right and left were similar boxes. On the stage three men were performing on trapezes. But Duroy paid no heed to them, his eyes finding more to interest them in the grand promenade. Forestier remarked upon the motley appearance of the throng, but Duroy did not listen to him. A woman, leaning her arms upon the edge of her *loge,* was staring at him. She was a tall, voluptuous brunette, her face whitened with enamel, her black eyes penciled, and her lips painted. With a movement of her head, she summoned a friend who was passing, a blonde with auburn hair, likewise inclined to *embonpoint,* and said to her in a whisper intended to be heard: "There is a nice fellow!"

Forestier heard it, and said to Duroy with a smile: "You are lucky, my dear boy. My congratulations!"

The *ci-devant* soldier blushed and mechanically fingered the two pieces of gold in his pocket.

The curtain fell—the orchestra played a *valse*— and Duroy said:

"Shall we walk around the gallery?"

"If you like."

Soon they were carried along in the current of promenaders. Duroy drank in with delight the air, vitiated as it was by tobacco and cheap perfume, but Forestier perspired, panted, and coughed.

"Let us go into the garden," he said. Turning to the left, they entered a kind of covered garden in which two large fountains were playing. Under the yews, men and women sat at tables drinking.

"Another glass of beer?" asked Forestier.

"Gladly."

They took their seats and watched the promenaders. Occasionally a woman would stop and ask with a coarse smile: "What have you to offer, sir?"

Forestier's invariable answer was: "A glass of water from the fountain." And the woman would mutter, "Go along," and walk away.

At last the brunette reappeared, arm-in-arm with the blonde. They made a handsome couple. The former smiled on perceiving Duroy, and taking a chair she calmly seated herself in front of him, and said in a clear voice: "Waiter, two glasses."

In astonishment, Forestier exclaimed: "You are not at all bashful!"

She replied: "Your friend has bewitched me; he is such a fine fellow. I believe he has turned my head."

Duroy said nothing.

The waiter brought the beer, which the women swallowed rapidly; then they rose, and the brunette, nodding her head and tapping Duroy's arm with her fan, said to him: "Thank you, my dear! However, you are not very talkative."

As they disappeared, Forestier laughed and said: "Tell, me, old man, did you know that you had a charm for the weaker sex? You must be careful."

Without replying, Duroy smiled. His friend asked: "Shall you remain any longer? I am going; I have had enough."

Georges murmured: "Yes, I will stay a little longer: it is not late."

Forestier arose: "Very well, then, good-bye until to-morrow. Do not forget: 17 Rue Fontaine at seven thirty."

"I shall not forget. Thank you."

The friends shook hands and the journalist left Duroy to his own devices.

Forestier once out of sight, Duroy felt free, and again he joyously touched the gold pieces in his pocket; then rising, he mingled with the crowd.

He soon discovered the blonde and the brunette. He went toward them, but when near them dared not address them.

The brunette called out to him: "Have you found your tongue?"

He stammered: "Zounds!" too bashful to say another word. A pause ensued, during which the brunette took his arm and together they left the hall.

CHAPTER II.

MADAME FORESTIER

"WHERE does M. Forestier live?"
"Third floor on the left,"
said the porter pleasantly,
on learning Duroy's destination.

Georges ascended the staircase.
He was somewhat embarrassed and
ill-at-ease. He had on a new suit but
he was uncomfortable. He felt that it
was defective; his boots were not glossy,
he had bought his shirt that same evening at the Louvre for four francs fifty, his
trousers were too wide and betrayed their
cheapness in their fit, or rather, misfit, and
his coat was too tight.

Slowly he ascended the stairs, his heart beating,
his mind anxious. Suddenly before him stood a well-
dressed gentleman staring at him. The person resembled Duroy so close that the latter retreated, then
stopped, and saw that it was his own image reflected
in a pier-glass! Not having anything but a small
mirror at home, he had not been able to see himself
entirely, and had exaggerated the imperfections of his

toilette. When he saw his reflection in the glass, he did not even recognize himself; he took himself for some one else, for a man-of-the-world, and was really satisfied with his general appearance. Smiling to himself, Duroy extended his hand and expressed his astonishment, pleasure, and approbation. A door opened on the staircase. He was afraid of being surprised and began to ascend more rapidly, fearing that he might have been seen posing there by some of his friend's invited guests.

On reaching the second floor, he saw another mirror, and once more slackened his pace to look at himself. He likewise paused before the third glass, twirled his mustache, took off his hat to arrange his hair, and murmured half aloud, a habit of his: "Hall mirrors are most convenient."

Then he rang the bell. The door opened almost immediately, and before him stood a servant in a black coat, with a grave, shaven face, so perfect in his appearance that Duroy again became confused as he compared the cut of their garments.

The lackey asked:

"Whom shall I announce, Monsieur?" He raised a portière and pronounced the name.

Duroy lost his self-possession upon being ushered into a world as yet strange to him. However, he advanced. A young, fair woman received him alone in a large, well-lighted room. He paused, disconcerted. Who was that smiling lady? He remembered that Forestier was married, and the thought that the handsome blonde was his friend's wife rendered him awkward and ill-at-ease. He stammered out:

"Madame, I am —"

She held out her hand. "I know, Monsieur—Charles told me of your meeting last night, and I am very glad that he asked you to dine with us to-day."

Duroy blushed to the roots of his hair, not knowing how to reply; he felt that he was being inspected from his head to his feet. He half thought of excusing himself, of inventing an explanation of the carelessness of his toilette, but he did not know how to touch upon that delicate subject.

He seated himself upon a chair she pointed out to him, and as he sank into its luxurious depths, it seemed to him that he was entering a new and charming life, that he would make his mark in the world, that he was saved. He glanced at Mme. Forestier. She wore a gown of pale blue cashmere which clung gracefully to her supple form and rounded outlines; her arms and throat rose in lily-white purity from the mass of lace which ornamented the corsage and short sleeves. Her hair was dressed high and curled on the nape of her neck.

Duroy grew more at his ease under her glance, which recalled to him, he knew not why, that of the girl he had met the preceding evening at the Folies-Bergères. Mme. Forestier had gray eyes, a small nose, full lips, and a rather heavy chin, an irregular, attractive face, full of gentleness and yet of malice.

After a short silence, she asked: "Have you been in Paris a long time?"

Gradually regaining his self-possession, he replied: "Only a few months, Madame. I am in the railroad

employ, but my friend Forestier has encouraged me
to hope that, thanks to him, I can enter into journalism."

She smiled kindly and murmured in a low voice:
"I know."

The bell rang again and the servant announced:
"Mme. de Marelle." She was a dainty brunette, attired in a simple, dark robe; a red rose in her black
tresses seemed to accentuate her special character,
and a young girl, or rather a child, for such she was,
followed her.

Mme. Forestier said: "Good evening, Clotilde."

"Good evening, Madeleine."

They embraced each other, then the child offered
her forehead with the assurance of an adult, saying:

"Good evening, cousin."

Mme. Forestier kissed her, and then made the in-
troductions:

"M. Georges Duroy, an old friend of Charles.
Mme. de Marelle, my friend, a relative in fact." She
added: "Here, you know, we do not stand on ceremony."

Duroy bowed. The door opened again and a short
man entered, upon his arm a tall, handsome woman,
taller than he and much younger, with distinguished
manners and a dignified carriage. It was M. Walter,
deputy, financier, a moneyed man, and a man of business, manager of "La Vie Française," with his wife,
née Basile Ravalade, daughter of the banker of that
name.

Then came Jacques Rival, very elegant, followed
by Norbert de Varenne. The latter advanced with

the grace of the old school and taking Mme. Forestier's hand kissed it; his long hair falling upon his hostess's bare arm as he did so.

Forestier now entered, apologizing for being late; he had been detained.

The servant announced dinner, and they entered the dining-room. Duroy was placed between Mme. de Marelle and her daughter. He was again rendered uncomfortable for fear of committing some error in the conventional management of his fork, his spoon, or his glasses, of which he had four. Nothing was said during the soup; then Norbert de Varenne asked a general question: "Have you read the Gauthier case? How droll it was!"

Then followed a discussion of the subject in which the ladies joined. Then a duel was mentioned and Jacques Rival led the conversation; that was his province. Duroy did not venture a remark, but occasionally glanced at his neighbor. A diamond upon a slight, golden thread depended from her ear; from time to time she uttered a remark which evoked a smile upon his lips. Duroy sought vainly for some compliment to pay her; he busied himself with her daughter, filled her glass, waited upon her, and the child, more dignified than her mother, thanked him gravely saying, "You are very kind, Monsieur," while she listened to the conversation with a reflective air. The dinner was excellent and everyone was delighted with it.

The conversation returned to the colonization of Algeria. M. Walter uttered several jocose remarks; Forestier alluded to the article he had prepared for the morrow; Jacques Rival declared himself in favor of a military government with grants of land to all the officers after thirty years of colonial service.

"In that way," said he, "you can establish a strong colony, familiar with and liking the country, knowing its language and able to cope with all those local yet grave questions which invariably confront newcomers.

Norbert de Varenne interrupted: "Yes, they would know everything, except agriculture. They would speak Arabic, but they would not know how to transplant beet-root, and how to sow wheat. They would be strong in fencing, but weak in the art of farming. On the contrary, the new country should be opened to everyone. Intelligent men would make positions for themselves; the others would succumb. It is a natural law."

A pause ensued. Everyone smiled. Georges Duroy, startled at the sound of his own voice, as if he had never heard it, said:

"What is needed the most down there is good soil. Really fertile land costs as much as it does in France and is bought by wealthy Parisians. The real colonists, the poor, are generally cast out into the desert, where nothing grows for lack of water."

All eyes turned upon him. He colored. M. Walter asked: "Do you know Algeria, sir?"

He replied: "Yes, sir, I was there twenty-eight months." Leaving the subject of colonization, Norbert de Varenne questioned him as to some of the Algerian customs. Georges spoke with animation; excited by the wine and the desire to please, he related anecdotes of the regiment, of Arabian life, and of the war.

Mme. Walter murmured to him in her soft tones: "You could write a series of charming articles."

Forestier took advantage of the situation to say to M. Walter: "My dear sir, I spoke to you a short while since of M. Georges Duroy and asked you to permit me to include him on the staff of political reporters. Since Marambot has left us, I have had no one to take urgent and confidential reports, and the paper is suffering by it."

M. Walter put on his spectacles in order to examine Duroy. Then he said: "I am convinced that M. Duroy is original, and if he will call upon me to-morrow at three o'clock, we will arrange matters." After a pause, turning to the young man, he said: "You may write us a short sketch on Algeria, M. Duroy. Simply relate your experiences; I am sure they will interest our readers. But you must do it quickly."

Mme. Walter added with her customary, serious grace: "You will have a charming title: 'Souvenirs of a Soldier in Africa.' Will he not, M. Norbert?"

The old poet, who had attained renown late in life, disliked and mistrusted newcomers. He replied dryly: "Yes, excellent, provided that it is written in the right key, for there lies the great difficulty."

Mme. Forestier cast upon Duroy a protecting and smiling glance which seemed to say: "You shall succeed." The servant filled the glasses with wine, and Forestier proposed the toast: "To the long prosperity of 'La Vie Française.'" Duroy felt superhuman strength within him, infinite hope, and invincible resolution. He was at his ease now among these people; his eyes rested upon their faces with renewed assur-

ance, and for the first time he ventured to address
his neighbor:

"You have the most beautiful earrings I have
ever seen."

She turned toward him with a smile: "It is a
fancy of mine to wear diamonds like this, simply on
a thread."

He murmured in reply, trembling at his audacity:
"It is charming—but the ear increases the beauty of
the ornament."

She thanked him with a glance. As he turned
his head, he met Mme. Forestier's eyes, in which
he fancied he saw a mingled expression of gaiety, malice, and encouragement. All the men were
talking at the same time; their discussion was animated.

When the party left the dining-room, Duroy offered his arm to the little girl. She thanked him
gravely and stood upon tiptoe in order to lay her
hand upon his arm. Upon entering the drawing-
room, the young man carefully surveyed it. It was
not a large room; but there were no bright colors,
and one felt at ease; it was restful. The walls were
draped with violet hangings covered with tiny em-
broidered flowers of yellow silk. The portières were
of a grayish blue and the chairs were of all shapes,
of all sizes; scattered about the room were couches
and large and small easy-chairs, all covered with
Louis XVI. brocade, or Utrecht velvet, a cream colored ground with garnet flowers.

"Do you take coffee, M. Duroy?" Mme. Forestier
offered him a cup, with the smile that was always
upon her lips.

"Yes, Madame, thank you." He took the cup,
and as he did so, the young woman whispered to
him: "Pay Mme. Walter some attention." Then
she vanished before he could reply.

First he drank his coffee, which he feared he
should let fall upon the carpet; then he sought a pretext for approaching the manager's wife and com-
mencing a conversation. Suddenly he perceived that
she held an empty cup in her hand, and as she was
not near a table, she did not know where to put it.
He rushed toward her:

"Allow me, Madame."

"Thank you, sir."

He took away the cup and returned: "If you but
knew, Madame, what pleasant moments 'La Vie
Française' afforded me, when I was in the desert!
It is indeed the only paper one cares to read outside
of France; it contains everything."

She smiled with amiable indifference as she replied: "M. Walter had a great deal of trouble in
producing the kind of journal which was required."

They talked of Paris, the suburbs, the Seine, the
delights of summer, of everything they could think
of. Finally M. Norbert de Varenne advanced, a glass
of liqueur in his hand, and Duroy discreetly withdrew. Mme. de Marelle, who was chatting with her
hostess, called him: "So, sir," she said bluntly,
"you are going to try journalism?" That question
led to a renewal of the interrupted conversation with
Mme. Walter. In her turn Mme. de Marelle related
anecdotes, and becoming familiar, laid her hand upon
Duroy's arm. He felt that he would like to devote
himself to her, to protect her—and the slowness

with which he replied to her questions indicated his preoccupation. Suddenly, without any cause, Mme. de Marelle called: "Laurine!" and the girl came to her. "Sit down here, my child, you will be cold near the window."

Duroy was seized with an eager desire to embrace the child, as if part of that embrace would revert to the mother. He asked in a gallant, yet paternal tone: "Will you permit me to kiss you, Mademoiselle?" The child raised her eyes with an air of surprise. Mme. de Marelle said with a smile: "Reply."

"I will allow you to-day, Monsieur, but not all the time."

Seating himself, Duroy took Laurine upon his knee, and kissed her lips and her fine wavy hair. Her mother was surprised: "Well, that is strange! Ordinarily she only allows ladies to caress her, You are irresistible, Monsieur!"

Duroy colored, but did not reply.

When Mme. Forestier joined them, a cry of astonishment escaped her: "Well, Laurine has become sociable; what a miracle!"

The young man rose to take his leave, fearing he might spoil his conquest by some awkward word. He bowed to the ladies, clasped and gently pressed their hands, and then shook hands with the men. He observed that Jacques Rival's was dry and warm and responded cordially to his pressure; Norbert de Varenne's was moist and cold and slipped through his fingers; Walter's was cold and soft, without life, expressionless; Forestier's fat and warm.

His friend whispered to him: "To-morrow at three o'clock; do not forget."

"Never fear!"

When he reached the staircase, he felt like running down, his joy was so great; he went down two steps at a time, but suddenly on the second floor, in the large mirror, he saw a gentleman hurrying on, and he slackened his pace, as much ashamed as if he had been surprised in a crime.

He surveyed himself some time with a complacent smile; then taking leave of his image, he bowed low, ceremoniously, as if saluting some grand personage.

CHAPTER III.

First Attempts

WHEN Georges Duroy reached the street, he hesitated as to what he should do. He felt inclined to stroll along, dreaming of the future and inhaling the soft night air; but the thought of the series of articles ordered by M. Walter occurred to him, and he decided to return home at once and begin work. He walked rapidly along until he came to Rue Boursault. The tenement in which he lived was occupied by twenty families — families of workingmen — and as he mounted the staircase he experienced a sensation of disgust and a desire to live as wealthy men do. Duroy's room was on the fifth floor. He entered it, opened his window, and looked out: the view was anything but prepossessing.

He turned away, thinking: "This won't do. I must go to work." So he placed his light upon the table and began to write. He dipped his pen into the ink and wrote at the head of his paper in a bold hand: "Souvenirs of a Soldier in Africa." Then he cast about for the first phrase. He rested his head

(24)

upon his hand and stared at the blank sheet before
him. What should he say? Suddenly he thought:
"I must begin with my departure," and he wrote:
"In 1874, about the fifteenth of May, when exhausted
France was recruiting after the catastrophe of the
terrible years—" Here he stopped short, not knowing how to introduce his subject. After a few minutes' reflection, he decided to lay aside that page
until the following day, and to write a description of
Algiers. He began: "Algiers is a very clean city—"
but he could not continue. After an effort he
added: "It is inhabited partly by Arabs." Then he
threw his pen upon the table and arose. He glanced
around his miserable room; mentally he rebelled
against his poverty and resolved to leave the next
day.

Suddenly the desire to work came on him, and
he tried to begin the article again; he had vague
ideas of what he wanted to say, but he could not
express his thoughts in words. Convinced of his in-
ability he arose once more, his blood coursing rapidly
through his veins. He turned to the window just as
the train was coming out of the tunnel, and his
thoughts reverted to his parents. He saw their tiny
home on the heights overlooking Rouen and the
valley of the Seine. His father and mother kept an
inn, La Belle-Vue, at which the citizens of the *fau-
bourgs* took their lunches on Sundays. They had
wished to make a "gentleman" of their son and had
sent him to college. His studies completed, he
had entered the army with the intention of becoming
an officer, a colonel, or a general. But becoming disgusted with military life, he determined to try his

fortune in Paris. When his time of service had ex-
pired, he went thither, with what results we have
seen. He awoke from his reflections as the locomotive whistled shrilly, closed his window, and began to
disrobe, muttering: "Bah, I shall be able to work
better to-morrow morning. My brain is not clear
to-night. I have drunk a little too much. I can't
work well under such circumstances." He extinguished his light and fell asleep.

He awoke early, and, rising, opened his window
to inhale the fresh air. In a few moments he seated
himself at his table, dipped his pen in the ink, rested
his head upon his hand and thought—but in vain!
However, he was not discouraged, but in thought
reassured himself: "Bah, I am not accustomed to
it! It is a profession that must be learned like all
professions. Some one must help me the first time.
I'll go to Forestier. He'll start my article for me in
ten minutes."

When he reached the street, Duroy decided that
it was rather early to present himself at his friend's
house, so he strolled along under the trees on one
of the boulevards for a time. On arriving at Forestier's door, he found his friend going out.

"You here—at this hour! Can I do anything for
you?"

Duroy stammered in confusion: "I—I—cannot
write that article on Algeria that M. Walter wants.
It is not very surprising, seeing that I have never
written anything. It requires practice. I could write
very rapidly, I am sure, if I could make a beginning.
I have the ideas but I cannot express them." He
paused and hesitated.

Forestier smiled maliciously: "I understand that."

Duroy continued: "Yes, anyone is liable to have that trouble at the beginning; and, well — I have come to ask you to help me. In ten minutes you can set me right. You can give me a lesson in style; without you I can do nothing."

The other smiled gaily. He patted his companion's arm and said to him: "Go to my wife; she will help you better than I can. I have trained her for that work. I have not time this morning or I would do it willingly."

But Duroy hesitated: "At this hour I cannot inquire for her."

"Oh, yes, you can; she has risen. You will find her in my study."

"I will go, but I shall tell her you sent me!"

Forestier walked away, and Duroy slowly ascended the stairs, wondering what he should say and what kind of a reception he would receive.

The servant who opened the door said: "Monsieur has gone out."

Duroy replied: "Ask Mme. Forestier if she will see me, and tell her that M. Forestier, whom I met on the street, sent me."

The lackey soon returned and ushered Duroy into Madame's presence. She was seated at a table and extended her hand to him.

"So soon?" said she. It was not a reproach, but a simple question.

He stammered: "I did not want to come up, Madame, but your husband, whom I met below, insisted — I dare scarcely tell you my errand — I worked late last night and early this morning, to write the

article on Algeria which M. Walter wants—and I did
not succeed—I destroyed all my attempts—I am not
accustomed to the work—and I came to ask Forestier to assist me—this once."

She interrupted with a laugh: "And he sent you
to me?"

"Yes, Madame. He said you could help me better than he—but—I dared not—I did not like to."

She rose.

"It will be delightful to work together that way.
I am charmed with your idea. Wait, take my chair,
for they know my handwriting on the paper—we
will write a successful article."

She took a cigarette from the mantelpiece and
lighted it. "I cannot work without smoking," she
said; "what are you going to say?"

He looked at her in astonishment. "I do not
know; I came here to find that out."

She replied: "I will manage it all right. I will
make the sauce but I must have the dish." She
questioned him in detail and finally said:

"Now, we will begin. First of all we will suppose that you are addressing a friend, which will allow us scope for remarks of all kinds. Begin this
way: 'My dear Henry, you wish to know something
about Algeria; you shall.'"

Then followed a brilliantly worded description of
Algeria and of the port of Algiers, an excursion to
the province of Oran, a visit to Saida, and an adventure with a pretty Spanish maid employed in
a factory.

When the article was concluded, he could find no
words of thanks; he was happy to be near her,

grateful for and delighted with their growing intimacy. It seemed to him that everything about him was a part of her, even to the books upon the shelves. The chairs, the furniture, the air — all were permeated with that delightful fragrance peculiar to her.

She asked bluntly: "What do you think of my friend Mme. de Marelle?"

"I think her very fascinating," he said; and he would have liked to add: "But not as much so as you." He had not the courage to do so.

She continued: "If you only knew how comical, original, and intelligent she is! She is a true Bohemian. It is for that reason that her husband no longer loves her. He only sees her defects and none of her good qualities."

Duroy was surprised to hear that Mme. de Marelle was married.

"What," he asked, "is she married? What does her husband do?"

Mme. Forestier shrugged her shoulders. "Oh, he is superintendent of a railroad. He is in Paris a week out of each month. His wife calls it 'Holy Week,' or 'The week of duty.' When you get better acquainted with her, you will see how witty she is! Come here and see her some day."

As she spoke, the door opened noiselessly, and a gentleman entered unannounced. He halted on seeing a man. For a moment Mme. Forestier seemed confused; then she said in a natural voice, though her cheeks were tinged with a blush:

"Come in, my dear sir; allow me to present to you an old comrade of Charles, M. Georges Duroy, a future journalist." Then in a different tone, she said: "Our best and dearest friend, Count de Vaudrec."

The two men bowed, gazed into one another's eyes, and then Duroy took his leave. Neither tried to detain him.

On reaching the street he felt sad and uncomfortable. Count de Vaudrec's face was constantly before him. It seemed to him that the man was displeased at finding him *tête-à-tête* with Mme. Forestier, though why he should be, he could not divine.

To while away the time until three o'clock, he lunched at Duval's, and then lounged along the boulevard. When the clock chimed the hour of his appointment, he climbed the stairs leading to the office of "La Vie Française."

Duroy asked: "Is M. Walter in?"

"M. Walter is engaged," was the reply. "Will you please take a seat?"

Duroy waited twenty minutes, then he turned to the clerk and said: "M. Walter had an appointment with me at three o'clock. At any rate, see if my friend M. Forestier is here."

He was conducted along a corridor and ushered into a large room in which four men were writing at a table. Forestier was standing before the fireplace, smoking a cigarette. After listening to Duroy's story he said:

"Come with me; I will take you to M. Walter, or else you might remain here until seven o'clock."

They entered the manager's room. Norbert de Varenne was writing an article, seated in an easy-chair; Jacques Rival, stretched upon a divan, was smoking a cigar. The room had the peculiar odor

familiar to all journalists. When they approached
M. Walter, Forestier said: "Here is my friend Duroy."

The manager looked keenly at the young man
and asked:

"Have you brought my article?"

Duroy drew the sheets of manuscript from his
pocket.

"Here they are, Monsieur."

The manager seemed delighted and said with a
smile: "Very good. You are a man of your word.
Need I look over it, Forestier?"

But Forestier hastened to reply: "It is not necessary, M. Walter; I helped him in order to initiate
him into the profession. It is very good." Then
bending toward him, he whispered: "You know
you promised to engage Duroy to replace Marambot.
Will you allow me to retain him on the same
terms?"

"Certainly."

Taking his friend's arm, the journalist drew him
away, while M. Walter returned to the game of
écarté he had been engaged in when they entered.
Forestier and Duroy returned to the room in which
Georges had found his friend. The latter said to his
new reporter:

"You must come here every day at three o'clock,
and I will tell you what places to go to. First of
all, I shall give you a letter of introduction to the
chief of the police, who will in turn introduce you to
one of his employees. You can arrange with him for
all important news, official and semiofficial. For details you can apply to Saint-Potin, who is posted;

you will see him to-morrow. Above all, you must learn to make your way everywhere in spite of closed doors. You will receive two hundred francs a months, two sous a line for original matter, and two sous a line for articles you are ordered to write on different subjects."

"What shall I do to-day?" asked Duroy.

"I have no work for you to-day; you can go if you wish to."

"And our — our article?"

"Oh, do not worry about it; I will correct the proofs. Do the rest to-morrow and come here at three o'clock as you did to-day."

And after shaking hands, Duroy descended the staircase with a light heart.

CHAPTER IV.

DUROY LEARNS SOMETHING

GEORGES DUROY did not sleep well, so anxious was he to see his article in print. He rose at daybreak, and was on the street long before the newsboys. When he secured a paper and saw his name at the end of a column in large letters, he became very much excited. He felt inclined to enact the part of a newsboy and cry out to the hurrying throng: "Buy this! it contains an article by me!" He strolled along to a *café* and seated himself in order to read the article through; that done he decided to go to the railroad office, draw his salary, and hand in his resignation.

With great pomposity he informed the chief clerk that he was on the staff of "La Vie Française," and by that means was avenged for many petty insults which had been offered him. He then had some cards written with his new calling beneath his name, made several purchases, and repaired to the office of "La Vie Française." Forestier received him loftily as one would an inferior.

7 G. de M.—3

"Ah, here you are! Very well; I have several things for you to do. Just wait ten minutes till I finish this work." He continued writing.

At the other end of the table sat a short, pale man, very stout and bald. Forestier asked him, when his letter was completed, "Saint-Potin, at what time shall you interview those people?'

"At four o'clock."

"Take Duroy, who is here, with you and initiate him into the business."

"Very well."

Then turning to his friend, Forestier added: "Have you brought the other paper on Algeria? The article this morning was very successful."

Duroy stammered: "No, I thought I should have time this afternoon. I had so much to do — I could not."

The other shrugged his shoulders. "If you are not more careful, you will spoil your future. M. Walter counted on your copy. I will tell him it will be ready to-morrow. If you think you will be paid for doing nothing, you are mistaken." After a pause, he added: "You should strike while the iron is hot."

Saint-Potin rose: "I am ready," said he.

Forestier turned around in his chair and said to Duroy: "Listen. The Chinese general Li-Theng-Fao, stopping at the Continental, and Rajah Taposahib Ramaderao Pali, stopping at Hotel Bishop, have been in Paris two days. You must interview them." Addressing Saint-Potin, he said: "Do not forget the principal points I indicated to you. Ask the general and the rajah their opinions on the dealings of England in the extreme East, their ideas of their system of colonization and government, their hopes relative to the intervention of Europe and of France in particular." To Duroy he said: "Observe what Saint-Potin says; he is an excellent reporter, and try to learn how to draw out a man in five minutes." Then he resumed his work.

The two men walked down the boulevard together, while Saint-Potin gave Duroy a sketch of all the officials connected with the paper, sparing no one in his criticism. When he mentioned Forestier, he said: "As for him, he was fortunate in marrying his wife."

Duroy asked: "What about his wife?"

Saint-Potin rubbed his hands. "Oh, she is beloved by an old fellow named Vaudrec — he dotes upon her."

Duroy felt as if he would like to box Saint-Potin's ears. To change the subject he said: "It seems to me that it is late, and we have two noble lords to call upon!"

Saint-Potin laughed: "You are very innocent! Do you think that I am going to interview that Chinese and that Indian? As if I did not know better than they do what they should think to please the readers of 'La Vie Française'! I have interviewed five hundred Chinese, Prussians, Hindoos, Chilians, and Japanese. They all say the same thing. I need only copy my article on the last comer, word for word, changing the heading, names, titles, and ages: in that there must be no error, or I shall be hauled over the coals by the 'Figaro' or 'Gaulois.' But on that subject the porter of the hotels will post me in five minutes. We will smoke our cigars and stroll

in that direction.   Total — one hundred sous for cab-
fare.   That is the way, my dear fellow."

When they arrived at the Madeleine, Saint-Potin
said to his companion: "If you have anything to
do, I do not need you."

Duroy shook hands with him and walked away.
The thought of the article he had to write that evening haunted him.   Mentally he collected the material
as he wended his way to the *café* at which he dined.
Then he returned home and seated himself at his
table to work.   Before his eyes was the sheet of
blank paper, but all the material he had amassed had
escaped him.   After trying for an hour, and after fill-
ing five pages with sentences which had no connection one with the other, he said: "I am not yet
familiar with the work.   I must take another lesson."

At ten o'clock the following morning he rang the
bell, at his friend's house.   The servant who opened
the door, said: "Monsieur is busy."

Duroy had not expected to find Forestier at home.
However he said: "Tell him it is M. Duroy on important business."

In the course of five minutes he was ushered into
the room in which he had spent so happy a morning.   In the place Mme. Forestier had occupied, her
husband was seated writing, while Mme. Forestier
stood by the mantelpiece and dictated to him, a cigarette between her lips.

Duroy paused upon the threshold and murmured:
"I beg your pardon, I am interrupting you."

His friend growled angrily: "What do you want
again?   Make haste; we are busy."

Georges stammered: "It is nothing."

But Forestier persisted: "Come, we are losing time; you did not force your way into the house for the pleasure of bidding us good morning."

Duroy, in confusion, replied: "No, it is this: I cannot complete my article, and you were — so — so kind the last time that I hoped — that I dared to come —"

Forestier interrupted with: "So you think I will do your work and that you have only to take the money. Well, that is fine!" His wife smoked on without interfering.

Duroy hesitated: "Excuse me. I believed — I — thought —" Then, in a clear voice, he said: "I beg a thousand pardons, Madame, and thank you very much for the charming article you wrote for me yesterday." Then he bowed, and said to Charles: "I will be at the office at three o'clock."

He returned home saying to himself: "Very well, I will write it alone and they shall see." Scarcely had he entered than he began to write, anger spurring him on. In an hour he had finished an article, which was a chaos of absurd matter, and took it boldly to the office. Duroy handed Forestier his manuscript. "Here is the rest of Algeria."

"Very well, I will hand it to the manager. That will do."

When Duroy and Saint-Potin, who had some political information to look up, were in the hall, the latter asked: "Have you been to the cashier's room?"

"No, why?"

"Why? To get your pay? You should always get your salary a month in advance. One cannot tell what might happen. I will introduce you to the cashier."

Duroy drew his two hundred francs together with twenty-eight francs for his article of the preceding day, which, in addition to what remained to him of his salary from the railroad office, left him three hundred and forty francs. He had never had so much, and he thought himself rich for an indefinite time. Saint-Potin took him to the offices of four or five rival papers, hoping that the news he had been commissioned to obtain had been already received by them and that he could obtain it by means of his diplomacy.

When evening came, Duroy, who had nothing more to do, turned toward the Folies-Bergères, and walking up to the office, he said: "My name is Georges Duroy. I am on the staff of 'La Vie Française.' I was here the other night with M. Forestier, who promised to get me a pass. I do not know if he remembered it."

The register was consulted, but his name was not inscribed upon it. However, the cashier, a very affable man, said to him: "Come in, M. Duroy, and speak to the manager yourself; he will see that everything is all right."

He entered and almost at once came upon Rachel, the woman he had seen there before. She approached him: "Good evening, my dear; are you well?"

"Very well; how are you?"

"I am not ill. I have dreamed of you twice since the other night."

Duroy smiled. "What does that mean?"

"That means that I like you"; she raised her eyes
to the young man's face, took his arm and leaning
upon it, said: "Let us drink a glass of wine and
then take a walk. I should like to go to the opera
like this, with you, to show you off."

*   *   *   *   *   *   *

At daybreak he again sallied forth to obtain a
"Vie Française." He opened the paper feverishly;
his article was not there. On entering the office
several hours later, he said to M. Walter: "I was
very much surprised this morning not to see my second article on Algeria."

The manager raised his head and said sharply:
"I gave it to your friend, Forestier, and asked him
to read it; he was dissatisfied with it; it will have
to be done over."

Without a word, Duroy left the room, and entering his friend's office, brusquely asked: "Why did
not my article appear this morning?"

The journalist, who was smoking a cigar, said
calmly: "The manager did not consider it good, and
bade me return it to you to be revised. There it is."
Duroy revised it several times, only to have it rejected. He said nothing more of his "souvenirs,"
but gave his whole attention to reporting. He became acquainted behind the scenes at the theaters,
and in the halls and corridors of the chamber of
deputies; he knew all the cabinet ministers, generals,
police agents, princes, ambassadors, men of the
world, Greeks, cabmen, waiters at *cafés*, and many
others. In short he soon became a remarkable reporter, of great value to the paper, so M. Walter said.

But as he only received ten centimes a line in addition to his fixed salary of two hundred francs and as his expenses were large, he never had a sou. When he saw certain of his associates with their pockets full of money, he wondered what secret means they employed in order to obtain it. He determined to penetrate that mystery, to enter into the association, to obtrude himself upon his comrades, and make them share with him. Often at evening, as he watched the trains pass his window, he dreamed of the conduct he might pursue.

CHAPTER V.

THE FIRST INTRIGUE

Two months elapsed. It was September. The fortune which Duroy had hoped to make so rapidly seemed to him slow in coming. Above all he was dissatisfied with the mediocrity of his position; he was appreciated, but was treated according to his rank. Forestier himself no longer invited him to dinner, and treated him as an inferior. Often he had thought of making Mme. Forestier a visit, but the remembrance of their last meeting restrained him. Mme. de Marelle had invited him to call, saying: "I am always at home about three o'clock." So one afternoon, when he had nothing to do, he proceeded toward her house. She lived on Rue Verneuil, on the fourth floor. A maid answered his summons, and said: "Yes, Madame is at home, but I do not know whether she has risen." She conducted Duroy into the drawing-room, which was large, poorly furnished, and somewhat untidy. The shabby, threadbare chairs were ranged along the walls according to the servant's fancy, for there was not a trace visible of the

(41)

care of a woman who loves her home. Duroy took a seat and waited some time. Then a door opened and Mme. de Marelle entered hastily, clad in a Japanese dressing-gown. She exclaimed:

"How kind of you to come to see me. I was positive you had forgotten me." She held out her hand to him with a gesture of delight; and Duroy, quite at his ease in that shabby apartment, kissed it as he had seen Norbert de Varenne do.

Examining him from head to foot, she cried: "How you have changed! Well, tell me the news."

They began to chat at once as if they were old acquaintances, and in five minutes an intimacy, a mutual understanding, was established between those two beings alike in character and kind. Suddenly the young woman said in surprise: "It is astonishing how I feel with you. It seems to me as if I had known you ten years. We shall undoubtedly become good friends; would that please you?"

He replied: "Certainly," with a smile more expressive than words. He thought her very bewitching in her pretty gown. When near Mme. Forestier, whose impassive, gracious smile attracted yet held at a distance, and seemed to say: "I like you, yet take care," he felt a desire to cast himself at her feet, or to kiss the hem of her garment. When near Mme. de Marelle, he felt a more passionate desire.

A gentle rap came at the door through which Mme. de Marelle had entered, and she cried: "You may come in, my darling."

The child entered, advanced to Duroy and offered him her hand. The astonished mother murmured: "That is a conquest." The young man, having kissed the child, seated her by his side, and with a serious air questioned her as to what she had done since they last met. She replied in a flute-like voice and with the manner of a woman. The clock struck three; the journalist rose.

"Come often," said Mme. de Marelle; "it has been a pleasant *causerie*. I shall always be glad to welcome you. Why do I never meet you at the Forestiers?"

"For no particular reason. I am very busy. I hope, however, that we shall meet there one of these days."

In the course of a few days he paid another visit to the enchantress. The maid ushered him into the drawing-room and Laurine soon entered; she offered him not her hand but her forehead, and said: "Mamma wishes me to ask you to wait for her about fifteen minutes, for she is not dressed. I will keep you company."

Duroy, who was amused at the child's ceremonious manner, replied: "Indeed, Mademoiselle, I shall be enchanted to spend a quarter of an hour with you." When the mother entered they were in the midst of an exciting game, and Mme. de Marelle paused in amazement, crying: "Laurine playing? You are a sorcerer, sir!" He placed the child, whom he had caught in his arms, upon the floor, kissed the lady's hand, and they seated themselves, the child between them. They tried to converse, but Laurine, usually so silent, monopolized the conversation, and her mother was compelled to send her to her room.

When they were alone, Mme. de Marelle lowered her voice and said: "I have a great project. It is this: As I dine every week at the Forestiers', I return it from time to time by inviting them to a restaurant. I do not like to have company at home; I am not so situated that I can have any. I know nothing about housekeeping or cooking. I prefer a life free from care; therefore I invite them to the *café* occasionally; but it is not lively when we are only three. I am telling you this in order to explain such an informal gathering. I should like you to be present at our Saturdays at the Café Riche at seven-thirty. Do you know the house?"

Duroy accepted gladly. He left her in a transport of delight and impatiently awaited the day of the dinner. He was the first to arrive at the place appointed and was shown into a small private room, in which the table was laid for four; that table looked very inviting with its colored glasses, silver, and candelabra.

Duroy seated himself upon a low bench. Forestier entered and shook hands with him with a cordiality he never evinced at the office.

"The two ladies will come together," said he. "These dinners are truly delightful."

Very soon the door opened and Mesdames Forestier and De Marelle appeared, heavily veiled, surrounded by the charming mystery necessary to a rendezvous in a place so public. As Duroy greeted the former, she took him to task for not having been to see her; then she added with a smile: "Ah, you prefer Mme. de Marelle; the time passes more pleasantly with her."

When the waiter handed the wine-list to Forestier, Mme. de Marelle exclaimed: "Bring the gentle-

men whatever they want; as for us, we want nothing
but champagne."

Forestier, who seemed not to have heard her,
asked: "Do you object to my closing the window?
My cough has troubled me for several days."

"Not at all."

His wife did not speak. The various courses
were duly served and then the guests began to chat.
They discussed a scandal which was being circulated
about a society belle. Forestier was very much
amused by it. Duroy said with a smile: "How many
would abandon themselves to a caprice, a dream of
love, if they did not fear that they would pay for a
brief happiness with tears and an irremediable scandal?"

Both women glanced at him approvingly. Forestier cried with a sceptical laugh: "The poor husbands!" Then they talked of love. Duroy said:
"When I love a woman, everything else in the
world is forgotten."

Mme. Forestier murmured: "There is no happiness comparable to that first clasp of the hand, when
one asks: 'Do you love me?' and the other replies:
'Yes, I love you.'" Mme. de Marelle cried gaily as
she drank a glass of champagne: "I am less Platonic."

Forestier, lying upon the couch, said in serious
tone: "That frankness does you honor and proves
you to be a practical woman. But might one ask,
What is M. de Marelle's opinion?"

She shrugged her shoulders disdainfully and said:
"M. de Marelle has no opinion on that subject."

The conversation grew slow. Mme. de Marelle
seemed to offer provocation by her remarks, while
Mme. Forestier's charming reserve, the modesty in

her voice, in her smile, all seemed to extenuate the bold sallies which issued from her lips. The dessert came and then followed the coffee. The hostess and her guests lighted cigarettes, but Forestier suddenly began to cough. When the attack was over, he growled angrily: "These parties are not good for me; they are stupid. Let us go home."

Mme. de Marelle summoned the waiter and asked for her bill. She tried to read it, but the figures danced before her eyes; she handed the paper to Duroy.

"Here, pay it for me; I cannot see." At the same time, she put her purse in his hand.

The total was one hundred and thirty francs. Duroy glanced at the bill and when it was settled, whispered: "How much shall I give the waiter?"

"Whatever you like; I do not know."

He laid five francs upon the plate and handed the purse to its owner, saying: "Shall I escort you home?"

"Certainly; I am unable to find the house."

They shook hands with the Forestiers and were soon rolling along in a cab side by side. Duroy could think of nothing to say; he felt impelled to clasp her in his arms. "If I should dare, what would she do?" thought he. The recollection of their conversation at dinner emboldened, but the fear of scandal restrained him. Mme. de Marelle reclined silently in her corner. He would have thought her asleep, had he not seen her eyes glisten whenever a ray of light penetrated the dark recesses of the carriage. Of what was she thinking? Suddenly she moved her foot, nervously, impatiently. That movement caused him to tremble, and turning quickly, he cast himself upon her, seeking her lips with his. She uttered a cry, attempted to repulse him and then yielded to his caresses as if she had not the strength to resist.

The carriage stopped at her door, but she did not rise; she did not move, stunned by what had just taken place. Fearing that the cabman would mistrust something, Duroy alighted from the cab first and offered his hand to the young woman. Finally she got out, but in silence. Georges rang the bell, and when the door was opened, he asked timidly: "When shall I see you again?"

She whispered so low that he could barely hear her: "Come and lunch with me to-morrow." With those words she disappeared.

Duroy gave the cabman a five-franc piece, and turned away with a triumphant, joyful air. He had at last conquered a married woman! A woman of the world! A Parisian! How easy it had been!

He was somewhat nervous the following day as he ascended Mme. de Marelle's staircase. How would she receive him? Suppose she forbade him to enter her house? If she had told — but no, she could not tell anything without telling the whole truth! He was master of the situation!

The little maid-servant opened the door. She was as pleasant as usual. Duroy felt reassured and asked: "Is Madame well?"

"Yes, sir; as well as she always is," was the reply, and he was ushered into the salon. He walked to the mantelpiece to see what kind of an appearance he presented: he was readjusting his cravat when he saw in the mirror the young woman stand-

ing on the threshold looking at him. He pretended
not to have seen her, and for several moments they
gazed at one another in the mirror. Then he turned.
She had not moved; she seemed to be waiting. He
rushed toward her crying: "How I love you!" He
clasped her to his breast. He thought: "It is easier
than I thought it would be. All is well." He looked
at her with a smile, without uttering a word, trying
to put into his glance a wealth of love. She too
smiled and murmured: "We are alone. I sent Laurine to lunch with a friend."

He sighed, and kissing her wrists said: "Thanks;
I adore you." She took his arm as if he had been
her husband, and led him to a couch, upon which they
seated themselves side by side. Duroy stammered,
incoherently: "You do not care for me."

She laid her hand upon his lips. "Be silent!"

"How I love you!" said he.

She repeated: "Be silent!"

They could hear the servant laying the table in
the dining-room. He rose: "I cannot sit so near
you. I shall lose my head."

The door opened: "Madame is served!"

He offered her his arm gravely. They lunched
without knowing what they were eating. The servant came and went without seeming to notice anything. When the meal was finished, they returned
to the drawing-room and resumed their seats on the
couch side by side. Gradually he drew nearer her
and tried to embrace her.

"Be careful, some one might come in."

He whispered: "When can I see you alone to
tell you how I love you?"

She leaned toward him and said softly: "I will
pay you a visit one of these days."

He colored. "My rooms—are—are—very modest."

She smiled: "That makes no difference. I shall
come to see you and not your rooms."

He urged her to tell him when she would come.
She fixed a day in the following week, while he be-
sought her with glowing eyes to hasten the day. She
was amused to see him implore so ardently and
yielded a day at a time. He repeated: "To-morrow,
say—to-morrow." Finally she consented. "Yes, to-
morrow at five o'clock."

He drew a deep breath; then they chatted together
as calmly as if they had known one another for
twenty years. A ring caused them to start; they
separated. She murmured: "It is Laurine."

The child entered, paused in surprise, then ran
toward Duroy clapping her hands, delighted to see
him, and crying: "Ah, 'Bel-Ami!'"

Mme. de Marelle laughed. "Bel-Ami! Laurine has
christened you. It is a pretty name. I shall call you
Bel-Ami, too!"

He took the child upon his knee. At twenty minutes of three he rose to go to the office; at the half-
open door he whispered: "To-morrow, five o'clock."
The young woman replied: "Yes," with a smile and
disappeared.

After he had finished his journalistic work, he tried
to render his apartments more fit to receive his expected visitor. He was well satisfied with the results
of his efforts and retired, lulled to rest by the whistling of the trains. Early the next morning he bought

7 G. de M.—4

a cake and a bottle of Madeira. He spread the collation on his dressing-table which was covered with a napkin. Then he waited. She came at a quarter past five and exclaimed as she entered: "Why, it is nice here. But there were a great many people on the stairs."

He took her in his arms and kissed her hair. An hour and a half later he escorted her to a cab-stand on the Rue de Rome. When she was seated in the cab, he whispered: "Tuesday, at the same hour."

She repeated his words, and as it was night, she kissed him. Then as the cabman started up his horse, she cried: "Adieu, Bel-Ami!" and the old *coupé* rumbled off.

For three weeks Duroy received Mme. de Marelle every two or three days, sometimes in the morning, sometimes in the evening.

As he was awaiting her one afternoon, a noise on the staircase drew him to his door. A child screamed. A man's angry voice cried: "What is the brat howling about?"

A woman's voice replied: "Nicolas has been tripped up on the landing-place by the journalist's sweetheart."

Duroy retreated, for he heard the rustling of skirts. Soon there was a knock at his door, which he opened, and Mme. de Marelle rushed in, crying: "Did you hear?" Georges feigned ignorance of the matter.

"No; what?"

"How they insulted me?"

"Who?"

"Those miserable people below."

"Why, no; what is it? Tell me."

She sobbed and could not speak. He was forced to place her upon his bed and to lay a damp cloth upon her temples. When she grew calmer, anger succeeded her agitation. She wanted Duroy to go downstairs at once, to fight them, to kill them.

He replied: "They are working-people. Just think, it would be necessary to go to court where you would be recognized; one must not compromise oneself with such people."

She said: "What shall we do? I cannot come here again."

He replied: "That is very simple. I will move."

She murmured: "Yes, but that will take some time."

Suddenly she said: "Listen to me, I have found a means; do not worry about it. I will send you a 'little blue' to-morrow morning." She called a telegram a "little blue."

She smiled with delight at her plans, which she would not reveal. She was, however, very much affected as she descended the staircase and leaned with all her strength upon her lover's arm. They met no one.

He was still in bed the following morning when the promised telegram was handed him. Duroy opened it and read:

"Come at five o'clock to Rue de Constantinople, No. 127. Ask for the room rented by Mme. Duroy.   Clo."

At five o'clock precisely he entered a large furnished house and asked the janitor: "Has Mme. Duroy hired a room here?"

"Yes, sir."

"Will you show me to it, if you please?"

The man, accustomed no doubt to situations in which it was necessary to be prudent, looked him straight in the eyes; then selecting a key, he asked: "Are you M. Duroy?"

"Certainly."

He opened a small suite, comprising two rooms on the ground floor.

Duroy thought uneasily: "This will cost a fortune. I shall have to run into debt. She has done a very foolish thing."

The door opened and Clotilde rushed in. She was enchanted. "Is it not fine? There are no stairs to climb; it is on the ground floor! One could come and go through the window without the porter seeing one."

He embraced her nervously, not daring to ask the question that hovered upon his lips. She had placed a large package on the stand in the center of the room. Opening it she took out a tablet of soap, a bottle of Lubin's extract, a sponge, a box of hairpins, a button-hook, and curling-tongs. Then she amused herself by finding places in which to put them.

She talked incessantly as she opened the drawers: "I must bring some linen in order to have a change. We shall each have a key, besides the one at the lodge, in case we should forget ours. I rented the apartments for three months — in your name, of course, for I could not give mine."

Then he asked: "Will you tell me when to pay?"

She replied simply: "It is paid, my dear."

He made a pretense of being angry: "I cannot permit that."

She laid her hand upon his shoulder and said in a supplicatory tone: "Georges, it will give me pleasure to have the nest mine. Say that you do not care, dear Georges," and he yielded. When she had left him, he murmured: "She is kind-hearted, anyway."

Several days later he received a telegram which read:

"My husband is coming home this evening. We shall therefore not meet for a week. What a bore, my dearest!

"Your Clo."

Duroy was startled; he had not realized the fact that Mme. de Marelle was married. He impatiently awaited her husband's departure. One morning he received the following telegram:

"Five o'clock.—Clo."

When they met, she rushed into his arms, kissed him passionately, and asked: "After a while will you take me to dine?"

"Certainly, my darling, wherever you wish to go."

"I should like to go to some restaurant frequented by the working-classes."

They repaired to a wine merchant's where meals were also served. Clotilde's entrance caused a sensation on account of the elegance of her dress. They partook of a ragout of mutton and left that place to enter a ball-room in which she pressed more closely to his side. In fifteen minutes her curiosity was satisfied and he conducted her home. Then followed a series of visits to all sorts of places of amusement. Duroy soon began to tire of those expeditions, for he had exhausted all his resources and all means of obtaining money. In addition to that he owed Forestier a hundred francs, Jacques Rival three hundred, and he was hampered with innumerable petty debts ranging from twenty francs to one hundred sous.

On the fourteenth of December, he was left without a sou in his pocket. As he had often done before, he did not lunch, and spent the afternoon working at the office. At four o'clock he received a telegram from Mme. de Marelle, saying: "Shall we dine together and afterward have a frolic?"

He replied at once: "Impossible to dine," then he added: "But I will expect you at our apartments at nine o'clock." Having sent a boy with the note in order to save the money for a telegram, he tried to think of some way by which he could obtain his evening meal. He waited until all of his associates had gone and when he was alone, he rang for the porter, put his hand in his pocket and said: "Foucart, I have left my purse at home and I have to dine at the Luxembourg. Lend me fifty sous to pay for my cab."

The man handed him three francs and asked:

"Is that enough?"

"Yes, thank you." Taking the coins, Duroy rushed down the staircase and dined at a cookshop.

At nine o'clock, Mme. de Marelle, whom he awaited in the tiny salon, arrived. She wished to take a walk and he objected. His opposition irritated her.

"I shall go alone, then. Adieu!"

Seeing that the situation was becoming grave, he seized her hands and kissed them, saying:

"Pardon me, darling; I am nervous and out of sorts this evening. I have been annoyed by business matters."

Somewhat appeased but still vexed, she replied:

"That does not concern me; I will not be the butt for your ill humor."

He clasped her in his arms and murmured his apologies. Still she persisted in her desire to go out.

"I beseech you, remain here by the fire with me. Say yes."

"No," she replied, "I will not yield to your caprices."

He insisted: "I have a reason, a serious reason—"

"If you will not go with me, I shall go alone. Adieu!"

She disengaged herself from his embrace and fled to the door. He followed her:

"Listen Clo, my little Clo, listen to me—"

She shook her head, evaded his caresses and tried to escape from his encircling arms.

"I have a reason—"

Looking him in the face, she said: "You lie! What is it?"

He colored, and in order to avoid a rupture, confessed in accents of despair: "I have no money!"

She would not believe him until he had turned all his pockets inside out, to prove his words. Then she fell upon his breast: "Oh, my poor darling! Had I known! How did it happen?"

He invented a touching story to this effect: That his father was in straitened circumstances, that he had given him not only his savings, but had run himself into debt.

"I shall have to starve for the next six months."

"Shall I lend you some?" she whispered.

He replied with dignity: "You are very kind, dearest; but do not mention that again; it wounds me."

She murmured: "You will never know how much I love you." On taking leave of him, she asked: "Shall we meet again the day after to-morrow?"

"Certainly."

"At the same time?"

"Yes, my darling."

They parted.

When Duroy opened his bedroom door and fumbled in his vest pocket for a match, he was amazed to find in it a piece of money — a twenty-franc piece! At first he wondered by what miracle it had got there; suddenly it occurred to him that Mme. de Marelle had given him alms! Angry and humiliated, he determined to return it when next they met. The next morning it was late when he awoke; he tried to overcome his hunger. He went out and as he passed the restaurants he could scarcely resist their temptations. At noon he said: "Bah, I shall lunch upon Clotilde's twenty francs; that will not hinder me from returning the money to-morrow."

He ate his lunch, for which he paid two francs
fifty, and on entering the office of "La Vie Française" he repaid the porter the three francs he had
borrowed from him. He worked until seven o'clock,
then he dined, and he continued to draw upon the
twenty francs until only four francs twenty remained.
He decided to say to Mme. de Marelle upon her
arrival:

"I found the twenty-franc piece you slipped into
my pocket. I will not return the money to-day, but
I will repay you when we next meet."

When Madame came, he dared not broach the
delicate subject. They spent the evening together
and appointed their next meeting for Wednesday of
the following week, for Mme. de Marelle had a number of engagements. Duroy continued to accept
money from Clotilde and quieted his conscience by
assuring himself: "I will give it back in a lump. It
is nothing but borrowed money anyway." So he kept
account of all that he received in order to pay it back
some day.

One evening, Mme. de Marelle said to him:
"Would you believe that I have never been to the
Folies-Bergères; will you take me there?"

He hesitated, fearing a meeting with Rachel. Then
he thought: "Bah, I am not married after all. If she
should see me, she would take in the situation and
not accost me. Moreover, we would have a box."

When they entered the hall, it was crowded; with
difficulty they made their way to their seats. Mme.
de Marelle did not look at the stage; she was interested in watching the women who were prome-
nading, and she felt an irresistible desire to touch

them, to see of what those beings were made. Suddenly she said:

"There is a large brunette who stares at us all the time. I think every minute she will speak to us. Have you seen her?"

He replied: "No, you are mistaken."

He told an untruth, for he had noticed the woman, who was no other than Rachel, with anger in her eyes and violent words upon her lips.

Duroy had passed her when he and Mme. de Marelle entered and she had said to him: "Good evening," in a low voice and with a wink which said "I understand." But he had not replied; for fear of being seen by his sweetheart he passed her coldly, disdainfully. The woman, her jealousy aroused, followed the couple and said in a louder key: "Good evening, Georges." He paid no heed to her. Then she was determined to be recognized and she remained near their box, awaiting a favorable moment. When she saw that she was observed by Mme. de Marelle, she touched Duroy's shoulder with the tip of her finger, and said:

"Good evening. How are you?"

But Georges did not turn his head.

She continued: "Have you grown deaf since Thursday?"

Still he did not reply. She laughed angrily and cried:

"Are you dumb, too? Perhaps Madame has your tongue?"

With a furious glance, Duroy then exclaimed: "How dare you accost me? Go along or I will have you arrested."

With flaming eyes, she cried: "Ah, is that so! Because you are with another is no reason that you cannot recognize me. If you had made the least sign of recognition when you passed me, I would not have molested you. You did not even say good evening to me when you met me."

During that tirade Mme. de Marelle in affright opened the door of the box and fled through the crowd seeking an exit. Duroy rushed after her. Rachel, seeing him disappear, cried: "Stop her! she has stolen my lover!"

Two men seized the fugitive by the shoulder, but Duroy, who had caught up with her, bade them desist, and together he and Clotilde reached the street.

They entered a cab. The cabman asked: "Where shall I drive to?" Duroy replied: "Where you will!"

Clotilde sobbed hysterically. Duroy did not know what to say or do. At length he stammered:

"Listen Clo — my dearest Clo, let me explain. It is not my fault. I knew that woman — long ago —"

She raised her head and with the fury of a betrayed woman, she cried disconnectedly: "Ah, you miserable fellow — what a rascal you are! Is it possible? What disgrace, oh, my God! You gave her my money — did you not? I gave him the money — for that woman — oh, the wretch!"

For several moments she seemed to be vainly seeking an epithet more forcible. Suddenly leaning forward she grasped the cabman's sleeve. "Stop!" she cried, and opening the door, she alighted. Georges was about to follow her but she commanded: "I forbid you to follow me," in a voice so loud that the passers-by crowded around her, and Duroy dared not stir for fear of a scandal.

She drew out her purse, and taking two francs fifty from it, she handed it to the cabman, saying aloud: "Here is the money for your hour.   Take that rascal to Rue Boursault at Batignolles!"

The crowd applauded; one man said: "Bravo, little one!" and the cab moved on, followed by the jeers of the bystanders.

CHAPTER VI.

A Step Upward

THE next morning Georges Duroy arose, dressed himself, and determined to have money; he sought Forestier. His friend received him in his study.

"What made you rise so early?" he asked.

"A very serious matter. I have a debt of honor."

"A gaming debt?"

He hesitated, then repeated: "A gaming debt."

"Is it large?"

"Five hundred francs." He only needed two hundred and eighty.

Forestier asked sceptically: "To whom do you owe that amount?"

Duroy did not reply at once. "To—to—a—M. de Carleville."

"Ah, where does he live?"

"Rue—Rue—"

Forestier laughed. "I know the gentleman! If you want twenty francs you can have them, but no more."

Duroy took the gold-piece, called upon more friends, and by five o'clock had collected eighty francs. As he required two hundred more, he kept what he had begged and muttered: "I shall not worry about it. I will pay it when I can."

For two weeks he lived economically, but at the end of that time, the good resolutions he had formed vanished, and one evening he returned to the Folies Bergères in search of Rachel; but the woman was implacable and heaped coarse insults upon him, until he felt his cheeks tingle and he left the hall.

Forestier, out of health and feeble, made Duroy's existence at the office insupportable. The latter did not reply to his rude remarks, but determined to be avenged. He called upon Mme. Forestier. He found her reclining upon a couch, reading. She held out her hand without rising and said: "Good morning, Bel-Ami!"

"Why do you call me by that name?"

She replied with a smile: "I saw Mme. de Marelle last week and I know what they have christened you at her house."

He took a seat near his hostess and glanced at her curiously; she was a charming blonde, fair and plump, made for caresses, and he thought: "She is certainly nicer than the other one." He did not doubt that he would only have to extend his hand in order to gather the fruit. As he gazed upon her she chided him for his neglect of her.

He replied: "I did not come because it was for the best —"

"How? Why?"

"Why? Can you not guess?"

"No!"

"Because I loved you; a little, only a little, and I did not wish to love you any more."

She did not seem surprised, nor flattered; she smiled indifferently and replied calmly: "Oh, you can come just the same; no one loves me long."

"Why not?"

"Because it is useless, and I tell them so at once. If you had confessed your fears to me sooner, I would have reassured you. My dear friend, a man in love is not only foolish but dangerous. I cease all intercourse with people who love me or pretend to; firstly, because they bore me, and secondly, because I look upon them with dread, as I would upon a mad dog. I know that your love is only a kind of appetite; while with me it would be a communion of souls. Now, look me in the face—" she no longer smiled. "I will never be your sweetheart; it is therefore useless for you to persist in your efforts. And now that I have explained, shall we be friends?"

He knew that that sentence was irrevocable, and delighted to be able to form such an alliance as she proposed, he extended both hands, saying:

"I am yours, Madame, to do with as you will."

He kissed her hands and raising his head said: "If I had found a woman like you, how gladly would I have married her."

She was touched by those words, and in a soft voice, placing her hand upon his arm, she said: "I am going to begin my offices at once. You are not diplomatic—" she hesitated. "May I speak freely?"

"Yes."

"Call upon Mme. Walter who has taken a fancy to you. But be guarded as to your compliments, for she is virtuous. You will make a better impression there by being careful in your remarks. I know that your position at the office is unsatisfactory, but do not worry; all their employees are treated alike."

He said: "Thanks; you are an angel — a guardian angel."

As he took his leave, he asked again: "Are we friends — is it settled?"

"It is."

Having observed the effect of his last compliment, he said: "If you ever become a widow, I have put in my application!" Then he left the room hastily in order not to allow her time to be angry.

Duroy did not like to call on Mme. Walter, for he had never been invited, and he did not wish to commit a breach of etiquette. The manager had been kind to him, appreciated his services, employed him to do difficult work, why should he not profit by that show of favor to call at his house? One day, therefore, he repaired to the market and bought twenty-five pears. Having carefully arranged them in a basket to make them appear as if they came from a distance he took them to Mme. Walter's door with his card on which was inscribed:

"Georges Duroy begs Mme. Walter to accept the fruit which he received this morning from Normandy."

The following day he found in his letter-box at the office an envelope containing Mme. Walter's card on which was written:

"Mme. Walter thanks M. Georges Duroy very much, and is at home on Saturdays."

The next Saturday he called. M. Walter lived on Boulevard Malesherbes in a double house which he owned. The reception-rooms were on the first floor. In the antechamber were two footmen; one took Duroy's overcoat, the other his cane, put it aside, opened a door and announced the visitor's name. In the large mirror in the apartment Duroy could see the reflection of people seated in another room. He passed through two drawing-rooms and entered a small boudoir in which four ladies were gathered around a tea-table. Notwithstanding the assurance he had gained during his life in Paris, and especially since he had been thrown in contact with so many noted personages, Duroy felt abashed. He stammered:

"Madame, I took the liberty."

The mistress of the house extended her hand and said to him: "You are very kind, M. Duroy, to come to see me." She pointed to a chair. The ladies chatted on. Visitors came and went. Mme. Walter noticed that Duroy said nothing, that no one addressed him, that he seemed disconcerted, and she drew him into the conversation which dealt with the admission of a certain M. Linet to the Academy. When Duroy had taken his leave, one of the ladies said: "How odd he is! Who is he?"

Mme. Walter replied: "One of our reporters; he only occupies a minor position, but I think he will advance rapidly."

In the meantime, while he was being discussed, Duroy walked gaily down Boulevard Malesherbes.

7 G. de M.—5

The following week he was appointed editor of the "Echoes," and invited to dine at Mme. Walter's. The "Echoes" were, M. Walter said, the very pith of the paper. Everything and everybody should be remembered, all countries, all professions, Paris and the provinces, the army, the arts, the clergy, the schools, the rulers, and the courtiers. The man at the head of that department should be wide awake, always on his guard, quick to judge of what was best to be said and best to be omitted, to divine what would please the public and to present it well. Duroy was just the man for the place.

He was enjoying the fact of his promotion, when he received an engraved card which read:

"M. and Mme. Walter request the pleasure of M. Georges Duroy's company at dinner on Thursday, January 20."

He was so delighted that he kissed the invitation as if it had been a love-letter.

Then he sought the cashier to settle the important question of his salary. At first twelve hundred francs were allowed Duroy, who intended to save a large share of the money. He was busy two days getting settled in his new position, in a large room, one end of which he occupied, and the other end of which was allotted to Boisrenard, who worked with him.

The day of the dinner-party he left the office in good season, in order to have time to dress, and was walking along Rue de Londres when he saw before him a form which resembled Mme. de Marelle's. He felt his cheeks glow and his heart throb. He crossed the street in order to see the lady's face; he was mistaken, and breathed more freely. He had often wondered what he should do if he met Clotilde face to face. Should he bow to her or pretend not to see her? "I should not see her," thought he.

When Duroy entered his rooms he thought: "I must change my apartments; these will not do any longer." He felt both nervous and gay, and said aloud to himself: "I must write to my father." Occasionally he wrote home, and his letters always delighted his old parents. As. he tied his cravat at the mirror he repeated: "I must write home to-morrow. If my father could see me this evening in the house to which I am going, he would be surprised. Sacristi, I shall soon give a dinner which has never been equaled!"

Then he recalled his old home, the faces of his father and mother. He saw them seated at their homely board, eating their soup. He remembered every wrinkle on their old faces, every movement of their hands and heads; he even knew what they said to each other every evening as they supped. He thought: "I will go to see them some day." His toilette completed, he extinguished his light and descended the stairs.

On reaching his destination, he boldly entered the antechamber, lighted by bronze lamps, and gave his cane and his overcoat to the two lackeys who approached him. All the salons were lighted. Mme. Walter received in the second, the largest. She greeted Duroy with a charming smile, and he shook hands with two men who arrived after him, M. Firmin and M. Laroche-Mathieu; the latter had especial authority at the office on account of his influence in the chamber of deputies.

Then the Forestiers arrived, Madeleine looking charming in pink. Charles had become very much emaciated and coughed incessantly.

Norbert de Varenne and Jacques Rival came together. A door opened at the end of the room, and M. Walter entered with two tall young girls of sixteen and seventeen; one plain, the other pretty. Duroy knew that the manager was a *paterfamilias,* but he was astonished. He had thought of the manager's daughters as one thinks of a distant country one will never see. Then, too, he had fancied them children, and he saw women. They shook hands upon being introduced and seated themselves at a table set apart for them. One of the guests had not arrived, and that embarrassing silence which precedes dinners in general reigned supreme.

Duroy happening to glance at the walls, M. Walter said: "You are looking at my pictures? I will show them all to you." And he took a lamp that they might distinguish all the details. There were landscapes by Guillemet; "A Visit to the Hospital," by Gervex; "A Widow," by Bouguereau; "An Execution," by Jean Paul Laurens, and many others.

Duroy exclaimed: "Charming, charming, char—" but stopped short on hearing behind him the voice of Mme. de Marelle who had just entered. M. Walter continued to exhibit and explain his pictures; but Duroy saw nothing—heard without comprehending. Mme. de Marelle was there, behind him. What should he do? If he greeted her, might she not turn her back upon him or utter some insulting remark?

If he did not approach her, what would people think?
He was so ill at ease that at one time he thought he
should feign indisposition and return home.

The pictures had all been exhibited. M. Walter
placed the lamp on the table and greeted the last
arrival, while Duroy recommenced alone an examina-
tion of the canvas, as if he could not tear himself
away. What should he do? He heard their voices
and their conversation. Mme. Forestier called him;
he hastened toward her. It was to introduce him to
a friend who was on the point of giving a *fête,* and
who wanted a description of it in "La Vie Française."

He stammered: "Certainly, Madame, certainly."

Madame de Marelle was very near him; he dared
not turn to go away. Suddenly to his amazement,
she exclaimed: "Good evening, Bel-Ami; do you not
remember me?"

He turned upon his heel hastily; she stood before
him smiling, her eyes overflowing with roguishness
and affection. She offered him her hand; he took it
doubtfully, fearing some perfidy. She continued
calmly: "What has become of you? One never
sees you!"

Not having regained his self-possession, he murmured: "I have had a great deal to do, Madame, a
great deal to do. M. Walter has given me another
position and the duties are very arduous."

"I know, but that is no excuse for forgetting your
friends."

Their conversation was interrupted by the entrance
of a large woman, *décolletée,* with red arms. red
cheeks, and attired in gay colors. As she was re-

ceived with effusion, Duroy asked Mme. Forestier:
"Who is that person?"

"Viscountess de Percemur, whose *nom de plume*
is 'Patte Blanche.'"

He was surprised and with difficulty restrained a
burst of laughter.

"Patte Blanche? I fancied her a young woman
like you. Is that Patte Blanche? Ah, she is handsome, very handsome!"

A servant appeared at the door and announced:
"Madame is served."

Duroy was placed between the manager's plain
daughter, Mlle. Rose, and Mme. de Marelle. The
proximity of the latter embarrassed him somewhat,
although she appeared at ease and conversed with her
usual spirit. Gradually, however, his assurance returned, and before the meal was over, he knew that
their relations would be renewed. Wishing, too, to
be polite to his employer's daughter, he addressed
her from time to time. She responded as her mother
would have done, without any hesitation as to what
she should say. At M. Walter's right sat Viscountess
de Percemur, and Duroy, looking at her with a smile,
asked Mme. de Marelle in a low voice: "Do you
know the one who signs herself 'Domino Rose'?"

"Yes, perfectly; Baroness de Livar."

"Is she like the Countess?"

"No. But she is just as comical. She is sixty
years old, has false curls and teeth, wit of the time
of the Restoration, and toilettes of the same period."

When the guests returned to the drawing-room,
Duroy asked Mme. de Marelle: "May I escort you
home?"

"No."

"Why not?"

"Because M. Laroche-Mathieu, who is my neighbor, leaves me at my door every time that I dine here."

"When shall I see you again?"

"Lunch with me to-morrow."

They parted without another word. Duroy did not remain late; as he descended the staircase, he met Norbert de Varenne, who was likewise going away. The old poet took his arm; fearing no rivalry on the newspaper, their work being essentially different, he was very friendly to the young man.

"Shall we walk along together?"

"I shall be pleased to," replied Duroy.

The streets were almost deserted that night. At first the two men did not speak. Then Duroy, in order to make some remark, said: "That M. Laroche-Mathieu looks very intelligent."

The old poet murmured: "Do you think so?"

The younger man hesitated in surprise: "Why, yes! Is he not considered one of the most capable men in the Chamber?"

"That may be. In a kingdom of blind men the blind are kings. All those people are divided between money and politics; they are pedants to whom it is impossible to speak of anything that is familiar to us. Ah, it is difficult to find a man who is liberal in his ideas! I have known several, they are dead. Still, what difference does a little more or a little less genius make, since all must come to an end?" He paused, and Duroy said with a smile:

"You are gloomy to-night, sir!"

The poet replied: "I always am, my child; you will be too in a few years. While one is climbing the ladder, one sees the top and feels hopeful; but when one has reached that summit, one sees the descent and the end which is death. It is slow work ascending, but one descends rapidly. At your age one is joyous; one hopes for many things which never come to pass. At mine, one expects nothing but death."

Duroy laughed: "Egad, you make me shudder."

Norbert de Varenne continued: "You do not understand me now, but later on you will remember what I have told you. We breathe, sleep, drink, eat, work, and then die! The end of life is death. What do you long for? Love? A few kisses and you will be powerless. Money? What for? To gratify your desires. Glory? What comes after it all? Death! Death alone is certain."

He stopped, took Duroy by his coat collar and said slowly: "Ponder upon all that, young man; think it over for days, months, and years, and you will see life from a different standpoint. I am a lonely, old man. I have neither father, mother, brother, sister, wife, children, nor God. I have only poetry. Marry, my friend; you do not know what it is to live alone at my age. It is so lonesome. I seem to have no one upon earth. When one is old it is a comfort to have children."

When they reached Rue de Bourgogne, the poet halted before a high house, rang the bell, pressed Duroy's hand and said: "Forget what I have said to you, young man, and live according to your age. Adieu!" With those words he disappeared in the dark corridor.

Duroy felt somewhat depressed on leaving Varenne, but on his way a perfumed damsel passed
by him and recalled to his mind his reconciliation
with Mme. de Marelle. How delightful was the
realization of one's hopes!

The next morning he arrived at his lady-love's
door somewhat early; she welcomed him as if there
had been no rupture, and said as she kissed him:

"You do not know how annoyed I am, my beloved; I anticipated a delightful honeymoon and now
my husband has come home for six weeks. But I
could not let so long a time go by without seeing
you, especially after our little disagreement, and this
is how I have arranged matters: Come to dinner
Monday. I will introduce you to M. de Marelle, I
have already spoken of you to him."

Duroy hesitated in perplexity; he feared he might
betray something by a word, a glance. He stammered:

"No, I would rather not meet your husband."

"Why not? How absurd! Such things happen
every day. I did not think you so foolish."

"Very well, I will come to dinner Monday."

"To make it more pleasant, I will have the
Forestiers, though I do not like to receive company
at home."

On Monday as he ascended Mme. de Marelle's
staircase, he felt strangely troubled; not that he disliked to take her husband's hand, drink his wine, and
eat his bread, but he dreaded something, he knew
not what. He was ushered into the salon and he
waited as usual. Then the door opened, and a tall
man with a white beard, grave and precise, advanced
toward him and said courteously:

"My wife has often spoken of you, sir; I am charmed to make your acquaintance."

Duroy tried to appear cordial and shook his host's proffered hand with exaggerated energy. M. de Marelle put a log upon the fire and asked:

"Have you been engaged in journalism a long time?"

Duroy replied: "Only a few months." His embarrassment wearing off, he began to consider the situation very amusing. He gazed at M. de Marelle, serious and dignified, and felt a desire to laugh aloud. At that moment Mme. de Marelle entered and approached Duroy, who in the presence of her husband dared not kiss her hand. Laurine entered next, and offered her brow to Georges. Her mother said to her:

"You do not call M. Duroy Bel-Ami to-day."

The child blushed as if it were a gross indiscretion to reveal her secret.

When the Forestiers arrived, Duroy was startled at Charles's appearance. He had grown thinner and paler in a week and coughed incessantly; he said they would leave for Cannes on the following Thursday at the doctor's orders. They did not stay late; after they had left, Duroy said, with a shake of his head:

"He will not live long."

Mme. de Marelle replied calmly: "No, he is doomed! He was a lucky man to obtain such a wife."

Duroy asked: "Does she help him very much?"

"She does all the work; she is well posted on every subject, and she always gains her point, as she wants it, and when she wants it! Oh, she is as maneuvering as anyone! She is a treasure to a man who wishes to succeed."

Georges replied: "She will marry very soon again, I have no doubt."

"Yes! I should not even be surprised if she had some one in view — a deputy! but I do not know anything about it."

M. de Marelle said impatiently: "You infer so many things that I do not like! We should never interfere in the affairs of others. Everyone should make that a rule."

Duroy took his leave with a heavy heart. The next day he called on the Forestiers, and found them in the midst of packing. Charles lay upon a sofa and repeated: "I should have gone a month ago." Then he proceeded to give Duroy innumerable orders, although everything had been arranged with M. Walter. When Georges left him, he pressed his comrade's hand and said:

"Well, old fellow, we shall soon meet again."

Mme. Forestier accompanied him to the door and he reminded her of their compact. "We are friends and allies, are we not? If you should require my services in any way, do not hesitate to call upon me. Send me a dispatch or a letter and I will obey."

She murmured: "Thank you, I shall not forget."

As Duroy descended the staircase, he met M. de Vaudrec ascending. The Count seemed sad — perhaps at the approaching departure.

The journalist bowed, the Count returned his salutation courteously but somewhat haughtily.

On Thursday evening the Forestiers left town.

CHAPTER VII.

A Duel with an End

CHARLES'S absence gave Duroy a more important position on "La Vie Française." Only one matter arose to annoy him, otherwise his sky was cloudless.

An insignificant paper, "La Plume," attacked him constantly, or rather attacked the editor of the "Echoes" of "La Vie Française."

Jacques Rival said to him one day: "You are very forbearing."

"What should I do? It is no direct attack."

But, one afternoon when he entered the office, Boisrenard handed him a number of "La Plume."

"See, here is another unpleasant remark for you."

"Relative to what?"

"To the arrest of one Dame Aubert."

Georges took the paper and read a scathing personal denunciation. Duroy, it seems, had written an item claiming that Dame Aubert who, as the editor of "La Plume," claimed, had been put under arrest, was a myth. The latter retaliated by accusing Duroy of receiving bribes and of suppressing matter that should be published.

As Saint-Potin entered, Duroy asked him: "Have you seen the paragraph in 'La Plume'?"

"Yes, and I have just come from Dame Aubert's; she is no myth, but she has not been arrested; that report has no foundation."

Duroy went at once to M. Walter's office. After hearing the case, the manager bade him go to the woman's house himself, find out the details, and reply to the article.

Duroy set out upon his errand and on his return to the office, wrote the following:

"An anonymous writer in 'La Plume' is trying to pick a quarrel with me on the subject of an old woman who, he claims, was arrested for disorderly conduct, which I deny. I have myself seen Dame Aubert, who is sixty years old at least; she told me the particulars of her dispute with a butcher as to the weight of some cutlets, which dispute necessitated an explanation before a magistrate. That is the whole truth in a nutshell. As for the other insinuations I scorn them. One never should reply to such things, moreover, when they are written under a mask.　　　　　GEORGES DUROY."

M. Walter and Jacques Rival considered that sufficient, and it was decided that it should be published in that day's issue.

Duroy returned home rather agitated and uneasy. What would this opponent reply? Who was he? Why that attack? He passed a restless night. When he re-read his article in the paper the next morning, he thought it more aggressive in print than it was in writing. He might, it seemed to him, have softened certain terms. He was excited all day and feverish

during the night. He rose early to obtain an issue
of "La Plume" which should contain the reply to his
note. He ran his eyes over the columns and at first
saw nothing. He was beginning to breathe more
freely when these words met his eye:

"M. Duroy of 'La Vie Française' gives us the lie! In doing so,
he lies. He owns, however, that a woman named Aubert exists, and
that she was taken before a magistrate by an agent. Two words
only remain to be added to the word 'agent,' which are 'of morals'
and all is told. But the consciences of certain journalists are on a par
with their talents.   I sign myself,
                                   "Louis Langremont."

Georges's heart throbbed violently, and he returned
home in order to dress himself. He had been insulted
and in such a manner that it was impossible to hesitate. Why had he been insulted? For nothing! On
account of an old woman who had quarreled with
her butcher.

He dressed hastily and repaired to M. Walter's
house, although it was scarcely eight o'clock. M.
Walter was reading "La Plume."

"Well," he said gravely, on perceiving Duroy, "you
cannot let that pass." The young man did not reply.

The manager continued: "Go at once in search
of Rival, who will look after your interests."

Duroy stammered several vague words and set out
for Rival's house. Jacques was still in bed, but he
rose when the bell rang, and having read the insulting paragraph, said: "Whom would you like to
have besides me?"

"I do not know."

"Boisrenard?"

"Yes."

"Are you a good swordsman?"

"No."

"A good shot?"

"I have used a pistol a good deal."

"Good! Come and exercise while I attend to everything. Wait a moment."

He entered his dressing-room and soon reappeared, washed, shaven, and presentable.

"Come with me," said he. He lived on the ground floor, and he led Duroy into a cellar converted into a room for the practice of fencing and shooting. He produced a pair of pistols and began to give his orders as briefly as if they were on the dueling ground. He was well satisfied with Duroy's use of the weapons, and told him to remain there and practice until noon, when he would return to take him to lunch and tell him the result of his mission. Left to his own devices, Duroy aimed at the target several times and then sat down to reflect.

Such affairs were abominable anyway! What would a respectable man gain by risking his life? And he recalled Norbert de Varenne's remarks, made to him a short while before. "He was right!" he declared aloud. It was gloomy in that cellar, as gloomy as in a tomb. What o'clock was it? The time dragged slowly on. Suddenly he heard footsteps, voices, and Jacques Rival reappeared accompanied by Boisrenard. The former cried on perceiving Duroy: "All is settled!"

Duroy thought the matter had terminated with a letter of apology; his heart gave a bound and he stammered: "Ah—thank you!"

Rival continued: "M. Langremont has accepted every condition. Twenty-five paces, fire when the pistol is leveled and the order given." Then he added: "Now let us lunch; it is past twelve o'clock."

They repaired to a neighboring restaurant. Duroy was silent. He ate that they might not think he was frightened, and went in the afternoon with Boisrenard to the office, where he worked in an absent, mechanical manner. Before leaving, Jacques Rival shook hands with him and warned him that he and Boisrenard would call for him in a carriage the next morning at seven o'clock to repair to the wood at Vesinet, where the meeting was to take place.

All had been settled without his saying a word, giving his opinion, accepting or refusing, with such rapidity that his brain whirled and he scarcely knew what was taking place. He returned home about nine o'clock in the evening after having dined with Boisrenard, who had not left him all day. When he was alone, he paced the floor; he was too confused to think. One thought alone filled his mind and that was: a duel to-morrow! He sat down and began to meditate. He had thrown upon his table his adversary's card brought him by Rival. He read it for the twentieth time that day:

"Louis Langremont,
"176 Rue Montmartre."

Nothing more! Who was the man? How old was he? How tall? How did he look? How odious that a total stranger should without rhyme or reason, out of pure caprice, annoy him thus on account of

an old woman's quarrel with her butcher! He said
aloud: "The brute!" and glared angrily at the card.

He began to feel nervous; the sound of his voice
made him start; he drank a glass of water and laid
down. He turned from his right side to his left uneasily. He was thirsty; he rose, he felt restless·
"Am I afraid?" he asked himself.

Why did his heart palpitate so wildly at the
slightest sound? He began to reason philosophically
on the possibility of being afraid. No, certainly he
was not, since he was ready to fight. Still he felt
so deeply moved that he wondered if one could be
afraid in spite of oneself. What would happen if
that state of things should exist? If he should tremble or lose his presence of mind? He lighted his
candle and looked in the glass; he scarcely recognized his own face, it was so changed.

Suddenly he thought: "To-morrow at this time
I may be dead." He turned to his couch and saw
himself stretched lifeless upon it. He hastened to the
window and opened it; but the night air was so
chilly that he closed it, lighted a fire, and began to
pace the floor once more, saying mechanically: "I
must be more composed. I will write to my parents,
in case of accident." He took a sheet of paper and
after several attempts began:

"MY DEAR FATHER AND MOTHER:
"At daybreak I am going to fight a duel, and as something
might happen—"

He could write no more, he rose with a shudder.
It seemed to him that notwithstanding his efforts, he
would not have the strength necessary to face the

7 G. de M.—6

meeting. He wondered if his adversary had ever fought before; if he were known? He had never heard his name. However, if he had not been a remarkable shot, he would not have accepted that dangerous weapon without hesitation. He ground his teeth to prevent his crying aloud. Suddenly he remembered that he had a bottle of brandy; he fetched it from the cupboard and soon emptied it. Now he felt his blood course more warmly through his veins. "I have found a means," said he.

Day broke. He began to dress; when his heart failed him, he took more brandy. At length there was a knock at the door. His friends had come; they were wrapped in furs. After shaking hands, Rival said: "It is as cold as Siberia. Is all well?"

"Yes."

"Are you calm?"

"Very calm."

"Have you eaten and drunk something?"

"I do not need anything."

They descended the stairs. A gentleman was seated in the carriage. Rival said: "Dr. Le Brument." Duroy shook hands with him and stammered: "Thank you," as he entered the carriage. Jacques Rival and Boisrenard followed him, and the coachman drove off. He knew where to go.

The conversation flagged, although the doctor related a number of anecdotes. Rival alone replied to him. Duroy tried to appear self-possessed, but he was haunted continually by the fear of showing his feelings or of losing his self-possession. Rival addressed him, saying: "I took the pistols to Gastine Renette. He loaded them. The box is sealed."

Duroy replied mechanically: "Thank you."

Then Rival proceeded to give him minute directions, that he might make no mistakes. Duroy repeated those directions as children learn their lessons in order to impress them upon his memory. As he muttered the phrases over and over, he almost prayed that some accident might happen to the carriage; if he could only break his leg!

At the end of a glade he saw a carriage standing and four gentlemen stamping their feet in order to keep them warm, and he was obliged to gasp in order to get breath. Rival and Boisrenard alighted first, then the doctor and the combatant.

Rival took the box of pistols, and with Boisrenard approached the two strangers, who were advancing toward them. Duroy saw them greet one another ceremoniously, then walk through the glade together as they counted the paces.

Dr. Le Brument asked Duroy: "Do you feel well? Do you not want anything?"

"Nothing, thank you." It seemed to him that he was asleep, that he was dreaming. Was he afraid? He did not know. Jacques Rival returned and said in a low voice: "All is ready. Fortune has favored us in the drawing of the pistols." That was a matter of indifference to Duroy. They helped him off with his overcoat, led him to the ground set apart for the duel, and gave him his pistol. Before him stood a man, short, stout, and bald, who wore glasses. That was his adversary. A voice broke the silence—a voice which came from afar: "Are you ready, sirs?"

Georges cried: "Yes."

The same voice commanded: "Fire!"

Duroy heard nothing more, saw nothing more; he only knew that he raised his arm and pressed with all his strength upon the trigger. Soon he saw a little smoke before him; his opponent was still standing in the same position, and there was a small white cloud above his head. They had both fired. All was over! His second and the doctor felt him, unbuttoned his garments, and asked anxiously: "Are you wounded?" He replied: "No, I think not."

Langremont was not wounded either, and Jacques Rival muttered discontentedly: "That is always the way with those cursed pistols, one either misses or kills one's opponent."

Duroy was paralyzed with surprise and joy. All was over! He felt that he could fight the entire universe. All was over! What bliss! He felt brave enough to provoke anyone. The seconds consulted several moments, then the duelists and their friends entered the carriages and drove off. When the official report was drawn up, it was handed to Duroy who was to insert it in the "Echoes." He was surprised to find that two balls had been fired.

He said to Rival: "We only fired once!"

The latter smiled: "Yes—once—once each—that makes twice!"

And Duroy, satisfied with that explanation, asked no more questions. M. Walter embraced him.

"Bravo! you have defended the colors of 'La Vie Française'! Bravo!"

The following day at eleven o'clock in the forenoon, Duroy received a telegram:

"My God! I have been frightened. Come at once to Rue de Constantinople that I may embrace you, my love. How brave you are. I adore you. CLO."

He repaired to the place appointed, and Mme. de Marelle rushed into his arms, covering him with kisses.

"Oh, my darling, if you only knew how I felt when I read the morning papers! Tell me, tell me all about it."

Duroy was obliged to give her a detailed account.

"You must have had a terrible night before the duel!"

"Why, no; I slept very well."

"I should not have closed my eyes. Tell me what took place on the ground."

Forthwith he proceeded to give her a graphic description of the duel. When he had concluded, she said to him: "I cannot live without you! I must see you, and with my husband in Paris it is not very convenient. I often have an hour early in the morning when I could come and embrace you, but I cannot enter that horrible house of yours! What can we do?"

He asked abruptly: "How much do you pay here?"

"One hundred francs a month."

"Very well, I will take the apartments on my own account, and I will move at once. Mine are not suitable anyway for me now."

She thought a moment and then replied: "No I do not want you to."

He asked in surprise: "Why not?"

"Because!"

"That is no reason. These rooms suit me very well. I am here; I shall remain." He laughed. "Moreover, they were hired in my name!"

But she persisted: "No, no, I do not wish you to."

"Why not, then?"

She whispered softly, tenderly: "Because you would bring others here, and I do not wish you to."

Indignantly he cried: "Never, I promise you!"

"You would do so in spite of your promise."

"I swear I will not."

"Truly?"

"Truly—upon my word of honor. This is our nest—ours alone!"

She embraced him in a transport of delight. "Then I agree, my dearest. But if you deceive me once—just once, that will end all between us forever."

He protested, and it was agreed that he should settle in the rooms that same day. She said to him:

"You must dine with us Sunday. My husband thinks you charming."

He was flattered. "Indeed?"

"Yes, you have made a conquest. Did you not tell me that your home was in the country?"

"Yes; why?"

"Then you know something about agriculture?"

"Yes."

"Very well; talk to him of gardening and crops; he enjoys those subjects."

"All right. I shall not forget."

She left him, after lavishing upon him innumerable caresses.

CHAPTER VIII.

DEATH AND A PROPOSAL

DUROY moved his effects to the apartments in Rue de Constantinople. Two or three times a week, Mme. de Marelle paid him visits. Duroy, to counterbalance them, dined at her house every Thursday, and delighted her husband by talking agriculture to him.

It was almost the end of February. Duroy was free from care. One night, when he returned home, he found a letter under his door. He examined the postmark; it was from Cannes. Having opened it, he read:

"CANNES, Villa Jolie.

"DEAR SIR AND FRIEND: You told me, did you not, that I could count upon you at any time? Very well. I have a favor to ask of you; it is to come and help me — not to leave me alone during Charles's last moments. He may not live through the week, although he is not confined to his bed, but the doctor has warned me. I have not the strength nor the courage to see that agony day and night, and I think with terror of the approaching end. I can only ask such a thing of you, for my husband has no relatives. You were his comrade; he helped you to your position; come, I beg of you; I have no one else to ask. Your friend,

"MADELEINE FORESTIER."

(87)

Georges murmured: "Certainly I will go. Poor Charles!"

The manager, to whom he communicated the contents of that letter, grumblingly gave his consent. He repeated: "But return speedily, you are indispensable to us."

Georges Duroy left for Cannes the next day by the seven o'clock express, after having warned Mme. de Marelle by telegram. He arrived the following day at four o'clock in the afternoon. A *commissionnaire* conducted him to Villa Jolie. The house was small and low, and of the Italian style of architecture.

A servant opened the door and cried: "Oh, sir, Madame is awaiting you patiently."

Duroy asked: "How is your master?"

"Not very well, sir. He will not be here long."

The floor of the drawing-room which the young man entered was covered with a Persian rug; the large windows looked upon the village and the sea.

Duroy murmured: "How cozy it is here! Where the deuce do they get the money from?"

The rustling of a gown caused him to turn. Mme. Forestier extended both her hands, saying:

"How kind of you to come."

She was a trifle paler and thinner, but still as bright as ever, and perhaps prettier for being more delicate. She whispered: "It is terrible—he knows he cannot be saved and he tyrannizes over me. I have told him of your arrival. But where is your trunk?"

Duroy replied: "I left it at the station, not knowing which hotel you would advise me to stop at, in order to be near you."

She hesitated, then said: "You must stop here, at the villa. Your chamber is ready. He might die any moment, and if it should come in the night, I would be alone. I will send for your luggage."

He bowed. "As you will."

"Now, let us go upstairs," said she; he followed her. She opened a door on the first floor, and Duroy saw a form near a window, seated in an easy-chair, and wrapped in coverlets. He divined that it was his friend, though he scarcely recognized him. Forestier raised his hand slowly and with difficulty, saying:

"You are here; you have come to see me die. I am much obliged."

Duroy forced a smile. "To see you die? That would not be a very pleasant sight, and I would not choose that occasion on which to visit Cannes. I came here to rest."

"Sit down," said Forestier, and he bowed his head as if deep in hopeless meditation. Seeing that he did not speak, his wife approached the window and pointing to the horizon, said, "Look at that? Is it not beautiful?"

In spite of himself Duroy felt the grandeur of the closing day and exclaimed: "Yes, indeed, it is magnificent."

Forestier raised his head and said to his wife: "Give me more air."

She replied: "You must be careful; it is late, the sun is setting; you will catch more cold and that would be a serious thing in your condition."

He made a feeble gesture of anger with his right hand, and said: "I tell you I am suffocating! What difference does it make if I die a day sooner or later, since I must die?"

She opened the window wide. The air was soft and balmy. Forestier inhaled it in feverish gasps. He grasped the arms of his chair and said in a low voice: "Shut the window. I would rather die in a cellar."

His wife slowly closed the window, then leaned her brow against the pane and looked out. Duroy, ill at ease, wished to converse with the invalid to reassure him, but he could think of no words of comfort. He stammered: "Have you not been better since you are here?"

His friend shrugged his shoulders impatiently: "You will see very soon." And he bowed his head again.

Duroy continued: "At home it is still wintry. It snows, hails, rains, and is so dark that they have to light the lamps at three o'clock in the afternoon."

Forestier asked: "Is there anything new at the office?"

"Nothing. They have taken little Lacrin of the 'Voltaire,' to fill your place, but he is incapable. It is time you came back."

The invalid muttered: "I? I will soon be writing under six feet of sod." A long silence ensued.

Mme. Forestier did not stir; she stood with her back to the room, her face toward the window. At length Forestier broke the silence in a gasping voice, heartrending to listen to: "How many more sunsets shall I see — eight — ten — fifteen — twenty — or perhaps thirty — no more. You have more time, you two — as for me — all is at an end. And everything will go on when I am gone as if I were here." He paused a few moments, then continued: "Everything that I see reminds me that I shall not see them long. It is horrible. I shall no longer see the smallest objects—the glasses—the dishes—the beds on which we rest—the carriages. It is fine to drive in the evening. How I loved all that."

Again Norbert de Varenne's words occurred to Duroy. The room grew dark. Forestier asked irritably:

"Are we to have no lamp to-night? That is what is called caring for an invalid!"

The form outlined against the window disappeared and an electric bell was heard to ring. A servant soon entered and placed a lamp upon the mantelpiece. Mme. Forestier asked her husband: "Do you wish to retire, or will you go downstairs to dinner?"

"I will go down to dinner."

The meal seemed to Duroy interminable, for there was no conversation, only the ticking of a clock broke the silence. When they had finished, Duroy, pleading fatigue, retired to his room and tried in vain to invent some pretext for returning home as quickly as possible. He consoled himself by saying: "Perhaps it will not be for long."

The next morning Georges rose early and strolled down to the beach. When he returned the servant said to him: "Monsieur has asked for you two or three times. Will you go upstairs?"

He ascended the stairs. Forestier appeared to be asleep in a chair; his wife, reclining upon a couch, was reading. The invalid raised his head. Duroy asked:

"Well, how are you? You look better this morning."

Forestier murmured: "Yes, I am better and stronger. Lunch as hastily as you can with Madeleine, because we are going to take a drive."

When Mme. Forestier was alone with Duroy, she said to him: "You see, to-day he thinks he is better! He is making plans for to-morrow. We are now going to Gulf Juan to buy pottery for our rooms in Paris. He is determined to go, but he cannot stand the jolting on the road."

The carriage arrived, Forestier descended the stairs, step by step, supported by his servant. When he saw the closed landau, he wanted it uncovered. His wife opposed him: "It is sheer madness! You will take cold."

He persisted: "No, I am going to be better, I know it."

They first drove along a shady road and then took the road by the sea. Forestier explained the different points of interest. Finally they arrived at a pavilion over which were these words: "Gulf Juan Art Pottery," and the carriage drew up at the door. Forestier wanted to buy a vase to put on his bookcase. As he could not leave the carriage, they brought the pieces to him one by one. It took him a long time to choose, consulting his wife and Duroy: "You know it is for my study. From my easy-chair I can see it constantly. I prefer the ancient form — the Greek."

At length he made his choice. "I shall return to Paris in a few days," said he.

On their way home along the gulf a cool breeze suddenly sprang up, and the invalid began to cough. At first it was nothing, only a slight attack, but it grew worse and turned to a sort of hiccough — a rattle. Forestier choked, and every time he tried to breathe he coughed violently. Nothing quieted him. He had to be carried from the landau to his room. The heat of the bed did not stop the attack, which lasted until midnight. The first words the sick man uttered were to ask for a barber, for he insisted on being shaved every morning. He rose to be shaved, but was obliged to go to bed at once, and began to breathe so painfully that Mme. Forestier in affright woke Duroy and asked him to fetch the doctor. He returned almost immediately with Dr. Gavant who prescribed for the sick man. When the journalist asked him his opinion, he said: "It is the final stage. He will be dead to-morrow morning. Prepare that poor, young wife and send for a priest. I can do nothing more. However, I am entirely at your disposal."

Duroy went to Mme. Forestier. "He is going to die. The doctor advises me to send for a priest. What will you do?"

She hesitated a moment and then said slowly:

"I will go and tell him that the curé wishes to see him. Will you be kind enough to procure one who will require nothing but the confession, and who will not make much fuss?"

The young man brought with him a kind, old priest who accommodated himself to circumstances. When he had entered the death chamber, Mme. Forestier went out and seated herself with Duroy in an adjoining room.

"That has upset him," said she. "When I mentioned the priest to him, his face assumed a scared expression. He knew that the end was near. I shall never forget his face."

At that moment they heard the priest saying to him: "Why no, you are not so low as that. You are ill, but not in danger. The proof of that is that I came as a friend, a neighbor." They could not hear his reply. The priest continued: "No, I shall not administer the sacrament. We will speak of that when you are better. If you will only confess, I ask no more. I am a pastor; I take advantage of every occasion to gather in my sheep."

A long silence followed. Then suddenly the priest said, in the tone of one officiating at the altar:

"The mercy of God is infinite; repeat the 'Confiteor,' my son. Perhaps you have forgotten it; I will help you. Repeat with me: '*Confiteor Deo omnipotenti; Beatæ Mariæ semper virgini.*'" He paused from time to time to permit the dying man to catch up to him.

Then he said: "Now, confess." The sick man murmured something. The priest repeated: "You have committed sins: of what kind, my son?"

The young woman rose and said simply: "Let us go into the garden. We must not listen to his secrets."

They seated themselves upon a bench before the door, beneath a blossoming rosebush. After several moments of silence Duroy asked: "Will it be some time before you return to Paris?"

"No," she replied; "when all is over, I will go back."

"In about ten days?"

"Yes, at most."

He continued: "Charles has no relatives then?"

"None, save cousins. His father and mother died when he was very young."

In the course of a few minutes, the servant came to tell them that the priest had finished, and together they ascended the stairs. Forestier seemed to have grown thinner since the preceding day. The priest was holding his hand.

"*Au revoir*, my son. I will come again to-morrow morning"; and he left. When he was gone, the dying man, who was panting, tried to raise his two hands toward his wife and gasped:

"Save me — save me, my darling. I do not want to die — oh, save me — go for the doctor. I will take anything. I do not want to die." He wept; the tears coursed down his pallid cheeks. Then his hands commenced to wander hither and thither continually, slowly, and regularly, as if gathering something on the coverlet. His wife, who was also weeping, sobbed:

"No, it is nothing. It is only an attack; you will be better to-morrow; you tired yourself with that drive."

Forestier drew his breath quickly and so faintly that one could scarcely hear him. He repeated:

"I do not want to die! Oh, my God — my God — what has happened to me? I cannot see. Oh, my God!" His staring eyes saw something invisible to the others; his hands plucked continually at the counterpane. Suddenly he shuddered and gasped: "The cemetery — me — my God!" He did not speak again. He lay there motionless and ghastly. The hours dragged on; the clock of a neighboring convent chimed noon.

Duroy left the room to obtain some food. He returned an hour later; Mme. Forestier would eat nothing. The invalid had not stirred. The young woman was seated in an easy-chair at the foot of the bed. Duroy likewise seated himself, and they watched in silence. A nurse, sent by the doctor, had arrived and was dozing by the window.

Duroy himself was almost asleep when he felt a presentiment that something was about to happen. He opened his eyes just in time to see Forestier close his. He coughed slightly, and two streams of blood issued from the corners of his mouth and flowed upon his night robe; his hands ceased their perpetual motion; he had breathed his last. His wife, perceiving it, uttered a cry and fell upon her knees by the bedside. Georges, in surprise and affright, mechanically made the sign of the cross.

The nurse, awakening, approached the bed and said: "It has come." Duroy, recovering his self-possession, murmured with a sigh of relief: "It was not as hard as I feared it would be."

That night Mme. Forestier and Duroy watched in the chamber of death. They were alone beside him who was no more. They did not speak, Georges's eyes seemed attracted to that emaciated face which the flickering light made more hollow. That was his friend, Charles Forestier, who the day before had spoken to him. For several years he had lived, eaten, laughed, loved, and hoped as did everyone—and now all was ended for him forever.

Life lasted a few months or years, and then fled! One was born, grew, was happy, and died. Adieu! man or woman, you will never return to earth! He thought of the insects which live several hours, of the beasts which live several days, of the men who live several years, of the worlds which last several centuries. What was the difference between one and the other? A few more dawns, that was all.

Duroy turned away his eyes in order not to see the corpse. Mme. Forestier's head was bowed; her fair hair enhanced the beauty of her sorrowful face. The young man's heart grew hopeful. Why should he lament when he had so many years still before him? He glanced at the handsome widow. How had she ever consented to marry that man? Then he pondered upon all the hidden secrets of their lives. He remembered that he had been told of a Count de Vaudrec who had dowered and given her in marriage. What would she do now? Whom would she marry? Had she projects, plans? He would have liked to know. Why that anxiety as to what she would do?

Georges questioned himself, and found that it was caused by a desire to win her for himself. Why should he not succeed? He was positive that she liked him; she would have confidence in him, for she knew that he was intelligent, resolute, tenacious. Had she not sent for him? Was not that a kind of avowal? He was impatient to question her, to find out her intentions. He would soon have to leave that villa, for he could not remain alone with the young widow; therefore he must find out her plans before returning to Paris, in order that she might not yield to another's entreaties. He broke the oppressive silence by saying:

"You must be fatigued."

7 G. de M.—7

"Yes, but above all I am grieved."

Their voices sounded strange in that room. They glanced involuntarily at the corpse as if they expected to see it move. Duroy continued:

"It is a heavy blow for you, and will make a complete change in your life."

She sighed deeply, but did not reply. He added:

"It is very sad for a young woman like you to be left alone." He paused; she still did not reply, and he stammered: "At any rate, you will remember the compact between us; you can command me as you will. I am yours."

She held out her hand to him and said mournfully and gently: "Thanks, you are very kind. If I can do anything for you, I say too: 'Count on me.'"

He took her proffered hand, gazed at it, and was seized with an ardent desire to kiss it. Slowly he raised it to his lips and then relinquished it. As her delicate fingers lay upon her knee the young widow said gravely:

"Yes, I shall be all alone, but I shall force myself to be brave."

He did not know how to tell her that he would be delighted to wed her. Certainly it was no time to speak to her on such a subject; however, he thought he might be able to express himself by means of some phrase which would have a hidden meaning and would infer what he wished to say. But that rigid corpse lay between them. The atmosphere became oppressive, almost suffocating. Duroy asked:

"Can we not open the window a little? The air seems to be impure."

"Certainly," she replied; "I have noticed it too."

He opened the window, letting in the cool night air. He turned: "Come and look out, it is delightful."

She glided softly to his side. He whispered: "Listen to me. Do not be angry that I broach the subject at such a time, but the day after to-morrow I shall leave here and when you return to Paris it might be too late. You know that I am only a poor devil, who has his position to make, but I have the will and some intelligence, and I am advancing. A man who has attained his ambition knows what to count on; a man who has his way to make does not know what may come — it may be better or worse. I told you one day that my most cherished dream was to have a wife like you.

"I repeat it to you to-day. Do not reply, but let me continue. This is no proposal — the time and place would render it odious. I only wish to tell you that by a word you can make me happy, and that you can make of me as you will, either a friend or a husband — for my heart and my body are yours. I do not want you to answer me now. I do not wish to speak any more on the subject here. When we meet in Paris, you can tell me your decision."

He uttered these words without glancing at her, and she seemed not to have heard them, for she stood by his side motionless, staring vaguely and fixedly at the landscape before her, bathed in moonlight.

At length she murmured: "It is rather chilly," and turned toward the bed. Duroy followed her. They did not speak but continued their watch. Toward midnight Georges fell asleep. At daybreak the

nurse entered and he started up. Both he and Mme.
Forestier retired to their rooms to obtain some rest.
At eleven o'clock they rose and lunched together;
while through the open window was wafted the
sweet, perfumed air of spring. After lunch, Mme.
Forestier proposed that they take a turn in the
garden; as they walked slowly along, she suddenly
said, without turning her head toward him, in a low,
grave voice:

"Listen to me, my dear friend; I have already reflected upon what you proposed to me, and I cannot
allow you to depart without a word of reply. I will,
however, say neither yes nor no. We will wait, we
will see; we will become better acquainted. You
must think it well over too. Do not yield to an impulse. I mention this to you before even poor
Charles is buried, because it is necessary, after what
you have said to me, that you should know me as I
am, in order not to cherish the hope you expressed
to me any longer, if you are not a man who can
understand and bear with me.

"Now listen carefully: Marriage, to me, is not a
chain but an association. I must be free, entirely
unfettered, in all my actions—my coming and my
going; I can tolerate neither control, jealousy, nor
criticism as to my conduct. I pledge my word, however, never to compromise the name of the man I
marry, nor to render him ridiculous in the eyes of
the world. But that man must promise to look upon
me as an equal, an ally, and not as an inferior, or as
an obedient, submissive wife. My ideas, I know, are
not like those of other people, but I shall never
change them. Do not answer me, it would be use-

less. We shall meet again and talk it all over later. Now take a walk; I shall return to him. Good-bye until to-night."

He kissed her hand and left her without having uttered a word. That night they met at dinner; directly after the meal they sought their rooms, worn out with fatigue.

Charles Forestier was buried the next day in the cemetery at Cannes without any pomp, and Georges returned to Paris by the express which left at one-thirty. Mme. Forestier accompanied him to the station. They walked up and down the platform awaiting the hour of departure and conversing on in-different subjects.

The train arrived, the journalist took his seat; a porter cried: "Marseilles, Lyons, Paris! All aboard!" The locomotive whistled and the train moved slowly out of the station.

The young man leaned out of the carriage, and looked at the youthful widow standing on the plat-form gazing after him. Just as she was disappearing from his sight, he threw her a kiss, which she re-turned with a more discreet wave of her hand.

CHAPTER IX.

MARRIAGE

GEORGES DUROY resumed his old habits. Installed in the cozy apartments on Rue de Constantinople, his relations with Mme. de Marelle became quite conjugal.

Mme. Forestier had not returned; she lingered at Cannes. He, however, received a letter from her announcing her return about the middle of April, but containing not a word as to their parting. He waited. He was resolved to employ every means to marry her if she seemed to hesitate; he had faith in his good fortune, in that power of attraction which he felt within him—a power so irresistible that all women yielded to it.

At length a short note admonished him that the decisive moment had arrived.

"I am in Paris. Come to see me.
"MADELEINE FORESTIER."

Nothing more. He received it at nine o'clock. At three o'clock of the same day he called at her house.

She extended both hands to him with a sweet smile, and they gazed into each other's eyes for several seconds, then she murmured:

"How kind of you to come!"

He replied: "I should have come, whensoever you bade me."

They sat down; she inquired about the Walters, his associates, and the newspaper.

"I miss that very much," said she. "I had become a journalist in spirit. I like the profession." She paused. He fancied he saw in her smile, in her voice, in her words, a kind of invitation, and although he had resolved not to hasten matters, he stammered:

"Well—why—why do you not resume—that profession—under—the name of Duroy?"

She became suddenly serious, and placing her hand on his arm, she said: "Do not let us speak of that yet."

Divining that she would accept him, he fell upon his knees, and passionately kissed her hands, saying:

"Thank you—thank you—how I love you."

She rose, she was very pale. Duroy kissed her brow. When she had disengaged herself from his embrace, she said gravely: "Listen, my friend, I have not yet fully decided; but my answer may be 'yes.' You must wait patiently, however, until I disclose the secret to you."

He promised and left her, his heart overflowing with joy. He worked steadily, spent little, tried to save some money that he might not be without a sou at the time of his marriage, and became as miserly as he had once been prodigal.

Summer glided by; then autumn, and no one suspected the tie existing between Duroy and Mme.
Forestier, for they seldom met in public.

One evening Madeleine said to him: "You have
not yet told Mme. de Marelle our plans?"

"No, my dear; as you wished them kept secret, I
have not mentioned them to a soul."

"Very well; there is plenty of time. I will tell
the Walters."

She turned away her head and continued: "If
you wish, we can be married the beginning of May."

"I obey you in all things joyfully."

"The tenth of May, which falls on Saturday,
would please me, for it is my birthday."

"Very well, the tenth of May."

"Your parents live near Rouen, do they not?"

"Yes, near Rouen, at Canteleu."

"I am very anxious to see them!"

He hesitated, perplexed: "But—they are—"
Then he added more firmly: "My dear, they are
plain, country people, innkeepers, who strained every
nerve to give me an education. I am not ashamed
of them, but their—simplicity—their rusticity might
annoy you."

She smiled sweetly. "No, I will love them very
much. We will visit them; I wish to. I, too, am
the child of humble parents—but I lost mine—I have
no one in the world"—she held out her hand to him
—"but you."

He was affected, conquered as he had never been
by any woman.

"I have been thinking of something," said she,
"but it is difficult to explain."

He asked: "What is it?"

"It is this: I am like all women. I have my— my weaknesses. I should like to bear a noble name. Can you not on the occasion of our marriage change your name somewhat?" She blushed as if she had proposed something indelicate.

He replied simply: "I have often thought of it, but it does not seem easy to me."

"Why not?"

He laughed. "Because I am afraid I should be ridiculed."

She shrugged her shoulders. "Not at all—not at all. Everyone does it, and no one laughs. Separate your name in this way: Du Roy. It sounds very well."

He replied: "No, that will not do; it is too common a proceeding. I have thought of assuming the name of my native place, first as a literary pseudonym and then as my surname in conjunction with Duroy, which might later on, as you proposed, be separated."

She asked: "Is your native place Canteleu?"

"Yes."

"I do not like the termination. Could we not modify it?"

She took a pen and wrote down the names in order to study them. Suddenly she cried: "Now I have it," and held toward him a sheet of paper on which was written: "Mme. Duroy de Cantel."

Gravely he replied: "Yes, it is very nice."

She was delighted, and repeated: "Duroy de Cantel. Mme. Duroy de Cantel. It is excellent, excellent!"

Then she added with an air of conviction: "You will see how easily it will be accepted by everyone! After to-morrow, sign your articles 'D. de Cantel,' and your 'Echoes' simply 'Duroy.' That is done on the press every day and no one will be surprised to see you take a *nom de plume*. What is your father's name?"

"Alexandre."

She murmured "Alexandre!" two or three times in succession; then she wrote upon a blank sheet:

"M. and Mme. Alexandre du Roy de Cantel announce the marriage of their son, M. Georges du Roy de Cantel with Mme. Forestier."

She examined her writing, and, charmed with the effect, exclaimed: "With a little method one can succeed in anything."

When Georges reached the street resolved to call himself, henceforth, "Du Roy," or even "Du Roy de Cantel," it seemed to him that he was of more importance. He swaggered more boldly, held his head more erect and walked as he thought gentlemen should. He felt a desire to inform the passers-by, "My name is Du Roy de Cantel."

Scarcely had he entered his apartments when the thought of Mme. de Marelle rendered him uneasy, and he wrote to her immediately, appointing a meeting for the following day.

"It will be hard," thought he. "There will be a quarrel surely."

The next morning he received a telegram from Madame, informing him that she would be with him at one o'clock. He awaited her impatiently, determined to confess at once and afterward to argue with her, to tell her that he could not remain a bachelor indefinitely, and that, as M. de Marelle persisted in living, he had been compelled to choose some one else as a legal companion. When the bell rang, his heart gave a bound.

Mme. de Marelle entered and cast herself into his arms, saying: "Good afternoon, Bel-Ami." Perceiving that his embrace was colder than usual, she glanced up at him and asked: "What ails you?"

"Take a seat," said he. "We must talk seriously."

She seated herself without removing her hat, and waited. He cast down his eyes; he was preparing to commence.

Finally he said slowly: "My dear friend, you see that I am very much perplexed, very sad, and very much embarrassed by what I have to confess to you. I love you; I love you with all my heart, and the fear of giving you pain grieves me more than what I have to tell you."

She turned pale, trembled, and asked: "What is it? Tell me quickly."

He said sadly but resolutely: "I am going to be married."

She sighed like one about to lose consciousness; then she gasped, but did not speak.

He continued: "You cannot imagine how much I suffered before taking that resolution. But I have neither position nor money. I am alone in Paris, I must have near me some one who can counsel, comfort, and support me. What I need is an associate, an ally, and I have found one!" He paused, hoping that she would reply, expecting an outburst of furious rage, reproaches, and insults. She pressed her hand to her heart and breathed with difficulty. He took the hand resting on the arm of the chair, but she drew it away and murmured as if stupefied: "Oh, my God!"

He fell upon his knees before her, without, however, venturing to touch her, more moved by her silence than he would have been by her anger.

"Clo, my little Clo, you understand my position. Oh, if I could have married you, what happiness it would have afforded me! But you were married! What could I do? Just think of it! I must make my way in the world and I can never do so as long as I have no domestic ties. If you knew. There are days when I should like to kill your husband." He spoke in a low, seductive voice. He saw two tears gather in Mme. de Marelle's eyes and trickle slowly down her cheeks. He whispered: "Do not weep, Clo, do not weep, I beseech you. You break my heart."

She made an effort to appear dignified and haughty, and asked, though somewhat unsteadily: "Who is it?"

For a moment he hesitated before he replied: "Madeleine Forestier!"

Mme. de Marelle started; her tears continued to flow. She rose. Duroy saw that she was going to leave him without a word of reproach or pardon, and he felt humbled, humiliated. He seized her gown and implored:

"Do not leave me thus."

She looked at him with that despairing, tearful glance so charming and so touching, which expresses all the misery pent-up in a woman's heart, and stammered: "I have nothing — to say; I can do nothing. You — you are right; you have made a good choice."

And disengaging herself she left the room.

With a sigh of relief at escaping so easily, he repaired to Mme. Forestier's, who asked him: "Have you told Mme. de Marelle?"

He replied calmly: "Yes."

"Did it affect her?"

"Not at all. On the contrary, she thought it an excellent plan."

The news was soon noised abroad. Some were surprised, others pretended to have foreseen it, and others again smiled, inferring that they were not at all astonished. The young man, who signed his articles, "D. de Cantel," his "Echoes," "Duroy," and his political sketches, "Du Roy," spent the best part of his time with his betrothed, who had decided that the date fixed for the wedding should be kept secret, that the ceremony should be celebrated in the presence of witnesses only, that they should leave the same evening for Rouen, and that the day following they should visit the journalist's aged parents and spend several days with them. Duroy had tried to persuade Madeleine to abandon that project, but not succeeding in his efforts he was finally compelled to submit.

The tenth of May arrived. Thinking a religious ceremony unnecessary, as they had issued no invitations, the couple were married at a magistrate's and took the six o'clock train for Normandy.

As the train glided along, Duroy seated in front of his wife, took her hand, kissed it, and said: "When we return we will dine at Chatou sometimes."

She murmured: "We shall have a great many things to do!" in a tone which seemed to say: "We must sacrifice pleasure to duty."

He retained her hand wondering anxiously how he could manage to caress her. He pressed her hand slightly, but she did not respond to the pressure.

He said: "It seems strange that you should be my wife."

She appeared surprised: "Why?"

"I do not know. It seems droll. I want to embrace you and I am surprised that I have the right."

She calmly offered him her cheek which he kissed as he would have kissed his sister's. He continued:

"The first time I saw you (you remember, at that dinner to which I was invited at Forestier's), I thought: 'Sacristi, if I could only find a wife like that!' And now I have one."

She glanced at him with smiling eyes.

He said to himself: "I am too cold. I am stupid. I should make more advances." And he asked: "How did you make Forestier's acquaintance?"

She replied with provoking archness: "Are we going to Rouen to talk of him?"

He colored. "I am a fool. You intimidate me."

She was delighted. "I? Impossible."

He seated himself beside her. She exclaimed: "Ah! a stag!" The train was passing through the forest of Saint-Germain and she had seen a frightened deer clear an alley at a bound. As she gazed out of the open window, Duroy bending over her, pressed a kiss upon her neck. For several moments she remained motionless, then raising her head, she said: "You tickle me, stop!"

But he did not obey her.

She repeated: "Stop, I say!"

He seized her head with his right hand, turned it toward him and pressed his lips to hers. She struggled, pushed him away and repeated: "Stop!"

He did not heed her. With an effort, she freed herself and rising, said: "Georges, have done. We are not children, we shall soon reach Rouen."

"Very well," said he, gaily, "I will wait."

Reseating herself near him she talked of what they would do on their return; they would keep the apartments in which she had lived with her first husband, and Duroy would receive Forestier's position on "La Vie Française." In the meantime, forgetting her injunctions and his promise, he slipped his arm around her waist, pressed her to him and murmured: "I love you dearly, my little Made."

The gentleness of his tone moved the young woman, and leaning toward him she offered him her lips; as she did so, a whistle announced the proximity of the station. Pushing back some stray locks upon her temples, she exclaimed:

"We are foolish."

He kissed her hands feverishly and replied:

"I adore you, my little Made."

On reaching Rouen they repaired to a hotel where they spent the night. The following morning, when they had drunk the tea placed upon the table in their room, Duroy clasped his wife in his arms and said: "My little Made, I feel that I love you very, very much."

She smiled trustfully and murmured as she returned his kisses: "I love you too—a little."

The visit to his parents worried Georges, although he had prepared his wife. He began again: "You know they are peasants, real, not sham, comic-opera peasants."

She smiled. "I know it, you have told me often enough."

"We shall be very uncomfortable. There is only a straw bed in my room; they do not know what hair mattresses are at Canteleu."

She seemed delighted. "So much the better. It would be charming to sleep badly — when — near you — and to be awakened by the crowing of the cocks."

He walked toward the window and lighted a cigarette. The sight of the harbor, of the river filled with ships, moved him and he exclaimed: "Egad, but that is fine!"

Madeleine joined him and placing both of her hands on her husband's shoulder, cried: "Oh, how beautiful! I did not know that there were so many ships!"

An hour later they departed in order to breakfast with the old couple, who had been informed several days before of their intended arrival. Both Duroy and his wife were charmed with the beauties of the landscape presented to their view, and the cabman halted in order to allow them to get a better idea of the panorama before them. As he whipped up his horse, Duroy saw an old couple not a hundred meters off, approaching, and he leaped from the carriage crying: "Here they are, I know them."

The man was short, corpulent, florid, and vigorous, notwithstanding his age; the woman was tall, thin, and melancholy, with stooping shoulders — a woman who had worked from childhood, who had never laughed nor jested.

Madeleine, too, alighted and watched the couple advance, with a contraction of her heart she had not anticipated. They did not recognize their son in that fine gentleman, and they would never have taken that handsome lady for their daughter-in-law. They walked along, passed the child they were expecting, without glancing at the "city folks."

Georges cried with a laugh: "Good day, Father Duroy."

Both the old man and his wife were struck dumb with astonishment; the latter recovered her self-possession first and asked: "Is it you, son?"

The young man replied: "Yes, it is I, Mother Duroy," and approaching her, he kissed her upon both cheeks and said: "This is my wife."

The two rustics stared at Madeleine as if she were a curiosity, with anxious fear, combined with a sort of satisfied approbation on the part of the father and of jealous enmity on that of the mother.

M. Duroy, senior, who was naturally jocose, made so bold as to ask with a twinkle in his eye: "May I kiss you too?" His son uttered an exclamation and Madeleine offered her cheek to the old peasant, who afterward wiped his lips with the back of his hand. The old woman, in her turn, kissed her daughter-in-law with hostile reserve. Her ideal was a stout, rosy, country lass, as red as an apple and as round.

The carriage preceded them with the luggage. The old man took his son's arm and asked him: "How are you getting on?"

"Very well."

7 G. de M.—8

"That is right. Tell me, has your wife any means?"

Georges replied: "Forty thousand francs."

His father whistled softly and muttered: "Whew!" Then he added: "She is a handsome woman." He admired his son's wife, and in his day had considered himself a connoisseur.

Madeleine and the mother walked side by side in silence; the two men joined them. They soon reached the village, at the entrance to which stood M. Duroy's tavern. A pine board fastened over the door indicated that thirsty people might enter. The table was laid. A neighbor, who had come to assist, made a low courtesy on seeing so beautiful a lady appear; then recognizing Georges, she cried: "Oh Lord, is it you?"

He replied merrily: "Yes, it is I, Mother Brulin," and he kissed her as he had kissed his father and mother. Then he turned to his wife:

"Come into our room," said he, "you can lay aside your hat."

They passed through a door to the right and entered a room paved with brick, with whitewashed walls and a bed with cotton hangings.

A crucifix above a holy-water basin and two colored prints, representing Paul and Virginia beneath a blue palm-tree, and Napoleon I. on a yellow horse, were the only ornaments in that neat, but bare room.

When they were alone, Georges embraced Madeleine.

"Good morning, Made! I am glad to see the old people once more. When one is in Paris one does not think of this place, but when one returns, one enjoys it just the same."

At that moment his father cried, knocking on the partition with his fist: "Come, the soup is ready."

They re-entered the large public-room and took their seats at the table. The meal was a long one, served in a truly rustic fashion. Father Duroy, enlivened by the cider and several glasses of wine, related many anecdotes, while Georges, to whom they were all familiar, laughed at them.

Mother Duroy did not speak, but sat at the board, grim and austere, glancing at her daughter-in-law with hatred in her heart.

Madeleine did not speak nor did she eat; she was depressed. Wherefore? She had wished to come; she knew that she was coming to a simple home; she had formed no poetical ideas of those peasants, but she had perhaps expected to find them somewhat more polished, refined. She recalled her own mother, of whom she never spoke to anyone — a governess who had been betrayed and who had died of grief and shame when Madeleine was twelve years old. A stranger had had the little girl educated. Her father without doubt. Who was he? She did not know positively, but she had vague suspicions.

The meal was not yet over when customers entered, shook hands with M. Duroy, exclaimed on seeing his son, and seating themselves at the wooden tables began to drink, smoke, and play dominoes. The smoke from the clay pipes and penny cigars filled the room.

Madeleine choked and asked: "Can we go out? I cannot remain here any longer."

Old Duroy grumbled at being disturbed. Madeleine rose and placed her chair at the door in order to wait until her father-in-law and his wife had finished their coffee and wine.

Georges soon joined her.

"Would you like to stroll down to the Seine?" he asked.

Joyfully she cried: "Yes."

They descended the hillside, hired a boat at Croisset, and spent the remainder of the afternoon beneath the willows in the soft, warm, spring air, and rocked gently by the rippling waves of the river. They returned at nightfall. The evening repast by candle-light was more painful to Madeleine than that of the morning. Neither Father Duroy nor his wife spoke. When the meal was over, Madeleine drew her husband outside in order not to have to remain in that room, the atmosphere of which was heavy with smoke and the fumes of liquor.

When they were alone, he said: "You are already weary."

She attempted to protest; he interrupted her:

"I have seen it. If you wish we will leave to-morrow."

She whispered: "I should like to go."

They walked along and entered a narrow path among high trees, hedged in on either side by impenetrable brushwood.

She asked: "Where are we?"

He replied: "In the forest — one of the largest in France."

Madeleine, on raising her head, could see the stars between the branches and hear the rustling of the

leaves.   She felt strangely nervous.   Why, she could
not tell.   She seemed to be lost, surrounded by perils,
abandoned, alone, beneath that vast vaulted sky.

She murmured: "I am afraid; I should like to
return."

"Very well, we will."

On their return they found the old people in bed.
The next morning Madeleine rose early and was
ready to leave at daybreak.   When Georges told his
parents that they were going to return home, they
guessed whose wish it was.

His father asked simply: "Shall I see you soon
again?"

"Yes—in the summer-time."

"Very well."

His mother grumbled: "I hope you will not regret what you have done."

Georges gave them two hundred francs to appease
them, and the cab arriving at ten o'clock, the couple
kissed the old peasants and set out.

As they were descending the side of the hill,
Duroy laughed.   "You see," said he, "I warned you.
I should, however, not have presented you to M. and
Mme. du Roy de Cantel, senior."

She laughed too and replied: "I am charmed *now!*
They are nice people whom I am beginning to like
very much.   I shall send them confections from Paris."
Then she murmured: "Du Roy de Cantel.   We will
say that we spent a week at your parents' estate,"
and drawing near him, she kissed him saying:

"Good morning, Georges."

He replied: "Good morning, Madeleine," as he
slipped his arm around her waist.

CHAPTER X.

T HE Du Roys had been in Paris two days and the journalist had resumed work; he had given up his own especial province to assume that of Forestier, and to devote himself entirely to politics. On this particular evening he turned his steps toward home with a light heart. As he passed a florist's on Rue Nôtre Dame de Lorette he bought a bouquet of half-open roses for Madeleine. Having forgotten his key, on arriving at his door, he rang and the servant answered his summons.

Georges asked: "Is Madame at home?"

"Yes, sir."

In the dining-room he paused in astonishment to see covers laid for three: the door of the salon being ajar, he saw Madeleine arranging in a vase on the mantelpiece a bunch of roses similar to his.

He entered the room and asked: "Have you invited anyone to dinner?"

She replied without turning her head and continuing the arrangement of her flowers: "Yes and no: it is my old friend, Count de Vaudrec, who is in the habit of dining here every Monday and who will come now as he always has."

Georges murmured: "Very well."

He stopped behind her, the bouquet in his hand, the desire strong within him to conceal it—to throw it away. However, he said:

"Here, I have brought you some roses!"

She turned to him with a smile and said: "Ah, how thoughtful of you!" and she kissed him with such evident affection that he felt consoled.

She took the flowers, inhaled their perfume, and put them in an empty vase. Then she said as she noted the effect: "Now I am satisfied; my mantelpiece looks pretty," adding with an air of conviction:

"Vaudrec is charming; you will become intimate with him at once,"

A ring announced the Count. He entered as if he were at home. After gallantly kissing Mme. Du Roy's hand, he turned to her husband and cordially offered his hand, saying: "How are you, my dear Du Roy?"

He had no longer that haughty air, but was very affable. One would have thought in the course of five minutes, that the two men had known one another for ten years. Madeleine, whose face was radiant, said: "I will leave you together. I have work to superintend in the kitchen." The dinner was excellent and the Count remained very late. When he was gone, Madeleine said to her husband: "Is he not nice? He improves, too, on acquaintance. He is a good, true, faithful friend. Ah, without him—"

She did not complete her sentence and Georges replied: "Yes, he is very pleasant. I think we shall understand each other well."

"You do not know," she said, "that we have work to do to-night before retiring. I did not have time to tell you before dinner, for Vaudrec came. Laroche-Mathieu brought me important news of Morocco. We must make a fine article of that. Let us set to work at once. Come, take the lamp."

He carried the lamp and they entered the study. Madeleine leaned against the mantelpiece, and having lighted a cigarette, told him the news and gave him her plan of the article. He listened attentively, making notes as she spoke, and when she had finished he raised objections, took up the question and, in his turn, developed another plan. His wife ceased smoking, for her interest was aroused in following Georges's line of thought. From time to time she murmured: "Yes, yes; very good — excellent — very forcible —" And when he had finished speaking, she said: "Now let us write."

It was always difficult for him to make a beginning and she would lean over his shoulder and whisper the phrases in his ear, then he would add a few lines; when their article was completed, Georges re-read it. Both he and Madeleine pronounced it admirable and kissed one another with passionate admiration.

The article appeared with the signature of "G. du Roy de Cantel," and made a great sensation. M. Walter congratulated the author, who soon became celebrated in political circles. His wife, too, surprised him by the ingenuousness of her mind, the cleverness of her wit, and the number of her acquaintances. At almost any time upon returning home he found in his salon a senator, a deputy, a magistrate, or a general, who treated Madeleine with grave familiarity.

Deputy Laroche-Mathieu, who dined at Rue Fontaine every Tuesday, was one of the largest stockholders of M. Walter's paper and the latter's colleague and associate in many business transactions. Du Roy hoped, later on, that some of the benefits promised by him to Forestier might fall to his share. They would be given to Madeleine's new husband — that was all — nothing was changed; even his associates sometimes called him Forestier, and it made Du Roy furious at the dead. He grew to hate the very name; it was to him almost an insult. Even at home the obsession continued; the entire house reminded him of Charles.

One evening Du Roy, who liked sweetmeats, asked: "Why do we never have sweets?"

His wife replied pleasantly: "I never think of it, because Charles disliked them."

He interrupted her with an impatient gesture: "Do you know I am getting tired of Charles? It is Charles here, Charles there, Charles liked this, Charles liked that. Since Charles is dead, let him rest in peace."

Madeleine ascribed her husband's burst of ill humor to puerile jealousy, but she was flattered and did not reply. On retiring, haunted by the same thought, he asked:

"Did Charles wear a cotton nightcap to keep the draft out of his ears?"

She replied pleasantly: "No, a lace one!"

Georges shrugged his shoulders and said scornfully: "What a bird!"

From that time Georges never called Charles anything but "poor Charles," with an accent of infinite pity. One evening as Du Roy was smoking a cigarette at his window, toward the end of June, the heat awoke in him a desire for fresh air. He asked:

"My little Made, would you like to go as far as the Bois?"

"Yes, certainly."

They took an open carriage and drove to the Avenue du Bois de Boulogne. It was a sultry evening; a host of cabs lined the drive, one behind another. When the carriage containing Georges and Madeleine reached the turning which led to the fortifications, they kissed one another and Madeleine stammered in confusion: "We are as childish as we were at Rouen."

The road they followed was not so much frequented, a gentle breeze rustled the leaves of the trees, the sky was studded with brilliant stars and Georges murmured, as he pressed his wife to his breast: "Oh, my little Made."

She said to him: "Do you remember how gloomy the forest at Canteleu was? It seemed to me that it was full of horrible beasts and that it was interminable, while here it is charming. One can feel the caressing breezes, and I know that Sèvres is on the other side."

He replied: "In our forests there are nothing but stags, foxes, roebucks, and boars, with here and there a forester's house." He paused for a moment and then asked: "Did you come here in the evening with Charles occasionally?"

She replied: "Frequently."

He felt a desire to return home at once. Forestier's image haunted him, however; he could think of nothing else. The carriage rolled on toward the Arc de Triomphe and joined the stream of carriages returning home. As Georges remained silent, his wife, who divined his thoughts, asked in her soft voice: "Of what are you thinking? For half an hour you have not uttered a word."

He replied with a sneer: "I am thinking of all those fools who kiss one another, and I believe truly that there is something else to be done in life."

She whispered: "Yes, but it is nice sometimes! It is nice when one has nothing better to do."

Georges' thoughts were busy with the dead; he said to himself angrily: "I am foolish to worry, to torment myself as I have done." After remonstrating thus with himself, he felt more reconciled to the thought of Forestier, and felt like exclaiming: "Good evening, old fellow!"

Madeleine, who was bored by his silence, asked: "Shall we go to Tortoni's for ices before returning home?"

He glanced at her from his corner and thought: "She is pretty; so much the better. Tit for tat, my comrade. But if they begin again to annoy me with you, it will get somewhat hot at the North Pole!"

Then he replied: "Certainly, my darling," and before she had time to think he kissed her. It seemed to Madeleine that her husband's lips were icy. However he smiled as usual and gave her his hand to assist her to alight at the *café*.

CHAPTER XI.

Madame Walter Takes a Hand

O N ENTERING the office the following day, Du Roy sought Boisrenard and told him to warn his associates not to continue the farce of calling him Forestier, or there would be war. When Du Roy returned an hour later, no one called him by that name. From the office he proceeded to his home, and hearing the sound of ladies' voices in the drawing-room, he asked the servant: "Who is here?"

"Mme. Walter and Mme. de Marelle," was the reply.

His heart pulsated violently as he opened the door. Clotilde was seated by the fireplace; it seemed to Georges that she turned pale on perceiving him.

Having greeted Mme. Walter and her two daughters seated like sentinels beside her, he turned to his former mistress. She extended her hand; he took and pressed it as if to say: "I love you still!" She returned the pressure.

He said: "Have you been well since we last met?"

"Yes; have you, Bel-Ami?" And turning to Madeleine she added: "Will you permit me to call him Bel-Ami?"

"Certainly, my dear; I will permit anything you wish."

A shade of irony lurked beneath those words, uttered so pleasantly.

Mme. Walter mentioned a fencing-match to be given at Jacques Rival's apartments, the proceeds to be devoted to charities, and in which many society ladies were going to assist. She said: "It will be very entertaining; but I am in despair, for we have no one to escort us, my husband having an engagement."

Du Roy offered his services at once. She accepted, saying: "My daughters and I shall be very grateful."

He glanced at the younger of the two girls and thought: "Little Suzanne is not at all bad, not at all."

She resembled a doll, being very small and dainty, with a well-proportioned form, a pretty, delicate face, blue-gray eyes, a fair skin, and curly, flaxen hair. Her elder sister, Rose, was plain — one of those girls to whom no attention is ever paid. Her mother rose, and turning to Georges, said: "I shall count on you next Thursday at two o'clock."

He replied: "Count upon me, Madame."

When the door closed upon Mme. Walter, Mme. de Marelle, in her turn, rose.

"*Au revoir*, Bel-Ami."

This time *she* pressed *his* hand and he was moved by that silent avowal. "I will go to see her to-morrow," thought he.

Left alone with his wife, she laughed, and looking into his eyes said: "Mme. Walter has taken a fancy to you!"

He replied incredulously: "Nonsense!"

"But I know it. She spoke of you to me with great enthusiasm. She said she would like to find two husbands like you for her daughters. Fortunately she is not susceptible herself."

He did not understand her and repeated: "Susceptible herself?"

She replied in a tone of conviction: "Oh, Mme. Walter is irreproachable. Her husband you know as well as I. But she is different. Still she has suffered a great deal in having married a Jew, though she has been true to him; she is a virtuous woman."

Du Roy was surprised: "I thought her a Jewess."

"She a Jewess! No, indeed! She is the prime mover in all the charitable movements at the Madeleine. She was even married by a priest. I am not sure but that M. Walter went through the form of baptism."

Georges murmured: "And—she—likes—me—"

"Yes. If you were not married I should advise you to ask for the hand of—Suzanne—would you not prefer her to Rose?"

He replied as he twisted his mustache: "Eh! the mother is not so bad!"

Madeleine replied: "I am not afraid of her. At her age one does not begin to make conquests—one should commence sooner."

Georges thought: "If I might have had Suzanne, ah!" Then he shrugged his shoulders: "Bah, it is absurd; her father would not have consented."

He determined to treat Mme. Walter very considerately in order to retain her regard. All that evening he was haunted by recollections of his love for Clotilde; he recalled their escapades, her kindness. He repeated to himself: "She is indeed nice. Yes, I shall call upon her to-morrow."

When he had lunched the following morning he repaired to Rue Verneuil. The same maid opened the door, and with the familiarity of an old servant she asked: "Is Monsieur well?"

He replied: "Yes, my child," and entered the drawing-room in which some one was practising scales. It was Laurine. He expected she would fall upon his neck. She, however, rose ceremoniously, bowed coldly, and left the room with dignity; her manner was so much like that of an outraged woman that he was amazed. Her mother entered. He kissed her hand.

"How much I have thought of you," said he.

"And I of you," she replied.

They seated themselves and smiled as they gazed into one another's eyes.

"My dear little Clo, I love you."

"And I love you."

"Still — still — you did not miss me."

"Yes and no. I was grieved, but when I heard your reason, I said to myself: 'Bah, he will return to me some day.'"

"I dared not come. I did not know how I should be received. I dared not, but I longed to come. Now, tell me what ails Laurine; she scarcely bade me good morning and left the room with an angry air."

"I do not know, but one cannot mention you to her since your marriage; I really believe she is jealous."

"Nonsense."

"Yes, my dear, she no longer calls you Bel-Ami, but M. Forestier instead."

Du Roy colored, then drawing nearer the young woman, he said: "Kiss me."

She obeyed him.

"Where can we meet again?" he asked.

"At Rue de Constantinople."

"Ah, are the apartments not rented?"

"No, I kept them."

"You did?"

"Yes, I thought you would return."

His heart bounded joyfully. She loved him then with a lasting love! He whispered: "I adore you." Then he asked: "Is your husband well?"

"Yes, very well. He has just been home for a month; he went away the day before yesterday."

Du Roy could not suppress a smile: "How opportunely that always happens!"

She replied naïvely: "Yes, it happens opportunely, but he is not in the way when he is here; is he?"

"That is true; he is a charming man!"

"How do you like your new life?"

"Tolerably; my wife is a comrade, an associate, nothing more; as for my heart—"

"I understand; but she is good."

"Yes, she does not trouble me."

He drew near Clotilde and murmured: "When shall we meet again?"

"To-morrow, if you will."

"Yes, to-morrow at two o'clock."

He rose to take his leave somewhat embarrassed.

"You know I intend to take back the rooms on Rue de Constantinople myself. I wish to; it is not necessary for you to pay for them."

She kissed his hands, saying: "You may do as you like. I am satisfied to have kept them until we met again." And Du Roy took his leave very well satisfied.

When Thursday came, he asked Madeleine: "Are you not going to the fencing-match at Rival's?"

"No, I do not care about it. I will go to the chamber of deputies."

Georges called for Mme. Walter in an open carriage, for the weather was delightful. He was surprised to find her looking so handsome and so young. Never had she appeared so fresh. Her daughter, Suzanne, was dressed in pink; her sister looked like her governess. At Rival's door was a long line of carriages. Du Roy offered his arm to Mme. Walter and they entered.

The entertainment was for the benefit of the orphans of the Sixth Ward under the patronage of all the wives of the senators and deputies who were connected with "La Vie Française."

Jacques Rival received the arrivals at the entrance to his apartments, then he pointed to a small staircase which led to the cellar in which were his shooting-gallery and fencing-room, saying: "Downstairs, ladies, downstairs. The match will take place in the subterranean apartments."

Pressing Du Roy's hand, he said: "Good evening, Bel-Ami."

Du Roy was surprised: "Who told you about that name?"

Rival replied: "Mme. Walter, who thinks it very pretty."

Mme. Walter blushed.

"Yes, I confess that if I knew you better, I should do as little Laurine, and I should call you Bel-Ami, too. It suits you admirably."

Du Roy laughed. "I beg you to do so, Madame."

She cast down her eyes. "No, we are not well enough acquainted."

He murmured: "Permit me to hope that we shall become so."

"Well, we shall see," said she.

They descended the stairs and entered a large room, which was lighted by Venetian lanterns and decorated with festoons of gauze. Nearly all the benches were filled with ladies, who were chatting as if they were at a theater. Mme. Walter and her daughters reached their seats in the front row.

Du Roy, having obtained their places for them, whispered: "I shall be obliged to leave you; men cannot occupy the seats."

Mme. Walter replied hesitatingly: "I should like to keep you, just the same. You could tell me the names of the participants. See, if you stand at the end of the seat, you will not annoy anyone." She raised her large, soft eyes to his and insisted: "Come, stay with us—Bel-Ami—we need you!"

He replied: "I obey with pleasure, Madame!"

Suddenly Jacques Rival's voice announced: "We will begin, ladies."

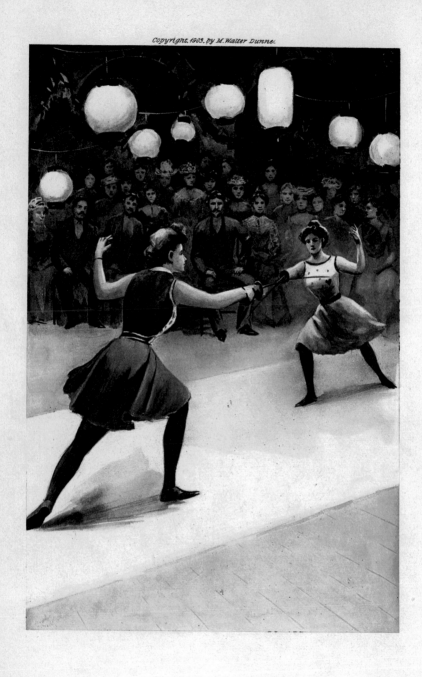

AFTER THE ORIGINAL DRAWING BY FERDINAND BAC.

"Then followed the fencing-match."

Then followed the fencing-match. Du Roy retained his place beside the ladies and gave them all
the necessary information. When the entertainment
was over and all expenses were paid, two hundred
and twenty francs remained for the orphans of the
Sixth Ward.

Du Roy, escorting the Walters, awaited his carriage. When seated face to face with Mme. Walter,
he met her troubled but caressing glance.

"Egad, I believe she is affected," thought he; and
he smiled as he recognized the fact that he was really
successful with the female sex, for Mme. de Marelle,
since the renewal of their relations, seemed to love
him madly.

With a light heart he returned home. Madeleine
was awaiting him in the drawing-room.

"I have some news," said she. "The affair with
Morocco is becoming complicated. France may send
an expedition out there in several months. In any
case the ministry will be overthrown and Laroche
will profit by the occasion."

Du Roy, in order to draw out his wife, pretended
not to believe it. "France would not be silly enough
to commence any folly with Tunis!"

She shrugged her shoulders impatiently. "I tell
you she will! You do not understand that it is a
question of money—you are as simple as Forestier."

Her object was to wound and irritate him, but he
only smiled and replied: "What! as simple as that
stupid fellow?"

She ceased and murmured: "Oh, Georges!"

He added: "Poor devil!" in a tone of profound
pity.

Madeleine turned her back upon him scornfully; after a moment of silence, she continued: "We shall have some company Tuesday. Mme. Laroche-Mathieu is coming here to dine with Viscountess de Percemur. Will you invite Rival and Norbert de Varenne? I shall go to Mmes. Walter and de Marelle to-morrow. Perhaps, too, we may have Mme. Rissolin."

Du Roy replied: "Very well, I will see to Rival and Norbert."

The following day he thought he would anticipate his wife's visit to Mme. Walter and attempt to find out if she really was in love with him. He arrived at Boulevard Malesherbes at two o'clock. He was ushered into the salon and waited. Finally Mme. Walter appeared and offered him her hand cordially. "What good wind blows you here?"

"No good wind, but a desire to see you. Some power has impelled me hither, I do not know why; I have nothing to say except that I have come; here I am! Pardon the morning call and the candor of my explanation."

He uttered those words with a smile upon his lips and a serious accent in his voice.

In her astonishment, she stammered with a blush: "But indeed—I do not understand—you surprise me."

He added: "It is a declaration made in jest in order not to startle you."

They were seated near each other. She took the matter as a jest. "Is it a declaration—seriously?"

"Yes, for a long time I have wished to make it, but I dared not; they say you are so austere, so rigid."

She had recovered her self-possession and replied:

"Why did you choose to-day?"

"I do not know." Then he lowered his voice: "Or rather because I have thought only of you since yesterday."

Suddenly turning pale, she gasped: "Come, enough of this childishness! Let us talk of something else."

But he fell upon his knees before her. She tried to rise; he prevented her by twining his arms about her waist, and repeated in a passionate voice: "Yes, it is true that I have loved you madly for some time. Do not answer me. I am mad—I love you. Oh, if you knew how I love you!"

She could utter no sound; in her agitation she repulsed him with both hands, for she could feel his breath upon her cheek. He rose suddenly and attempted to embrace her, but gaining her liberty for a moment, she escaped him and ran from chair to chair. He, considering such pursuit beneath his dignity, sank into a chair, buried his face in his hands, and feigned to sob convulsively. Then he rose, cried:

"Adieu, adieu!" and fled.

In the hall he took his cane calmly and left the house saying: "Cristi! I believe she loves me!"

He went at once to the telegraph office to send a message to Clotilde, appointing a rendezvous for the next day.

On entering the house at his usual time, he said to his wife: "Well, is everyone coming to dinner?"

She replied: "Yes, all but Mme. Walter, who is uncertain as to whether she can come. She acted very strangely. Never mind, perhaps she can manage it anyway."

He replied: "She will come."

He was not, however, certain and was rendered uneasy until the day of the dinner. That morning Madeleine received a message from Mme. Walter to this effect: "I have succeeded in arranging matters and I shall be with you, but my husband cannot accompany me."

Du Roy thought: "I did right not to return there. She has calmed down." Still he awaited her arrival anxiously.

She appeared very composed, somewhat reserved, and haughty. He was very humble, very careful, and submissive. Mmes. Laroche-Mathieu and Rissolin were accompanied by their husbands. Mme. de Marelle looked bewitching in an odd combination of yellow and black.

At Du Roy's right sat Mme. Walter, and he spoke to her only of serious matters with exaggerated respect. From time to time he glanced at Clotilde.

"She is really very pretty and fresh looking," thought he. But Mme. Walter attracted him by the difficulty of the conquest. She took her leave early.

"I will escort you," said he.

She declined his offer. He insisted: "Why do you not want me? You wound me deeply. Do not let me feel that I am not forgiven. You see that I am calm."

She replied: "You cannot leave your guests thus."

He smiled: "Bah! I shall be absent twenty minutes. No one will even notice it; if you refuse me, you will break my heart."

"Very well," she whispered, "I will accept."

When they were seated in the carriage, he seized her hand, and kissing it passionately said: "I love you, I love you. Let me tell it to you. I will not touch you. I only wish to repeat that I love you."

She stammered: "After what you promised me —it is too bad—too bad."

He seemed to make a great effort, then he continued in a subdued voice: "See, how I can control myself—and yet—let me only tell you this—I love you—yes, let me go home with you and kneel before you five minutes to utter those three words and gaze upon your beloved face."

She suffered him to take her hand and replied in broken accents: "No, I cannot—I do not wish to. Think of what my servants, my daughters, would say —no—no—it is impossible."

He continued: "I cannot live without seeing you; whether it be at your house or elsewhere, I must see you for only a moment each day that I may touch your hand, breathe the air stirred by your gown, contemplate the outlines of your form, and see your beautiful eyes."

She listened tremblingly to the musical language of love, and made answer: "No, it is impossible. Be silent!"

He spoke very low; he whispered in her ear, comprehending that it was necessary to win that simple woman gradually, to persuade her to appoint a meeting where she willed at first, and later on where he willed.

"Listen: I must see you! I will wait at your door like a beggar. If you do not come down, I will come to you, but I shall see you to-morrow."

She repeated: "No, do not come. I shall not receive you. Think of my daughters!"

"Then tell me where I can meet you—in the street—it matters not where—at any hour you wish —provided that I can see you. I will greet you; I will say, I love you; and then go away."

She hesitated, almost distracted. As the *coupé* stopped at the door, she whispered hastily: "I will be at La Trinité to-morrow, at half past three."

After alighting, she said to her coachman: "Take M. du Roy home."

When he returned, his wife asked: "Where have you been?"

He replied in a low voice: "I have been to send an important telegram."

Mme. de Marelle approached him: "You must take me home, Bel-Ami; you know that I only dine so far from home on that condition." Turning to Madeleine, she asked: "You are not jealous?"

Mme. du Roy replied slowly: "No, not at all."

The guests departed. Clotilde, enveloped in laces, whispered to Madeleine at the door: "Your dinner was perfect. In a short while you will have the best political salon in Paris."

When she was alone with Georges, she said: "Oh, my darling Bel-Ami, I love you more dearly every day."

The cab rolled on, and Georges' thoughts were with Mme. Walter.

CHAPTER XII.

A Meeting and the Result

THE July sun shone upon the Place de la Trinité, which was almost deserted. Du Roy drew out his watch. It was only three o'clock: he was half an hour too early. He laughed as he thought of the place of meeting. He entered the sacred edifice of La Trinité; the coolness within was refreshing. Here and there an old woman kneeled at prayer, her face in her hands. Du Roy looked at his watch again. It was not yet a quarter past three. He took a seat, regretting that he could not smoke. At the end of the church near the choir, he could hear the measured tread of a corpulent man whom he had noticed when he entered. Suddenly the rustle of a gown made him start. It was she. He arose and advanced quickly. She did not offer him her hand and whispered: "I have only a few minutes. You must kneel near me that no one will notice us."

She proceeded to a side aisle after saluting the Host on the High Altar, took a footstool, and kneeled down. Georges took one beside it and when they were in the attitude of prayer, he said: "Thank you, thank you. I adore you. I should like to tell you constantly how I began to love you, how I was conquered the first time I saw you. Will you permit me some day to unburden my heart, to explain all to you?"

She replied between her fingers: "I am mad to let you speak to me thus—mad to have come hither—mad to do as I have done, to let you believe that this—this adventure can have any results. Forget it, and never speak to me of it again." She paused.

He replied: "I expect nothing—I hope nothing—I love you—whatever you may do, I will repeat it so often, with so much force and ardor that you will finally understand me, and reply: 'I love you too.'"

He felt her frame tremble as she involuntarily repeated: "I love you too."

He was overcome by astonishment.

"Oh, my God!" she continued incoherently, "Should I say that to you? I feel guilty, despicable—I—who have two daughters—but I cannot—I cannot—I never thought—it was stronger than I—listen—listen—I have never loved—any other—but you—I swear it—I have loved you a year in secret—I have suffered and struggled—I can no longer; I love you." She wept and her bowed form was shaken by the violence of her emotion.

Georges murmured: "Give me your hand that I may touch, may press it."

She slowly took her hand from her face, he seized it saying: "I should like to drink your tears!"

Placing the hand he held upon his heart he asked:
"Do you feel it beat?"·

In a few moments the man Georges had noticed
before passed by them. When Mme. Walter heard
him near her, she snatched her fingers from Georges's
clasp and covered her face with them. After the man
had disappeared, Du Roy asked, hoping for another
place of meeting than La Trinité: "Where shall I
see you to-morrow?"

She did not reply; she seemed transformed into a
statue of prayer. He continued: "Shall I meet you
to-morrow at Park Monceau?"

She turned a livid face toward him and said unsteadily: "Leave me—leave me now—go—go away
—for only five minutes—I suffer too much near you.
I want to pray—go. Let me pray alone—five
minutes—let me ask God—to pardon me—to save
me—leave me—five minutes."

She looked so pitiful that he rose without a word
and asked with some hesitation: "Shall I return
presently?"

She nodded her head in the affirmative and he left
her. She tried to pray; she closed her eyes in order
not to see Georges. She could not pray; she could
only think of him. She would rather have died than
have fallen thus; she had never been weak. She
murmured several words of supplication; she knew
that all was over, that the struggle was in vain. She
did not however wish to yield, but she felt her weakness. Some one approached with a rapid step; she
turned her head. It was a priest. She rose, ran toward him, and clasping her hands, she cried: "Save
me, save me!"

He stopped in surprise.

"What do you want, Madame?"

"I want you to save me. Have pity on me. If you do not help me, I am lost!"

He gazed at her, wondering if she were mad.

"What can I do for you?" The priest was a young man somewhat inclined to corpulence.

"Receive my confession," said she, "and counsel me, sustain me, tell me what to do."

He replied: "I confess every Saturday from three to six."

Seizing his arm she repeated: "No, now, at once —at once! It is necessary! He is here! In this church! He is waiting for me."

The priest asked: "Who is waiting for you?"

"A man—who will be my ruin if you do not save me. I can no longer escape him—I am too weak—too weak."

She fell upon her knees sobbing: "Oh, father, have pity upon me. Save me, for God's sake, save me!" She seized his gown that he might not escape her, while he uneasily glanced around on all sides to see if anyone noticed the woman at his feet. Finally, seeing that he could not free himself from her, he said: "Rise; I have the key to the confessional with me."

*   *   *   *   *   *   *

Du Roy having walked around the choir, was sauntering down the nave, when he met the stout, bold man wandering about, and he wondered: "What can he be doing here?"

The man slackened his pace and looked at Georges with the evident desire to speak to him. When he was near him, he bowed and said politely:

"I beg your pardon, sir, for disturbing you; but
can you tell me when this church was built?"

Du Roy replied: "I do not know; I think it is
twenty or twenty-five years. It is the first time I
have been here. I have never seen it before." Feeling interested in the stranger, the journalist continued: "It seems to me that you are examining into it
very carefully."

The man replied: "I am not visiting the church;
I have an appointment." He paused and in a few
moments added: "It is very warm outside."

Du Roy looked at him and suddenly thought that
he resembled Forestier. "Are you from the provinces?" he asked.

"Yes, I am from Rennes. And did you, sir, enter
this church from curiosity?"

"No, I am waiting for a lady." And with a smile
upon his lips, he walked away.

He did not find Mme. Walter in the place in
which he had left her, and was surprised. She had
gone. He was furious. Then he thought she might
be looking for him, and he walked around the
church. Not finding her, he returned and seated
himself on the chair she had occupied, hoping that
she would rejoin him there. Soon he heard the sound
of a voice. He saw no one; whence came it? He
rose to examine into it, and saw in a chapel near by,
the doors of the confessionals. He drew nearer in
order to see the woman whose voice he heard. He
recognized Mme. Walter; she was confessing. At
first he felt a desire to seize her by the arm and drag
her away; then he seated himself near by and bided
his time. He waited quite a while. At length Mme.

Walter rose, turned, saw him and came toward him. Her face was cold and severe.

"Sir," said she, "I beseech you not to accompany me, not to follow me and not to come to my house alone. You will not be admitted. Adieu!" And she walked away in a dignified manner.

He permitted her to go, because it was against his principles to force matters. As the priest in his turn issued from the confessional, he advanced toward him and said: "If you did not wear a gown, I would give you a sound thrashing." Then he turned upon his heel and left the church whistling. In the doorway he met the stout gentleman. When Du Roy passed him, they bowed.

The journalist then repaired to the office of "La Vie Française." As he entered he saw by the clerks' busy air that something of importance was going on, and he hastened to the manager's room. The latter exclaimed joyfully as Du Roy entered: "What luck! here is Bel-Ami."

He stopped in confusion and apologized: "I beg your pardon, I am very much bothered by circumstances. And then I hear my wife and daughter call you Bel-Ami from morning until night, and I have acquired the habit myself. Are you displeased?"

Georges laughed. "Not at all."

M. Walter continued: "Very well, then I will call you Bel-Ami as everyone else does. Great changes have taken place. The ministry has been overthrown. Marrot is to form a new cabinet. He has chosen General Boutin d'Acre as minister of war, and our friend Laroche-Mathieu as minister of foreign affairs. We shall be very busy. I must write a leading article, a simple declaration of principles; then I must have something interesting on the Morocco question — you must attend to that."

Du Roy reflected a moment and then replied: "I have it. I will give you an article on the political situation of our African colony," and he proceeded to prepare M. Walter an outline of his work, which was nothing but a modification of his first article on "Souvenirs of a Soldier in Africa."

The manager having read the article said: "It is perfect; you are a treasure. Many thanks."

Du Roy returned home to dinner delighted with his day, notwithstanding his failure at La Trinité. His wife was awaiting him anxiously. She exclaimed on seeing him:

"You know that Laroche is minister of foreign affairs."

"Yes, I have just written an article on that subject."

"How?"

"Do you remember the first article we wrote on 'Souvenirs of a Soldier in Africa'? Well, I revised and corrected it for the occasion."

She smiled. "Ah, yes, that will do very well."

At that moment the servant entered with a dispatch containing these words without any signature:

"I was beside myself. Pardon me and come to-morrow at four o'clock to Park Monceau."

He understood the message, and with a joyful heart, slipped the telegram into his pocket. During dinner he repeated the words to himself; as he interpreted them, they meant, "I yield — I am yours where and when you will." He laughed.

Madeleine asked: "What is it?"

"Nothing much. I was thinking of a comical old priest I met a short while since."

     *   *   *   *   *   *   *

Du Roy arrived at the appointed hour the following day. The benches were all occupied by people trying to escape from the heat and by nurses with their charges.

He found Mme. Walter in a little antique ruin; she seemed unhappy and anxious. When he had greeted her, she said: "How many people there are in the garden!"

He took advantage of the occasion: "Yes, that is true; shall we go somewhere else?"

"Where?"

"It matters not where; for a drive, for instance. You can lower the shade on your side and you will be well concealed."

"Yes, I should like that better; I shall die of fear here."

"Very well, meet me in five minutes at the gate which opens on the boulevard. I will fetch a cab."

When they were seated in the cab, she asked: "Where did you tell the coachman to drive to?"

Georges replied: "Do not worry; he knows."

He had given the man his address on the Rue de Constantinople.

Mme. Walter said to Du Roy: "You cannot imagine how I suffer on your account—how I am tormented, tortured. Yesterday I was harsh, but I wanted to escape you at any price. I was afraid to remain alone with you. Have you forgiven me?"

He pressed her hand. "Yes, yes, why should I not forgive you, loving you as I do?"

She looked at him with a beseeching air: "Listen: You must promise to respect me, otherwise I could never see you again."

At first he did not reply; a smile lurked beneath his mustache; then he murmured: "I am your slave."

She told him how she had discovered that she loved him, on learning that he was to marry Madeleine Forestier. Suddenly she ceased speaking. The carriage stopped. Du Roy opened the door.

"Where are we?" she asked.

He replied: "Alight and enter the house. We shall be undisturbed there."

"Where are we?" she repeated.

"At my rooms; they are my bachelor apartments which I have rented for a few days that we might have a corner in which to meet."

She clung to the cab, startled at the thought of a *tête-à-tête*, and stammered: "No, no, I do not want to."

He said firmly: "I swear to respect you. Come, you see that people are looking at us, that a crowd is gathering around us. Make haste!" And he repeated, "I swear to respect you."

She was terror-stricken and rushed into the house. She was about to ascend the stairs. He seized her arm: "It is here, on the ground floor."

When he had closed the door, he showered kisses upon her neck, her eyes, her lips; in spite of herself, she submitted to his caresses and even returned them, hiding her face and murmuring in broken accents: "I swear that I have never had a lover"; while he thought: "That is a matter of indifference to me."

7 G. de M.—10

CHAPTER XIII.

MADAME DE MARELLE

AUTUMN had come. The Du Roys had spent the entire summer in Paris, leading a vigorous campaign in "La Vie Française," in favor of the new cabinet. Although it was only the early part of October, the chamber was about to resume its sessions, for affairs in Morocco were becoming menacing. The celebrated speech made by Count de Lambert Sarrazin had furnished Du Roy with material for ten articles on the Algerian colony. "La Vie Française" had gained considerable prestige by its connection with the power; it was the first to give political news, and every newspaper in Paris and the provinces sought information from it. It was quoted, feared, and began to be respected: it was no longer the organ of a group of political intriguers, but the avowed mouthpiece of the cabinet. Laroche-Mathieu was the soul of the journal and Du Roy his speaking-trumpet. M. Walter retired discreetly into the background. Madeleine's salon became an influential center in which several members of the cabinet met every week. The president of the council had even dined there twice; the minister of foreign affairs was quite at home at the Du Roys; he came at any hour, bringing dispatches or information, which he dictated either to the husband or wife as if they were his secretaries. After the minister had departed, when Du Roy was alone with Madeleine, he uttered threats and insinuations against the "parvenu," as he called him. His wife simply shrugged her shoulders scornfully, repeating: "Become a minister and you can do the same; until then, be silent."

His reply was: "No one knows of what I am capable; perhaps they will find out some day."

She answered philosophically: "He who lives will see."

The morning of the reopening of the Chamber, Du Roy lunched with Laroche-Mathieu in order to receive instructions from him, before the session, for a political article the following day in "La Vie Française," which was to be a sort of official declaration of the plans of the cabinet. After listening to Laroche-Mathieu's eloquence for some time with jealousy in his heart, Du Roy sauntered slowly toward the office to commence his work, for he had nothing to do until four o'clock, at which hour he was to meet Mme. de Marelle at Rue de Constantinople. They met there regularly twice a week, Mondays and Wednesdays.

On entering the office, he was handed a sealed dispatch; it was from Mme. Walter, and read thus:

"It is absolutely necessary that I should see you to-day. It is important. Expect me at two o'clock at Rue de Constantinople. I can render you a great service; your friend until death,

"VIRGINIE."

He exclaimed: "Heavens! what a bore!" and left the office at once, too much annoyed to work.

For six weeks he had ineffectually tried to break with Mme. Walter. At three successive meetings she had been a prey to remorse, and had overwhelmed her lover with reproaches. Angered by those scenes and already weary of the dramatic woman, he had simply avoided her, hoping that the affair would end in that way.

But she persecuted him with her affection, summoned him at all times by telegrams to meet her at street corners, in shops, or public gardens. She was very different from what he had fancied she would be, trying to attract him by actions ridiculous in one of her age. It disgusted him to hear her call him: "My rat—my dog—my treasure—my jewel—my blue-bird,"—and to see her assume a kind of childish modesty when he approached. It seemed to him that being the mother of a family, a woman of the world, she should have been more sedate, and have yielded with tears if she chose, but with the tears of a Dido and not of a Juliette. He never heard her call him "Little one," or "Baby," without wishing to reply "Old woman," to take his hat with an oath and leave the room.

At first they had often met at Rue de Constantinople, but Du Roy, who feared an encounter with Mme. de Marelle, invented a thousand and one pretexts in order to avoid that rendezvous. He was therefore obliged to either lunch or dine at her house daily, when she would clasp his hand under cover of the table or offer him her lips behind the doors. Above all, Georges enjoyed being thrown so much in

contact with Suzanne; she made sport of everything
and everybody with cutting appropriateness. At length,
however, he began to feel an unconquerable repug-
nance to the love lavished upon him by the mother;
he could no longer see her, hear her, nor think of
her without anger. He ceased calling upon her, replying to her letters, and yielding to her appeals. She
finally divined that he no longer loved her, and the discovery caused her unutterable anguish; but she watched
him, followed him in a cab with drawn blinds to the
office, to his house, in the hope of seeing him pass
by. He would have liked to strangle her, but he
controlled himself on account of his position on "La
Vie Française," and he endeavored by means of cold-
ness, and even at times harsh words, to make her
comprehend that all was at an end between them.

Then, too, she persisted in devising ruses for
summoning him to Rue de Constantinople, and he
was in constant fear that the two women would some
day meet face to face at the door.

On the other hand, his affection for Mme. de
Marelle had increased during the summer. They were
both Bohemians by nature; they took excursions together to Argenteuil, Bougival, Maisons, and Poissy,
and when he was forced to return and dine at Mme.
Walter's, he detested his mature mistress more
thoroughly, as he recalled the youthful one he had
just left. He was congratulating himself upon having
freed himself almost entirely from the former's clutches,
when he received the telegram above mentioned.

He re-read it as he walked along. He thought:
"What does that old owl want with me? I am
certain she has nothing to tell me except that she

adores me. However, I will see, perhaps there is some truth in it. Clotilde is coming at four, I must get rid of the other one at three or soon after, provided they do not meet. What jades women are!"

As he uttered those words he was reminded of his wife, who was the only one who did not torment him; she lived by his side and seemed to love him very much at the proper time, for she never permitted anything to interfere with her ordinary occupations of life. He strolled toward the appointed place of meeting, mentally cursing Mme. Walter.

"Ah, I will receive her in such a manner that she will not tell me anything. First of all, I will give her to understand that I shall never cross her threshold again."

He entered to await her. She soon arrived and, seeing him, exclaimed: "Ah, you received my dispatch! How fortunate!"

"Yes, I received it at the office just as I was setting out for the Chamber. What do you want?" he asked ungraciously.

She had raised her veil in order to kiss him, and approached him timidly and humbly with the air of a beaten dog.

"How unkind you are to me; how harshly you speak! What have I done to you? You do not know what I have suffered for you!"

He muttered: "Are you going to begin that again?"

She stood near him awaiting a smile, a word of encouragement, to cast herself into his arms, and whispered: "You need not have won me to treat me thus; you might have left me virtuous and happy.

Do you remember what you said to me in the church and how you forced me to enter this house? And now this is the way you speak to me, receive me! My God, my God, how you maltreat me!"

He stamped his foot and said violently: "Enough, be silent! I can never see you a moment without hearing that refrain. You were mature when you gave yourself to me. I am much obliged to you; I am infinitely grateful, but I need not be tied to your apron-strings until I die! You have a husband and I a wife. Neither of us is free; it was all a caprice, and now it is at an end!"

She said: "How brutal you are, how coarse and villainous! No, I was no longer a young girl, but I had never loved, never wavered in my dignity."

He interrupted her: "I know it, you have told me that twenty times; but you have had two children."

She drew back as if she had been struck: "Oh, Georges!" And pressing her hands to her heart, she burst into tears.

When she began to weep, he took his hat: "Ah, you are crying again! Good evening! Is it for this that you sent for me?"

She took a step forward in order to bar the way, and drawing a handkerchief from her pocket she wiped her eyes. Her voice grew steadier: "No, I came to — to give you — political news — to give you the means of earning fifty thousand francs — or even more if you wish to."

Suddenly softened he asked: "How?"

"By chance last evening I heard a conversation between my husband and Laroche. Walter advised the minister not to let you into the secret for you would expose it."

Du Roy placed his hat upon a chair and listened attentively.

"They are going to take possession of Morocco!"

"Why, I lunched with Laroche this morning, and he told me the cabinet's plans!"

"No, my dear, they have deceived you, because they feared their secret would be made known."

"Sit down," said Georges.

He sank into an armchair, while she drew up a stool and took her seat at his feet. She continued:

"As I think of you continually, I pay attention to what is talked of around me," and she proceeded to tell him what she had heard relative to the expedition to Tangiers which had been decided upon the day that Laroche assumed his office; she told him how they had little by little bought up, through agents who aroused no suspicions, the Moroccan loan, which had fallen to sixty-four or sixty-five francs; how when the expedition was entered upon the French government would guarantee the debt, and their friends would make fifty or sixty millions.

He cried: "Are you sure of that?"

She replied: "Yes, I am sure."

He continued: "That is indeed fine! As for that rascal of a Laroche, let him beware! I will get his ministerial carcass between my fingers yet!"

Then, after a moment's reflection, he muttered: "One might profit by that!"

"You too can buy some stock," said she; "it is only seventy-two francs."

He replied: "But I have no ready money."

She raised her eyes to his — eyes full of supplication.

"I have thought of that, my darling, and if you
love me a little, you will let me lend it to you."

He replied abruptly, almost harshly: "No, indeed."

She whispered imploringly: "Listen, there is something you can do without borrowing money. I intended buying ten thousand francs' worth of the
stock; instead, I will take twenty thousand and you
can have half. There will be nothing to pay at once.
If it succeeds, we will make seventy thousand francs;
if not, you will owe me ten thousand which you can
repay at your pleasure."

He said again: "No, I do not like those combina-
tions."

She tried to persuade him by telling him that she
advanced nothing — that the payments were made by
Walter's bank. She pointed out to him that he had
led the political campaign in "La Vie Française," and
that he would be very simple not to profit by the
results he had helped to bring about. As he still
hesitated, she added: "It is in reality Walter who
will advance the money, and you have done enough
for him to offset that sum."

"Very well," said he, "I will do it. If we lose
I will pay you back ten thousand francs."

She was so delighted that she rose, took his head
between her hands, and kissed him. At first he did
not repulse her, but when she grew more lavish with
her caresses, he said:

"Come, that will do."

She gazed at him sadly. "Oh, Georges, I can no
longer even embrace you."

"No, not to-day. I have a headache."

She reseated herself with docility at his feet and asked:

"Will you dine with us to-morrow? It would give me such pleasure."

He hesitated at first, but dared not refuse.

"Yes, certainly."

"Thank you, dearest." She rubbed her cheek against the young man's vest; as she did so, one of her long black hairs caught on a button; she twisted it tightly around, then she twisted another around another button and so on. When he rose, he would tear them out of her head, and would carry away with him unwittingly a lock of her hair. It would be an invisible bond between them. Involuntarily he would think, would dream of her; he would love her a little more the next day.

Suddenly he said: "I must leave you, for I am expected at the Chamber for the close of the session. I cannot be absent to-day."

She sighed: "Already!" Then adding resignedly: "Go, my darling, but you will come to dinner to-morrow"; she rose abruptly. For a moment she felt a sharp, stinging pain as if needles had been stuck into her head, but she was glad to have suffered for him.

"Adieu," said she.

He took her in his arms and kissed her eyes coldly; then she offered him her lips which he brushed lightly as he said: "Come, come, let us hurry; it is after three o'clock."

She passed out before him saying: "To-morrow at seven"; he repeated her words and they separated.

Du Roy returned at four o'clock to await his mistress. She was somewhat late because her husband had come home for a week. She asked:

"Can you come to dinner to-morrow? He will be delighted to see you."

"No; I dine at the Walters. We have a great many political and financial matters to talk over."

She took off her hat. He pointed to a bag on the mantelpiece: "I bought you some sweetmeats."

She clapped her hands. "What a darling you are!" She took them, tasted one, and said: "They are delicious. I shall not leave one. Come, sit down in the armchair, I will sit at your feet and eat my bonbons."

He smiled as he saw her take the seat a short while since occupied by Mme. Walter. She too, called him "darling, little one, dearest," and the words seemed to him sweet and caressing from her lips, while from Mme. Walter's they irritated and nauseated him.

Suddenly he remembered the seventy thousand francs he was going to make, and bluntly interrupting Mme. de Marelle's chatter, he said:

"Listen, my darling; I am going to intrust you with a message to your husband. Tell him from me to buy to-morrow ten thousand francs' worth of Moroccan stock which is at seventy-two, and I predict that before three months are passed he will have made eighty thousand francs. Tell him to maintain absolute silence. Tell him that the expedition to Tangiers is decided upon, and that the French government will guarantee the Moroccan debt. It is a state secret I am confiding to you, remember!"

She listened to him gravely and murmured:

"Thank you. I will tell my husband this evening. You may rely upon him; he will not speak of it; he can be depended upon; there is no danger."

She had eaten all of her bonbons and began to toy with the buttons on his vest. Suddenly she drew a long hair out of the buttonhole and began to laugh.

"See! Here is one of Madeleine's hairs; you are a faithful husband!" Then growing serious, she examined the scarcely perceptible thread more closely and said: "It is not Madeleine's, it is dark."

He smiled. "It probably belongs to the housemaid."

But she glanced at the vest with the care of a police-inspector and found a second hair twisted around a second button; then she saw a third; and turning pale and trembling somewhat, she exclaimed: "Oh, some woman has left hairs around all your buttons."

In surprise, he stammered: "Why you—you are mad."

She continued to unwind the hairs and cast them upon the floor. With her woman's instinct she had divined their meaning and gasped in her anger, ready to cry:

"She loves you and she wished you to carry away with you something of hers. Oh, you are a traitor." She uttered a shrill, nervous cry: "Oh, it is an old woman's hair—here is a white one—you have taken a fancy to an old woman now. Then you do not need me—keep the other one." She rose.

He attempted to detain her and stammered: "No —Clo—you are absurd—I do not know whose it is —listen—stay—see—stay—"

But she repeated: "Keep your old woman—keep her—have a chain made of her hair—of her gray hair—there is enough for that—"

Hastily she donned her hat and veil, and when he attempted to touch her she struck him in the face, and made her escape while he was stunned by the blow. When he found that he was alone, he cursed Mme. Walter, bathed his face, and went out vowing vengeance. That time he would not pardon. No, indeed.

He strolled to the boulevard and stopped at a jeweler's to look at a chronometer he had wanted for some time and which would cost eighteen hundred francs. He thought with joy: "If I make my seventy thousand francs, I can pay for it"—and he began to dream of all the things he would do when he got the money. First of all he would become a deputy; then he would buy the chronometer; then he would speculate on 'Change, and then, and then—he did not enter the office, preferring to confer with Madeleine before seeing Walter again and writing his article; he turned toward home. He reached Rue Drouot when he paused; he had forgotten to inquire for Count de Vaudrec, who lived on Chaussee d'-Antin. He retraced his steps with a light heart, thinking of a thousand things—of the fortune he would make, of that rascal of a Laroche, and of old Walter.

He was not at all uneasy as to Clotilde's anger, knowing that she would soon forgive him.

When he asked the janitor of the house in which Count de Vaudrec lived: "How is M. de Vaudrec? I have heard that he has been ailing of late," the man

replied: "The Count is very ill, sir; they think he
will not live through the night; the gout has reached
his heart."

Du Roy was so startled he did not know what to
do! Vaudrec dying! He stammered: "Thanks — I
will call again" — unconscious of what he was saying. He jumped into a cab and drove home. His
wife had returned. He entered her room out of
breath: "Did you know? Vaudrec is dying!"

She was reading a letter and turning to him asked:
"What did you say?"

"I said that Vaudrec is dying of an attack of
gout."

Then he added: "What shall you do?"

She rose; her face was livid; she burst into tears
and buried her face in her hands. She remained
standing, shaken by sobs, torn by anguish. Suddenly
she conquered her grief and wiping her eyes, said:
"I am going to him — do not worry about me — I do
not know what time I shall return — do not expect
me."

He replied: "Very well. Go."

They shook hands and she left in such haste that
she forgot her gloves. Georges, after dining alone,
began to write his article. He wrote it according to
the minister's instructions, hinting to the readers
that the expedition to Morocco would not take place.
He took it, when completed, to the office, conversed
several moments with M. Walter, and set out again,
smoking, with a light heart, he knew not why.

His wife had not returned. He retired and fell
asleep. Toward midnight Madeleine came home.
Georges sat up in bed and asked: "Well?"

He had never seen her so pale and agitated. She whispered: "He is dead!"

"Ah—and—he told you nothing?"

"Nothing. He was unconscious when I arrived."

Questions which he dared not ask arose to Georges' lips.

"Lie down and rest," said he.

She disrobed hastily and slipped into bed.

He continued: "Had he any relatives at his death-bed?"

"Only a nephew."

"Ah! Did he often see that nephew?"

"They had not met for ten years."

"Had he other relatives?"

"No, I believe not."

"Will that nephew be his heir?"

"I do not know."

"Was Vaudrec very rich?"

"Yes, very."

"Do you know what he was worth?"

"No, not exactly—one or two millions perhaps."

He said no more. She extinguished the light. He could not sleep. He looked upon Mme. Walter's promised seventy thousand francs as very insignificant. Suddenly he thought he heard Madeleine crying. In order to insure himself he asked: "Are you asleep?"

"No." Her voice was tearful and unsteady.

He continued: "I forgot to tell you that your minister has deceived us."

"How?"

He gave her a detailed account of the combination prepared by Laroche and Walter. When he concluded she asked: "How did you know that?"

He replied: "Pardon me if I do not tell you! You have your means of obtaining information into which I do not inquire; I have mine which I desire to keep. I can vouch at any rate for the truth of my statements."

She muttered: "It may be possible. I suspected that they were doing something without our knowledge."

As she spoke Georges drew near her; she paid no heed to his proximity, however, and turning toward the wall, he closed his eyes and fell asleep.

CHAPTER XIV.

The Will

THE church was draped in black, and over the door a large escutcheon surmounted by a coronet announced to the passers-by that a nobleman was being buried. The ceremony was just over; those present went out slowly, passing by the coffin, and by Count de Vaudrec's nephew, who shook hands and returned salutations.

When Georges du Roy and his wife left the church, they walked along side by side on their way home. They did not speak; they were both preoccupied. At length Georges said, as if talking to himself: "Truly it is very astonishing!"

Madeleine asked: "What, my friend?"

"That Vaudrec left us nothing."

She blushed and said: "Why should he leave us anything? Had he any reason for doing so?" Then after several moments of silence, she continued: "Perhaps there is a will at a lawyer's; we should not know of it."

7 G. de M.—11

He replied: "That is possible, for he was our best friend. He dined with us twice a week; he came at any time; he was at home with us. He loved you as a father; he had no family, no children, no brothers nor sisters, only a nephew. Yes, there should be a will. I would not care for much — a remembrance to prove that he thought of us — that he recognized the affection we felt for him. We should certainly have a mark of friendship."

She said with a pensive and indifferent air: "It is possible that there is a will."

When they entered the house, the footman handed Madeleine a letter. She opened it and offered it to her husband.

> "OFFICE OF M. LAMANEUR,
> "Notary.
> "17 Rue des Vosges.
>
> "MADAME: Kindly call at my office at a quarter past two o'clock Tuesday, Wednesday, or Thursday, on business which concerns you.   Yours respectfully,
> "LAMANEUR."

Georges, in his turn, colored.

"That is as it should be. It is strange, however, that he should write to you and not to me, for I am the head of the family legally."

"Shall we go at once?" she asked.

"Yes, I should like to."

After luncheon they set out for M. Lamaneur's office.

The notary was a short, round man — round all over. His head looked like a ball fastened to another ball, which was supported by legs so short that they too almost resembled balls.

He bowed, as Du Roy and his wife were shown into his office, pointed to seats, and said, turning to Madeleine: "Madame, I sent for you in order to inform you of Count de Vaudrec's will, which will be of interest to you."

Georges could not help muttering: "I suspected that."

The notary continued: "I shall read you the document which is very brief.

"'I, the undersigned, Paul Emile Cyprien Gontran, Count de Vaudrec, sound both in body and mind, here express my last wishes. As death might take me away at any moment, I wish to take the precaution of drawing up my will, to be deposited with M. Lamaneur.

"'Having no direct heirs, I bequeath all my fortune, comprising stocks and bonds for six hundred thousand francs and landed property for five hundred thousand, to Mme. Claire Madeleine du Roy unconditionally. I beg her to accept that gift from a dead friend as a proof of devoted, profound, and respectful affection.'"

The notary said: "That is all. That document bears the date of August last, and took the place of one of the same nature made two years ago in the name of Mme. Claire Madeleine Forestier. I have the first will, which would prove, in case of contestation on the part of the family, that Count de Vaudrec had not changed his mind."

Madeleine cast down her eyes; her cheeks were pale. Georges nervously twisted his mustache.

The notary continued after a moment's pause: "It is of course understood that Madame cannot accept that legacy without your consent."

Du Roy rose and said shortly: "I ask time for reflection."

The notary smiled, bowed, and replied pleasantly: "I comprehend the scruples which cause you to hesitate. I may add that M. de Vaudrec's nephew, who was informed this morning of his uncle's last wishes, expresses himself as ready to respect them if he be given one hundred thousand francs. In my opinion the will cannot be broken, but a lawsuit would cause a sensation which you would probably like to avoid. The world often judges uncharitably. Can you let me have your reply before Saturday?"

Georges bowed, and together with his wife left the office. When they arrived home, Du Roy closed the door and throwing his hat on the bed, asked: "What were the relations between you and Vaudrec?"

Madeleine, who was taking off her veil, turned around with a shudder: "Between us?"

"Yes, between you and him! One does not leave one's entire fortune to a woman unless—"

She trembled, and could scarcely take out the pins which fastened the transparent tissue. Then she stammered in an agitated manner: "You are mad — you are — you are — you did not think — he would leave you anything!"

Georges replied, emphazing each word: "Yes, he could have left me something; me, your husband, his friend; but not you, my wife and his friend. The distinction is material in the eyes of the world."

Madeleine gazed at him fixedly: "It seems to me that the world would have considered a legacy from him to you very strange."

"Why?"

"Because,"—she hesitated, then continued: "Because you are my husband; because you were not well acquainted; because I have been his friend so long; because his first will, made during Forestier's lifetime, was already in my favor."

Georges began to pace to and fro. He finally said: "You cannot accept that."

She answered indifferently: "Very well; it is not necessary then to wait until Saturday; you can inform M. Lamaneur at once."

He paused before her, and they gazed into one another's eyes as if by that mute and ardent interrogation they were trying to examine each other's consciences. In a low voice he murmured: "Come, confess your relations."

She shrugged her shoulders. "You are absurd. Vaudrec was very fond of me, very, but there was nothing more, never."

He stamped his foot. "You lie! It is not possible."

She replied calmly: "It is so, nevertheless."

He resumed his pacing to and fro; then pausing again, he said: "Explain to me, then, why he left all his fortune to you."

She did so with a nonchalant air: "It is very simple. As you said just now, we were his only friends, or rather, I was his only friend, for he knew me when a child. My mother was a governess in his father's house. He came here continually, and as he had no legal heirs, he selected me. It is possible that he even loved me a little. But what woman has never been loved thus? He brought me flowers every Monday. You were never surprised at that, and he never brought you any. To-day he leaves me his fortune for the same reason, because he had no one else to leave it to. It would on the other hand have been extremely surprising if he had left it to you."

"Why?"

"What are you to him?"

She spoke so naturally and so calmly that Georges hesitated before replying: "It makes no difference; we cannot accept that bequest under those conditions. Everyone would talk about it and laugh at me. My fellow-journalists are already too much disposed to be jealous of me and to attack me. I have to be especially careful of my honor and my reputation. I cannot permit my wife to accept a legacy of that kind from a man whom rumor has already assigned to her as her lover. Forestier might perhaps have tolerated that, but I shall not."

She replied gently: "Very well, my dear, we will not take it; it will be a million less in our pockets, that is all."

Georges paced the room and uttered his thoughts aloud, thus speaking to his wife without addressing her:

"Yes, a million — so much the worse. He did not think when making his will what a breach of etiquette he was committing. He did not realize in what a false, ridiculous position he was placing me. He should have left half of it to me — that would have made matters right."

He seated himself, crossed his legs and began to twist the ends of his mustache, as was his custom when annoyed, uneasy, or pondering over a weighty question.

Madeleine took up a piece of embroidery upon which she worked occasionally, and said: "I have nothing to say. You must decide."

It was some time before he replied; then he said hesitatingly: "The world would never understand how it was that Vaudrec constituted you his sole heiress and that I allowed it. To accept that legacy would be to avow guilty relations on your part and an infamous lack of self-respect on mine. Do you know how the acceptance of it might be interpreted? We should have to find some adroit means of palliating it. We should have to give people to suppose, for instance, that he divided his fortune between us, giving half to you and half to me."

She said: "I do not see how that can be done, since there is a formal will."

He replied: "Oh, that is very simple. We have no children; you can therefore deed me part of the inheritance. In that way we can silence malignant tongues."

She answered somewhat impatiently: "I do not see how we can silence malignant tongues since the will is there, signed by Vaudrec."

He said angrily: "Do you need to exhibit it, or affix it to the door? You are absurd! We will say that the fortune was left us jointly by Count de Vaudrec. That is all. You cannot, moreover, accept the legacy without my authority; I will only consent on the condition of a partition which will prevent me from becoming a laughing-stock for the world."

She glanced sharply at him: "As you will. I am ready."

He seemed to hesitate again, rose, paced the floor, and avoiding his wife's piercing gaze, he said: "No —decidedly no—perhaps it would be better to renounce it altogether—it would be more correct— more honorable. From the nature of the bequest even charitably-disposed people would suspect illicit relations."

He paused before Madeleine. "If you like, my darling, I will return to M. Lamaneur's alone, to consult him and to explain the matter to him. I will tell him of my scruples and I will add that we have agreed to divide it in order to avoid any scandal. From the moment that I accept a portion of the inheritance it will be evident that there is nothing wrong. I can say: 'My wife accepts it because I, her husband, accept'—I, who am the best judge of what she can do without compromising herself."

Madeleine simply murmured: "As you wish."

He continued: "Yes, it will be as clear as day if that is done. We inherit a fortune from a friend who wished to make no distinction between us, thereby showing that his liking for you was purely Platonic. You may be sure that if he had given it a thought, that is what he would have done. He did not reflect—he did not foresee the consequences. As you said just now, he offered you flowers every week, he left you his wealth."

She interrupted him with a shade of annoyance:

"I understand. No more explanations are necessary. Go to the notary at once."

He stammered in confusion: "You are right; I will go." He took his hat, and, as he was leaving the room, he asked: "Shall I try to compromise with the nephew for fifty thousand francs?"

She replied haughtily: "No. Give him the hundred thousand francs he demands, and take them from my share if you wish."

Abashed, he murmured: "No, we will share it. After deducting fifty thousand francs each we will still have a million net." Then he added: "Until later, my little Made."

He proceeded to the notary's to explain the arrangement decided upon, which he claimed originated with his wife. The following day they signed a deed for five hundred thousand francs, which Madeleine du Roy gave up to her husband.

On leaving the office, as it was pleasant, Georges proposed that they take a stroll along the boulevards. He was very tender, very careful of her, and laughed joyously while she remained pensive and grave.

It was a cold, autumn day. The pedestrians seemed in haste and walked along rapidly.

Du Roy led his wife to the shop into the windows of which he had so often gazed at the coveted chronometer.

"Shall I buy you some trinket?" he asked.

She replied indifferently: "As you like."

They entered the shop: "What would you prefer, a necklace, a bracelet, or earrings?"

The sight of the brilliant gems made her eyes sparkle in spite of herself, as she glanced at the cases filled with costly baubles.

Suddenly she exclaimed: "There is a lovely bracelet."

It was a chain, very unique in shape, every link of which was set with a different stone.

Georges asked: "How much is that bracelet?"

The jeweler replied: "Three thousand francs, sir."

"If you will let me have it for two thousand five hundred, I will take it."

The man hesitated, then replied: "No, sir, it is impossible."

Du Roy said: "See here—throw in this chronometer at fifteen hundred francs; that makes four thousand, and I will pay cash. If you do not agree, I will go somewhere else."

The jeweler finally yielded. "Very well, sir."

The journalist, after leaving his address, said: "You can have my initials G. R. C. interlaced below a baron's crown, engraved on the chronometer."

Madeleine, in surprise, smiled, and when they left the shop, she took his arm quite affectionately. She thought him very shrewd and clever. He was right; now that he had a fortune he must have a title.

They passed the Vaudeville on their way and, entering, secured a box. Then they repaired to Mme. de Marelle's at Georges' suggestion, to invite her to spend the evening with them. Georges rather dreaded the first meeting with Clotilde, but she did not seem to bear him any malice, or even to remember their disagreement. The dinner, which they took at a restaurant, was excellent, and the evening altogether enjoyable.

Georges and Madeleine returned home late. The gas was extinguished, and in order to light the way the journalist from time to time struck a match. On reaching the landing on the first floor they saw their reflections in the mirror. Du Roy raised his hand with the lighted match in it, in order to distinguish their images more clearly, and said, with a triumphant smile:

"The millionaires are passing by."

CHAPTER XV.

SUZANNE

MOROCCO had been conquered; France, the mistress of Tangiers, had guaranteed the debt of the annexed country. It was rumored that two ministers, Laroche-Mathieu being one of them, had made twenty millions.

As for Walter, in a few days he had become one of the masters of the world — a financier more omnipotent than a king. He was no longer the Jew, Walter, the director of a bank, the proprietor of a yellow newspaper; he was M. Walter the wealthy Israelite, and he wished to prove it.

Knowing the straitened circumstances of the Prince de Carlsbourg who owned one of the fairest mansions on Rue du Faubourg Saint-Honoré, he proposed to buy it. He offered three million francs for it. The prince, tempted by the sum, accepted his offer; the next day, Walter took possession of his new dwelling. Then another idea occurred to him — an idea of conquering all Paris — an idea *à la Bonaparte*.

At that time everyone was raving over a painting by the Hungarian, Karl Marcovitch, exhibited by

Jacques Lenoble and representing "Christ Walking
on the Water." Art critics enthusiastically declared
it to be the most magnificent painting of the age.
Walter bought it, thereby causing entire Paris to talk
of him, to envy him, to censure or approve his action. He issued an announcement in the papers
that everyone was invited to come on a certain evening to see it.

Du Roy was jealous of M. Walter's success. He
had thought himself wealthy with the five hundred
thousand francs extorted from his wife, and now he
felt poor as he compared his paltry fortune with the
shower of millions around him. His envious rage
increased daily. He cherished ill will toward everyone—toward the Walters, even toward his wife, and
above all toward the man who had deceived him,
made use of him, and who dined twice a week at
his house. Georges acted as his secretary, agent,
mouthpiece, and when he wrote at his dictation, he
felt a mad desire to strangle him. Laroche reigned
supreme in the Du Roy household, having taken the
place of Count de Vaudrec; he spoke to the servants as if he were their master. Georges submitted to it all, like a dog which wishes to bite and
dares not. But he was often harsh and brutal to
Madeleine, who merely shrugged her shoulders and
treated him as one would a fretful child. She was
surprised, too, at his constant ill humor, and said:
"I do not understand you. You are always complaining. Your position is excellent."

His only reply was to turn his back upon her.
He declared that he would not attend M. Walter's
fête—that he would not cross the miserable Jew's

threshold. For two months Mme. Walter had written to him daily, beseeching him to come to see
her, to appoint a meeting where he would, in order
that she might give him the seventy thousand francs
she had made for him. He did not reply and threw
her letters into the fire. Not that he would have refused to accept his share of the profits, but he enjoyed
treating her scornfully, trampling her under foot; she
was too wealthy; he would be inflexible.

The day of the exhibition of the picture, as Madeleine chided him for not going, he replied: "Leave
me in peace. I shall remain at home."

After they had dined, he said suddenly, "I suppose I shall have to go through with it. Get ready
quickly."

"I shall be ready in fifteen minutes," she said.

As they entered the courtyard of the Hôtel de
Carlsbourg it was one blaze of light. A magnificent carpet was spread upon the steps leading to the
entrance, and upon each one stood a man in livery,
as rigid as marble.

Du Roy's heart was torn with jealousy. He and
his wife ascended the steps and gave their wraps to
the footmen who approached them.

At the entrance to the drawing-room, two children,
one in pink, the other in blue, handed bouquets to the
ladies.

The rooms were already well filled. The major-
ity of the ladies were in street costumes, a proof
that they came thither as they would go to any exhibition. The few who intended to remain to the
ball which was to follow wore evening dress.

Mme. Walter, surrounded by friends, stood in the

second salon and received the visitors. Many did not know her, and walked through the rooms as if in a museum — without paying any heed to the host and hostess.

When Virginie perceived Du Roy, she grew livid and made a movement toward him; then she paused and waited for him to advance. He bowed ceremoniously, while Madeleine greeted her effusively. Georges left his wife near Mme. Walter and mingled with the guests. Five drawing-rooms opened one into the other; they were carpeted with rich, oriental rugs, and upon their walls hung paintings by the old masters. As he made his way through the throng, some one seized his arm, and a fresh, youthful voice whispered in his ear: "Ah, here you are at last, naughty Bel-Ami! Why do we never see you any more?"

It was Suzanne Walter, with her azure eyes and wealth of golden hair. He was delighted to see her, and apologized as they shook hands.

"I have been so busy for two months that I have been nowhere."

She replied gravely: "That is too bad. You have grieved us deeply, for mamma and I adore you. As for myself, I cannot do without you. If you are not here, I am bored to death. You see I tell you so frankly, that you will not remain away like that any more. Give me your arm; I will show you 'Christ Walking on the Water' myself; it is at the very end, behind the conservatory. Papa put it back there so that everyone would be obliged to go through the rooms. It is astonishing how proud papa is of this house."

As they walked through the rooms, all turned to look at that handsome man and that bewitching girl. A well-known painter said: "There is a fine couple." Georges thought: "If my position had been made, I would have married her. Why did I never think of it? How could I have taken the other one? What folly! One always acts too hastily— one never reflects sufficiently." And longing, bitter longing possessed him, corrupting all his pleasure, rendering life odious.

Suzanne said: "You must come often, Bel-Ami; we can do anything we like now papa is rich."

He replied: "Oh, you will soon marry—some prince, perhaps, and we shall never meet any more."

She cried frankly: "Oh, oh, I shall not! I shall choose some one I love very dearly. I am rich enough for two."

He smiled ironically and said: "I give you six months. By that time you will be Madame la Marquise, Madame la Duchesse, or Madame la Princesse, and you will look down upon me, Mademoiselle."

She pretended to be angry, patted his arm with her fan, and vowed that she would marry according to the dictates of her heart.

He replied: "We shall see; you are too wealthy."

"You, too, have inherited some money."

"Barely twenty thousand livres a year. It is a mere pittance nowadays."

"But your wife has the same."

"Yes, we have a million together; forty thousand a year. We cannot even keep a carriage on that."

They had, in the meantime, reached the last drawing-room, and before them lay the conservatory

with its rare shrubs and plants. To their left, under
a dome of palms, was a marble basin, on the edges
of which four large swans of delftware emitted the
water from their beaks.

The journalist stopped and said to himself: "This
is luxury; this is the kind of house in which to live.
Why can I not have one?"

His companion did not speak. He looked at her
and thought once more: "If I only had taken her!"

Suddenly Suzanne seemed to awaken from her
reverie. "Come," said she, dragging Georges through
a group which barred their way, and turning him to
the right. Before him, surrounded by verdure on all
sides, was the picture. One had to look closely at it
in order to understand it. It was a grand work—
the work of a master—one of those triumphs of art
which furnishes one for years with food for thought.

Du Roy gazed at it for some time, and then turned
away, to make room for others. Suzanne's tiny hand
still rested upon his arm. She asked:

"Would you like a glass of champagne? We will
go to the buffet; we shall find papa there."

Slowly they traversed the crowded rooms. Suddenly Georges heard a voice say: "That is Laroche
and Mme. du Roy."

He turned and saw his wife passing upon the
minister's arm. They were talking in low tones and
smiling into each other's eyes. He fancied he saw
some people whisper, as they gazed at them, and he
felt a desire to fall upon those two beings and smite
them to the earth. His wife was making a laughing-
stock of him. Who was she? A shrewd little par-
venue, that was all. He could never make his way

with a wife who compromised him.   She would be a
stumbling-block in his path.   Ah, if he had foreseen,
if he had known.   He would have played for higher
stakes.   What a brilliant match he might have made
with little Suzanne!   How could he have been so
blind?

They reached the dining-room with its marble
columns and walls hung with old Gobelins tapestry.
Walter spied his editor, and hastened to shake
hands.   He was beside himself with joy.   "Have you
seen everything?   Say, Suzanne, have you shown him
everything?   What a lot of people, eh?   Have you
seen Prince de Guerche? he just drank a glass of
punch."   Then he pounced upon Senator Rissolin
and his wife.

A gentleman greeted Suzanne — a tall, slender man
with fair whiskers and a worldly air.   Georges heard
her call him Marquis de Cazolles, and he was suddenly inspired with jealousy.   How long had she
known him?   Since she had become wealthy no
doubt.   He saw in him a possible suitor.   Some one
seized his arm.   It was Norbert de Varenne.   The
old poet said: "This is what they call amusing
themselves.   After a while they will dance, then
they will retire, and the young girls will be satisfied.
Take some champagne; it is excellent."

Georges scarcely heard his words.   He was looking for Suzanne, who had gone off with the Marquis
de Cazolles; he left Norbert de Varenne abruptly and
went in pursuit of the young girl.   The thirsty crowd
stopped him; when he had made his way through
it, he found himself face to face with M. and Mme.
de Marelle.   He had often met the wife, but he had

not met the husband for some time; the latter grasped both of his hands and thanked him for the message he had sent him by Clotilde relative to the stocks.

Du Roy replied: "In exchange for that service I shall take your wife, or rather offer her my arm. Husband and wife should always be separated."

M. de Marelle bowed. "Very well. If I lose you we can meet here again in an hour."

The two young people disappeared in the crowd, followed by the husband.

Mme. de Marelle said: "There are two girls who will have twenty or thirty millions each, and Suzanne is pretty in the bargain."

He made no reply; his own thought coming from the lips of another irritated him. He took Clotilde to see the painting. As they crossed the conservatory he saw his wife seated near Laroche-Mathieu, both of them almost hidden behind a group of plants. They seemed to say: "We are having a meeting in public, for we do not care for the world's opinion."

Mme. de Marelle admired Karl Marcovitch's painting, and they turned to repair to the other rooms. They were separated from M. de Marelle. He asked: "Is Laurine still vexed with me?"

"Yes. She refuses to see you and goes away when you are mentioned."

He did not reply. The child's sudden enmity grieved and annoyed him.

Suzanne met them at a door and cried: "Oh, here you are! Now, Bel-Ami, you are going to be left alone, for I shall take Clotilde to see my room." And

the two women glided through the throng. At that
moment a voice at his side murmured: "Georges!"

It was Mme. Walter. She continued in a low
voice: "How cruel you are! How needlessly you in-
flict suffering upon me. I bade Suzanne take that
woman away that I might have a word with you.
Listen: I must speak to you this evening — or — or —
you do not know what I shall do. Go into the conservatory. You will find a door to the left through
which you can reach the garden. Follow the walk
directly in front of you. At the end of it you will
see an arbor. Expect me in ten minutes. If you do
not meet me, I swear I will cause a scandal here at
once!"

He replied haughtily: "Very well, I shall be at
the place you named in ten minutes."

But Jacques Rival detained him. When he reached
the alley, he saw Mme. Walter in front of him; she
cried: "Ah, here you are! Do you wish to kill me?"

He replied calmly: "I beseech you, none of that,
or I shall leave you at once."

Throwing her arms around his neck, she exclaimed: "What have I done to you that you should
treat me so?"

He tried to push her away: "You twisted your
hair around my coat buttons the last time we met,
and it caused trouble between my wife and myself."

She shook her head: "Ah, your wife would not
care. It was one of your mistresses who made a
scene."

"I have none."

"Indeed! Why do you never come to see me?
Why do you refuse to dine with me even once a

week? I have no other thoughts than of you. I suffer terribly. You cannot understand that your image, always present, closes my throat, stifles me, and leaves me scarcely strength enough to move my limbs in order to walk. So I remain all day in my chair thinking of you."

He looked at her in astonishment. These were the words of a desperate woman, capable of anything. He, however, cherished a vague project and replied: "My dear, love is not eternal. One loves and one ceases to love. When it lasts it becomes a drawback. I want none of it! However, if you will be reasonable, and will receive and treat me as a friend, I will come to see you as formerly. Can you do that?"

She murmured: "I can do anything in order to see you."

"Then it is agreed that we are to be friends, nothing more."

She gasped: "It is agreed"; offering him her lips she cried in her despair: "One more kiss—one last kiss!"

He gently drew back. "No, we must adhere to our rules."

She turned her head and wiped away two tears, then drawing from her bosom a package of notes tied with pink ribbon, she held it toward Du Roy: "Here is your share of the profits in that Moroccan affair. I was so glad to make it for you. Here, take it."

He refused: "No, I cannot accept that money."

She became excited: "Oh, you will not refuse it now! It is yours, yours alone. If you do not take it, I will throw it in the sewer. You will not refuse it, Georges!"

He took the package and slipped it into his pocket. "We must return to the house; you will take cold."

"So much the better; if I could but die!"

She seized his hand, kissed it passionately, and fled toward the house. He returned more leisurely, and entered the conservatory with head erect and smiling lips. His wife and Laroche were no longer there. The crowd had grown thinner. Suzanne, leaning on her sister's arm, advanced toward him. In a few moments, Rose, whom they teased about a certain Count, turned upon her heel and left them.

Du Roy, finding himself alone with Suzanne, said in a caressing voice: "Listen, my dear little one; do you really consider me a friend?"

"Why, yes, Bel-Ami."

"You have faith in me?"

"Perfect faith."

"Do you remember what I said to you a while since?"

"About what?"

"About your marriage, or rather the man you would marry."

"Yes."

"Well, will you promise me one thing?"

"Yes; what is it?"

"To consult me when you receive a proposal and to accept no one without asking my advice."

"Yes, I will gladly."

"And it is to be a secret between us — not a word to your father or mother."

"Not a word."

Rival approached them saying: "Mademoiselle, your father wants you in the ballroom."

She said: "Come, Bel-Ami," but he refused, for he had decided to leave at once, wishing to be alone with his thoughts. He went in search of his wife, and found her drinking chocolate at the buffet with two strange men. She introduced her husband without naming them.

In a short while, he asked: "Shall we go?"

"Whenever you like."

She took his arm and they passed through the almost deserted rooms.

Madeleine asked: "Where is Mme. Walter; I should like to bid her good-bye."

"It is unnecessary. She would try to keep us in the ballroom, and I have had enough."

"You are right."

On the way home they did not speak. But when they had entered their room, Madeleine, without even taking off her veil, said to him with a smile: "I have a surprise for you."

He growled ill-naturedly: "What is it?"

"Guess."

"I cannot make the effort."

"The day after to-morrow is the first of January."

"Yes."

"It is the season for New Year's gifts."

"Yes."

"Here is yours, which Laroche handed me just now." She gave him a small black box which resembled a jewel-casket.

He opened it indifferently and saw the cross of the Legion of Honor. He turned a trifle pale, then smiled, and said: "I should have preferred ten millions. That did not cost him much."

She had expected a transport of delight and was irritated by his indifference.

"You are incomprehensible. Nothing seems to satisfy you."

He replied calmly: "That man is only paying his debts; he owes me a great deal more."

She was astonished at his tone, and said: "It is very nice, however, at your age."

He replied: "I should have much more."

He took the casket, placed it on the mantelpiece, and looked for some minutes at the brilliant star within it, then he closed it with a shrug of his shoulders and began to prepare to retire.

"L'Officiel" of January 1 announced that M. Prosper Georges du Roy had been decorated with the Legion of Honor for exceptional services. The name was written in two words, and that afforded Georges more pleasure than the decoration itself.

An hour after having read that notice, he received a note from Mme. Walter, inviting him to come and bring his wife to dine with them that evening, to celebrate his distinction.

At first he hesitated, then throwing the letter in the fire, he said to Madeleine: "We shall dine at the Walters' this evening."

In her surprise she exclaimed: "Why, I thought you would never set your foot in their house again."

His sole reply was: "I have changed my mind."

When they arrived at Rue du Faubourg Saint-Honoré, they found Mme. Walter alone in the dainty boudoir in which she received her intimate friends. She was dressed in black and her hair was powdered. At a distance she appeared like an old lady, in proximity, like a youthful one.

"Are you in mourning?" asked Madeleine.

She replied sadly: "Yes and no. I have lost none of my relatives, but I have arrived at an age when one should wear somber colors. I wear it to-day to inaugurate it; hitherto I have worn it in my heart."

The dinner was somewhat tedious. Suzanne alone talked incessantly. Rose seemed preoccupied. The journalist was overwhelmed with congratulations, after the meal, when all repaired to the drawing-rooms. Mme. Walter detained him as they were about to enter the salon, saying: "I will never speak of anything to you again, only come to see me, Georges. It is impossible for me to live without you. I see you, I feel you, in my heart all day and all night. It is as if I had drunk a poison which preyed upon me. I cannot bear it. I would rather be as an old woman to you. I powdered my hair for that reason to-night; but come here—come from time to time as a friend."

He replied calmly: "Very well. It is unnecessary to speak of it again. You see I came to-day on receipt of your letter."

Walter, who had preceded them, with his two daughters and Madeleine, awaited Du Roy near the picture of "Christ Walking on the Water."

"Only think," said he, "I found my wife yesterday kneeling before that painting as if in a chapel. She was praying!"

Mme. Walter replied in a firm voice, in a voice in which vibrated a secret exaltation: "That Christ will save my soul. He gives me fresh courage and strength every time that I look at Him." And pausing before the picture, she murmured: "How beautiful He is! How frightened those men are, and how they love Him! Look at His head, His eyes, how simple and supernatural He is at the same time!"

Suzanne cried: "Why, He looks like you, Bel-Ami! I am sure He looks like you. The resemblance is striking."

She made him stand beside the painting and everyone recognized the likeness. Du Roy was embarrassed. Walter thought it very singular; Madeleine, with a smile, remarked that Jesus looked more manly. Mme. Walter stood by motionless, staring fixedly at her lover's face, her cheeks as white as her hair.

CHAPTER XVI.

Divorce

During the remainder of the winter, the Du Roys often visited the Walters. Georges, too, frequently dined there alone, Madeleine pleading fatigue and preferring to remain at home. He had chosen Friday as his day, and Mme. Walter never invited anyone else on that evening; it belonged to Bel-Ami. Often in a dark corner or behind a tree in the conservatory, Mme. Walter embraced the young man and whispered in his ear: "I love you, I love you! I love you desperately!"

But he always repulsed her coldly, saying: "If you persist in that, I will not come again."

Toward the end of March people talked of the marriage of the two sisters: Rose was to marry, Dame Rumor said, Count de Latour-Ivelin and Suzanne, the Marquis de Cazolles. The subject of Suzanne's possible marriage had not been broached again between her and Georges until one morning, the latter having been brought home by M. Walter to lunch, he whispered to Suzanne: "Come, let us give the fish some bread."

They proceeded to the conservatory in which was the marble basin containing the fish. As Georges and Suzanne leaned over its edge, they saw their reflections in the water and smiled at them. Suddenly, he said in a low voice: "It is not right of you to keep secrets from me, Suzanne."

She asked:

"What secrets, Bel-Ami?"

"Do you remember what you promised me here the night of the *fête?*"

"No."

"To consult me every time you received a proposal."

"Well?"

"Well, you have received one!"

"From whom?"

"You know very well."

"No, I swear I do not."

"Yes, you do. It is from that fop of a Marquis de Cazolles."

"He is not a fop."

"That may be, but he is stupid. He is no match for you who are so pretty, so fresh, so bright!"

She asked with a smile: "What have you against him?"

"I? Nothing!"

"Yes, you have. He is not all that you say he is."

"He is a fool, and an intriguer."

She glanced at him: "What ails you?"

He spoke as if tearing a secret from the depths of his heart: "I am — I am jealous of him."

She was astonished.

"You?"

"Yes, I."

"Why?"

"Because I love you and you know it."

Then she said severely: "You are mad, Bel-Ami!"

He replied: "I know that I am! Should I confess it—I, a married man, to you, a young girl? I am worse than mad—I am culpable, wretched—I have no possible hope, and that thought almost destroys my reason. When I hear that you are going to be married, I feel murder in my heart. You must forgive me, Suzanne."

He paused. The young girl murmured half sadly, half gaily: "It is a pity that you are married; but what can you do? It cannot be helped."

He turned toward her abruptly and said: "If I were free would you marry me?"

She replied: "Yes, Bel-Ami, I would marry you because I love you better than any of the others."

He rose and stammering: "Thanks—thanks—do not, I implore you, say yes to anyone. Wait a while. Promise me."

Somewhat confused, and without comprehending what he asked, she whispered: "I promise."

Du Roy threw a large piece of bread into the water and fled, without saying adieu, as if he were beside himself. Suzanne, in surprise, returned to the salon.

When Du Roy arrived home, he asked Madeleine, who was writing letters: "Shall you dine at the Walters' Friday? I am going."

She hesitated: "No, I am not well. I prefer to remain here."

"As you like. No one will force you." Then he took up his hat and went out.

For some time he had watched and followed her, knowing all her actions. The time he had awaited had come at length.

On Friday he dressed early, in order, as he said, to make several calls before going to M. Walter's. At about six o'clock, after having kissed his wife, he went in search of a cab. He said to the cabman: "You can stop at No. 17 Rue Fontaine, and remain there until I order you to go on. Then you can take me to the restaurant Du Coq-Faisan, Rue Lafayette."

The cab rolled slowly on; Du Roy lowered the shades. When in front of his house, he kept watch of it. After waiting ten minutes, he saw Madeleine come out and go toward the boulevards. When she was out of earshot, he put his head out of the window and cried: "Go on!"

The cab proceeded on its way and stopped at the Coq-Faisan. Georges entered the dining-room and ate slowly, looking at his watch from time to time. At seven-thirty he left and drove to Rue La Rochefoucauld. He mounted to the third story of a house in that street, and asked the maid who opened the door: "Is M. Guibert de Lorme at home?"

"Yes, sir."

He was shown into the drawing-room, and after waiting some time, a tall man with a military bearing and gray hair entered. He was the police commissioner.

Du Roy bowed, then said: "As I suspected, my wife is with her lover in furnished apartments they have rented on Rue des Martyrs."

The magistrate bowed: "I am at your service, sir."

"Very well, I have a cab below." And with three other officers they proceeded to the house in which Du Roy expected to surprise his wife. One officer remained at the door to watch the exit; on the second floor they halted; Du Roy rang the bell and they waited. In two or three minutes Georges rang again several times in succession. They heard a light step approach, and a woman's voice, evidently disguised, asked:

"Who is there?"

The police officer replied: "Open in the name of the law."

The voice repeated: "Who are you?"

"I am the police commissioner. Open, or I will force the door."

The voice continued: "What do you want?"

Du Roy interrupted: "It is I; it is useless to try to escape us."

The footsteps receded and then returned. Georges said: "If you do not open, we will force the door."

Receiving no reply he shook the door so violently that the old lock gave way, and the young man almost fell over Madeleine, who was standing in the antechamber in her petticoat, her hair loosened, her feet bare, and a candle in her hand.

He exclaimed: "It is she. We have caught them," and he rushed into the room. The commissioner turned to Madeleine, who had followed them through the rooms, in one of which were the remnants of a supper, and looking into her eyes said: "You are Mme. Claire Madeleine du Roy, lawful wife of M. Prosper Georges du Roy, here present?"

She replied: "Yes, sir."

"What are you doing here?"

She made no reply. The officer repeated his question; still she did not reply. He waited several moments and then said: "If you do not confess, Madame, I shall be forced to inquire into the matter."

They could see a man's form concealed beneath the covers of the bed. Du Roy advanced softly and uncovered the livid face of M. Laroche-Mathieu.

The officer again asked: "Who are you?"

As the man did not reply, he continued: "I am the police commissioner and I call upon you to tell me your name. If you do not answer, I shall be forced to arrest you. In any case, rise. I will interrogate you when you are dressed."

In the meantime Madeleine had regained her composure, and seeing that all was lost, she was determined to put a brave face upon the matter. Her eyes sparkled with the audacity of bravado, and taking a piece of paper she lighted the ten candles in the candelabra as if for a reception. That done, she leaned against the mantelpiece, took a cigarette out of a case, and began to smoke, seeming not to see her husband.

In the meantime the man in the bed had dressed himself and advanced. The officer turned to him: "Now, sir, will you tell me who you are?"

He made no reply.

"I see I shall have to arrest you."

Then the man cried: "Do not touch me. I am inviolable."

Du Roy rushed toward him exclaiming: "I can have you arrested if I want to!" Then he added: "This man's name is Laroche-Mathieu, minister of foreign affairs."

The officer retreated and stammered: "Sir, will you tell me who you are?"

"For once that miserable fellow has not lied. I am indeed Laroche-Mathieu, minister," and pointing to Georges' breast, he added, "and that scoundrel wears upon his coat the cross of honor which I gave him."

Du Roy turned pale. With a rapid gesture he tore the decoration from his buttonhole and throwing it in the fire exclaimed: "That is what a decoration is worth which is given by a scoundrel of your order."

The commissioner stepped between them, as they stood face to face, saying: "Gentlemen, you forget yourselves and your dignity."

Madeleine smoked on calmly, a smile hovering about her lips. The officer continued: "Sir, I have surprised you alone with Mme. du Roy under suspicious circumstances; what have you to say?"

"Nothing; do your duty."

The commissioner turned to Madeleine: "Do you confess, Madame, that this gentleman is your lover?"

She replied boldly: "I do not deny it. That is sufficient."

The magistrate made several notes; when he had finished writing, the minister, who stood ready, coat upon arm, hat in hand, asked: "Do you need me any longer, sir? Can I go?"

Du Roy addressed him with an insolent smile: "Why should *you* go, we have finished; we will leave you alone together." Then, taking the officer's arm, he said: "Let us go, sir; we have nothing more to do in this place."

An hour later Georges du Roy entered the office of "La Vie Française." M. Walter was there; he raised his head and asked: "What, are you here? Why are you not dining at my house? Where have you come from?"

Georges replied with emphasis: "I have just found out something about the minister of foreign affairs."

"What?"

"I found him alone with my wife in hired apartments. The commissioner of police was my witness. The minister is ruined."

"Are you not jesting?"

"No, I am not. I shall even write an article on it."

"What is your object?"

"To overthrow that wretch, that public malefactor."

Georges placed his hat upon a chair and added: "Woe to those whom I find in my path. I never pardon."

The manager stammered: "But your wife?"

"I shall apply for a divorce at once."

"A divorce?"

"Yes, I am master of the situation. I shall be free. I have a stated income. I shall offer myself as a candidate in October in my native district, where I am known. I could not win any respect were I to be hampered with a wife whose honor was sullied. She took me for a simpleton, but since I have known her game, I have watched her, and now I shall get on, for I shall be free."

Georges rose.

"I will write the item; it must be handled prudently."

The old man hesitated, then said: "Do so: it serves those right who are caught in such scrapes."

CHAPTER XVII.

THE FINAL PLOT

THREE months had elapsed. Georges
du Roy's divorce had been obtained. His wife had resumed the
name of Forestier.

As the Walters were going to
Trouville on the fifteenth of July, they
decided to spend a day in the country
before starting.

The day chosen was Thursday, and they
set out at nine o'clock in the morning in
a large six-seated carriage drawn by four
horses. They were going to lunch at Saint-
Germain. Bel-Ami had requested that he might
be the only young man in the party, for he could
not bear the presence of the Marquis de Cazolles.
At the last moment, however, it was decided that
Count de Latour-Ivelin should go, for he and Rose
had been betrothed a month. The day was delightful. Georges, who was very pale, gazed at Suzanne
as they sat in the carriage and their eyes met.

Mme. Walter was contented and happy. The
luncheon was a long and merry one. Before leaving

for Paris, Du Roy proposed a walk on the terrace. They stopped on the way to admire the view; as they passed on, Georges and Suzanne lingered behind. The former whispered softly: "Suzanne, I love you madly."

She whispered in return: "I love you too, Bel-Ami."

He continued: "If I cannot have you for my wife, I shall leave the country."

She replied: "Ask papa. Perhaps he will consent."

He answered impatiently: "No, I repeat that it is useless; the door of the house would be closed against me. I would lose my position on the journal, and we would not even meet. Those are the consequences a formal proposal would produce. They have promised you to the Marquis de Cazolles; they hope you will finally say 'yes' and they are waiting."

"What can we do?"

"Have you the courage to brave your father and mother for my sake?"

"Yes."

"Truly?"

"Yes."

"Well! There is only one way. It must come from you and not from me. You are an indulged child; they let you say anything and are not surprised at any audacity on your part. Listen, then! This evening on returning home, go to your mother first, and tell her that you want to marry me. She will be very much agitated and very angry."

Suzanne interrupted him: "Oh, mamma would be glad."

He replied quickly: "No, no, you do not know her. She will be more vexed than your father. But you must insist, you must not yield; you must repeat that you will marry me and me alone. Will you do so?"

"I will."

"And on leaving your mother, repeat the same thing to your father very decidedly."

"Well, and then—"

"And then matters will reach a climax! If you are determined to be my wife, my dear, dear, little Suzanne, I will elope with you."

She clapped her hands, as all the charming adventures in the romances she had read occurred to her, and cried:

"Oh, what bliss! When will you elope with me?"

He whispered very low: "To-night!"

"Where shall we go?"

"That is my secret. Think well of what you are doing. Remember that after that flight you must become my wife. It is the only means, but it is dangerous—very dangerous—for you."

"I have decided. Where shall I meet you?"

"Meet me about midnight in the Place de la Concorde."

"I will be there."

He clasped her hand. "Oh, how I love you! How brave and good you are! Then you do not want to marry Marquis de Cazolles?"

"Oh, no!"

Mme. Walter, turning her head, called out: "Come, little one; what are you and Bel-Ami doing?"

They rejoined the others and returned by way of
Chatou. When the carriage arrived at the door of
the mansion, Mme. Walter pressed Georges to dine
with them, but he refused, and returned home to
look over his papers and destroy any compromising
letters. Then he repaired in a cab with feverish
haste to the place of meeting. He waited there some
time, and thinking his ladylove had played him
false, he was about to drive off, when a gentle voice
whispered at the door of his cab: "Are you there,
Bel-Ami?"

"Is it you, Suzanne?"

"Yes."

"Ah, get in." She entered the cab and he bade
the cabman drive on.

He asked: "Well, how did it all pass off?"

She murmured faintly:

"Oh, it was terrible, with mamma especially."

"Your mamma? What did she say? Tell me!"

"Oh, it was frightful! I entered her room and
made the little speech I had prepared. She turned
pale and cried: 'Never!' I wept, I protested that I
would marry only you; she was like a mad woman;
she vowed I should be sent to a convent. I never
saw her like that, never. Papa, hearing her agitated
words, entered. He was not as angry as she was,
but he said you were not a suitable match for me.
As they had vexed me, I talked louder than they, and
papa with a dramatic air bade me leave the room.
That decided me to fly with you. And here I am;
where shall we go?"

He replied, encircling her waist with his arm: "It
is too late to take the train; this cab will take us to

Sèvres where we can spend the night, and to-morrow we will leave for La Roche-Guyon. It is a pretty village on the banks of the Seine between Mantes and Bonnières."

The cab rolled on. Georges took the young girl's hand and kissed it respectfully. He did not know what to say to her, being unaccustomed to Platonic affection. Suddenly he perceived that she was weeping. He asked in affright:

"What ails you, my dear little one?"

She replied tearfully: "I was thinking that poor mamma could not sleep if she had found out that I was gone!"

  *   *   *   *   *   *   *

Her mother indeed was not asleep.

When Suzanne left the room, Mme. Walter turned to her husband and asked in despair: "What does that mean?"

"It means that that intriguer has influenced her. It is he who has made her refuse Cazolles. You have flattered and cajoled him, too. It was Bel-Ami here, Bel-Ami there, from morning until night. Now you are paid for it!"

"I?"

"Yes, you. You are as much infatuated with him as Madeleine, Suzanne, and the rest of them. Do you think that I did not see that you could not exist for two days without him?"

She rose tragically: "I will not allow you to speak to me thus. You forget that I was not brought up like you, in a shop."

With an oath, he left the room, banging the door behind him.

When he was gone, she thought over all that had taken place. Suzanne was in love with Bel-Ami, and Bel-Ami wanted to marry Suzanne! No, it was not true! She was mistaken; he would not be capable of such an action; he knew nothing of Suzanne's escapade. They would take Suzanne away for six months and that would end it.

She rose, saying: "I cannot rest in this uncertainty. I shall lose my reason. I will arouse Suzanne and question her."

She proceeded to her daughter's room. She entered; it was empty; the bed had not been slept in. A horrible suspicion possessed her and she flew to her husband. He was in bed, reading.

She gasped: "Have you seen Suzanne?"

"No — why?"

"She is — gone! she is not in her room."

With one bound he was out of bed; he rushed to his daughter's room; not finding her there, he sank into a chair. His wife had followed him.

"Well?" she asked.

He had not the strength to reply: he was no longer angry; he groaned: "He has her — we are lost."

"Lost, how?"

"Why, he must marry her now!"

She cried wildly: "Marry her, never! Are you mad?"

He replied sadly: "It will do no good to yell! He has disgraced her. The best thing to be done is to give her to him, and at once, too; then no one will know of this escapade."

She repeated in great agitation: "Never; he shall never have Suzanne."

Overcome, Walter murmured: "But he has her.
And he will keep her as long as we do not yield;
therefore, to avoid a scandal we must do so at once."

But his wife replied: "No, no, I will never consent."

Impatiently he returned: "It is a matter of necessity. Ah, the scoundrel—how he has deceived us!
But he is shrewd at any rate. She might have done
better as far as position, but not intelligence and
future, is concerned. He is a promising young man.
He will be a deputy or a minister some day."

Mme. Walter, however, repeated wildly: "I will
never let him marry Suzanne! Do you hear—never!"

In his turn he became incensed, and like a practical man defended Bel-Ami. "Be silent! I tell you
he must marry her! And who knows? Perhaps
we shall not regret it! With men of his stamp
one never knows what may come about. You saw
how he downed Laroche-Mathieu in three articles,
and that with a dignity which was very difficult to
maintain in his position as husband. So, we shall
see."

Mme. Walter felt a desire to cry aloud and tear
her hair. But she only repeated angrily: "He shall
not have her!"

Walter rose, took up his lamp, and said: "You
are silly, like all women! You only act on impulse.
You do not know how to accommodate yourself to
circumstances. You are stupid! I tell you he shall
marry her; it is essential." And he left the room.

Mme. Walter remained alone with her suffering,
her despair. If only a priest were at hand! She
would cast herself at his feet and confess all her

errors and her agony — he would prevent the marriage! Where could she find a priest? Where should she turn? Before her eyes floated, like a vision, the calm face of "Christ Walking on the Water," as she had seen it in the painting. He seemed to say to her: "Come unto Me. Kneel at My feet. I will comfort and instruct you as to what to do."

She took the lamp and sought the conservatory; she opened the door leading into the room which held the enormous canvas, and fell upon her knees before it. At first she prayed fervently, but as she raised her eyes and saw the resemblance to Bel-Ami, she murmured: "Jesus — Jesus —" while her thoughts were with her daughter and her lover. She uttered a wild cry, as she pictured them together — alone — and fell into a swoon. When day broke they found Mme. Walter still lying unconscious before the painting. She was so ill, after that, that her life was almost despaired of.

M. Walter explained his daughter's absence to the servants by saying to them that she had been sent to a convent for a short time. Then he replied to a long letter from Du Roy, giving his consent to his marriage with his daughter. Bel-Ami had posted that epistle when he left Paris, having prepared it the night of his departure. In it he said in respectful terms that he had loved the young girl a long time; that there had never been any understanding between them, but that as she came to him to say: "I will be your wife," he felt authorized in keeping her, in hiding her, in fact, until he had obtained a reply from her parents, whose wishes were to him of more value than those of his betrothed.

Georges and Suzanne spent a week at La Roche-Guyon. Never had the young girl enjoyed herself so thoroughly. As she passed for his sister, they lived in a chaste and free intimacy, a kind of loving companionship. He thought it wiser to treat her with respect, and when he said to her: "We will return to Paris to-morrow; your father has bestowed your hand upon me," she whispered naïvely: "Already? This is just as pleasant as being your wife."

CHAPTER XVIII.

ATTAINMENT

IT WAS dark in the apartments in the Rue de Constantinople, when Georges du Roy and Clotilde de Marelle, having met at the door, entered them. Without giving him time to raise the shades, the latter said:

"So you are going to marry Suzanne Walter?"

He replied in the affirmative, adding gently: "Did you not know it?"

She answered angrily: "So you are going to marry Suzanne Walter? For three months you have deceived me. Everyone knew of it but me. My husband told me. Since you left your wife you have been preparing for that stroke, and you made use of me in the interim. What a rascal you are!"

He asked: "How do you make that out? I had a wife who deceived me; I surprised her, obtained a divorce, and am now going to marry another. What is more simple than that?"

She murmured: "What a villain!"

He said with dignity: "I beg of you to be more careful as to what you say."

She rebelled at such words from him: "What! Would you like me to handle you with gloves? You have conducted yourself like a rascal ever since I have known you, and now you do not want me to speak of it. You deceive everyone; you gather pleasure and money everywhere, and you want me to treat you as an honest man."

He rose; his lips twitched: "Be silent or I will make you leave these rooms."

She cried: "Leave here—you will make me— you? You forget that it is I who have paid for these apartments from the very first, and you threaten to put me out of them. Be silent, good-for-nothing! Do you think I do not know how you stole a portion of Vaudrec's bequest from Madeleine? Do you think I do not know about Suzanne?"

He seized her by her shoulders and shook her. "Do not speak of that; I forbid you."

"I know you have ruined her!"

He would have taken anything else, but that lie exasperated him. He repeated: "Be silent—take care"— and he shook her as he would have shaken the bough of a tree. Still she continued: "You were her ruin, I know it." He rushed upon her and struck her as if she had been a man. Suddenly she ceased speaking, and groaned beneath his blows. Finally he desisted, paced the room several times in order to regain his self-possession, entered the bedroom, filled the basin with cold water and bathed his head. Then he washed his hands and returned to see what Clotilde was doing. She had not moved. She lay upon the floor weeping softly. He asked harshly:

"Will you soon have done crying?"

She did not reply. He stood in the center of the room, somewhat embarrassed, somewhat ashamed, as he saw the form lying before him. Suddenly he seized his hat. "Good evening. You can leave the key with the janitor when you are ready. I will not await your pleasure."

He left the room, closed the door, sought the porter, and said to him: "Madame is resting. She will go out soon. You can tell the proprietor that I have given notice for the first of October."

His marriage was fixed for the twentieth; it was to take place at the Madeleine. There had been a great deal of gossip about the entire affair, and many different reports were circulated. Mme. Walter had aged greatly; her hair was gray and she sought solace in religion.

In the early part of September "La Vie Française" announced that Baron du Roy de Cantel had become its chief editor, M. Walter reserving the title of manager. To that announcement were subjoined the names of the staff of art and theatrical critics, political reporters, and so forth. Journalists no longer sneered in speaking of "La Vie Française;" its success had been rapid and complete. The marriage of its chief editor was what was called a "Parisian event," Georges du Roy and the Walters having occasioned much comment for some time.

The ceremony took place on a clear, autumn day. At ten o'clock the curious began to assemble; at eleven o'clock, detachments of officers came to dis-

perse the crowd.   Soon after, the first guests arrived;
they were followed by others, women in rich costumes, men, grave and dignified.   The church slowly
began to fill.   Norbert de Varenne espied Jacques
Rival, and joined him.

"Well," said he, "sharpers always succeed."

His companion, who was not envious, replied:
"So much the better for him.   His fortune is made."

Rival asked: "Do you know what has become
of his wife?"

The poet smiled.   "Yes and no — she lives a very
retired life, I have been told, in the Montmartre
quarter.   But — there is a but — for some time I have
read political articles in 'La Plume,' which resemble
those of Forestier and Du Roy.   They are supposed
to be written by a Jean Le Dol, a young, intelligent,
handsome man — something like our friend Georges
— who has become acquainted with Mme. Forestier.
From that I have concluded that she likes beginners
and that they like her.   She is, moreover, rich;
Vaudrec and Laroche-Mathieu were not attentive to
her for nothing."

Rival asked: "Tell me, is it true that Mme. Walter and Du Roy do not speak?"

"Yes.   She did not wish to give him her daughter's hand.   But he threatened the old man with
shocking revelations.   Walter remembered Laroche-
Mathieu's fate and yielded at once; but his wife, obstinate like all women, vowed that she would never
address a word to her son-in-law.   It is comical to
see them together!   She looks like the statue of
vengeance, and he is very uncomfortable, although he
tries to appear at his ease."

Suddenly the beadle struck the floor three times with his staff. All the people turned to see what was coming, and the young bride appeared in the doorway leaning upon her father's arm. She looked like a beautiful doll, crowned with a wreath of orange blossoms. She advanced with bowed head. The ladies smiled and murmured as she passed them. The men whispered:

"Exquisite, adorable!"

M. Walter walked by her side with exaggerated dignity. Behind them came four maids of honor dressed in pink and forming a charming court for so dainty a queen.

Mme. Walter followed on the arm of Count de Latour-Ivelin's aged father. She did not walk; she dragged herself along, ready to faint at every step. She had aged and grown thinner.

Next came Georges du Roy with an old lady, a stranger. He held his head proudly erect and wore upon his coat, like a drop of blood, the red ribbon of the Legion of Honor.

He was followed by the relatives: Rose, who had been married six weeks, with a senator; Count de Latour-Ivelin with Viscountess de Percemur. Following them was a motley procession of associates and friends of Du Roy, country cousins of Mme. Walter's, and guests invited by her husband.

The tones of the organ filled the church; the large doors at the entrance were closed, and Georges kneeled beside his bride in the choir. The new bishop of Tangiers, cross in hand, miter on head, entered from the sacristy, to unite them in the name of the Almighty. He asked the usual questions, rings

were exchanged, words pronounced which bound
them forever, and then he delivered an address to the
newly married couple.

The sound of stifled sobs caused several to turn
their heads. Mme. Walter was weeping, her face
buried in her hands. She had been obliged to yield;
but since the day on which she had told Du Roy:
"You are the vilest man I know; never speak to me
again, for I will not answer you," she had suffered
intolerable anguish. She hated Suzanne bitterly; her
hatred was caused by unnatural jealousy. The bishop
was marrying a daughter to her mother's lover, before
her and two thousand persons, and she could say
nothing; she could not stop him. She could not cry:
"He is mine, that man is my lover. That union you
are blessing is infamous."

Several ladies, touched by her apparent grief, murmured: "How affected that poor mother is!"

The bishop said: "You are among the favored ones
of the earth. You, sir, who are raised above others
by your talent—you who write, instruct, counsel,
guide the people, have a grand mission to fulfill—a
fine example to set."

Du Roy listened to him proudly. A prelate of the
Roman Church spoke thus to him. A number of illustrious people had come thither on his account. It
seemed to him that an invisible power was impelling
him on. He would become one of the masters of the
country—he, the son of the poor peasants of Canteleu. He had given his parents five thousand francs
of Count de Vaudrec's fortune and he intended sending them fifty thousand more; then they could buy a
small estate and live happily.

The bishop had finished his harangue, a priest
ascended the altar, and the organ pealed forth. Suddenly the vibrating tones melted into delicate, melo-
dious ones, like the songs of birds; then again they
swelled into deep, full tones and human voices chanted
over their bowed heads. Vauri and Landeck of the
Opera were singing.

Bel-Ami, kneeling beside Suzanne, bowed his head.
At that moment he felt almost pious, for he was
filled with gratitude for the blessings showered upon
him. Without knowing just whom he was addressing, he offered up thanks for his success. When the
ceremony was over, he rose, and, giving his arm to
his wife, they passed into the sacristy. A stream of
people entered. Georges fancied himself a king whom
the people were coming to greet. He shook hands,
uttered words which signified nothing, and replied to
congratulations with the words: "You are very kind."

Suddenly he saw Mme. de Marelle, and the recollection of all the kisses he had given her and which
she had returned, of all their caresses, of the sound
of her voice, possessed him with the mad desire to
regain her. She was so pretty, with her bright eyes
and roguish air! She advanced somewhat timidly
and offered him her hand. He took, retained, and
pressed it as if to say: "I shall love you always, I
am yours."

Their eyes met, smiling, bright, full of love. She
murmured in her soft tones: "Until we meet again,
sir!" and he gaily repeated her words.

Others approached, and she passed on. Finally the
throng dispersed. Georges placed Suzanne's hand
upon his arm to pass through the church with her.

It was filled with people, for all had resumed their seats in order to see them leave the sacred edifice together. He walked along slowly, with a firm step, his head erect. He saw no one. He only thought of himself.

When they reached the threshold he saw a crowd gathered outside, come to gaze at him, Georges du Roy. The people of Paris envied him. Raising his eyes, he saw beyond the Place de la Concorde, the chamber of deputies, and it seemed to him that it was only a stone's throw from the portico of the Madeleine to that of the Palais Bourbon.

Leisurely they descended the steps between two rows of spectators, but Georges did not see them; his thoughts had returned to the past, and before his eyes, dazzled by the bright sunlight, floated the image of Mme. de Marelle, rearranging the curly locks upon her temples before the mirror in their apartments.

"Leisurely they descended the steps."

YVETTE

YVETTE

CHAPTER I.

THE INITIATION OF SAVAL

As THEY were leaving the Café Riche, Jean de Servigny said to Léon Saval: "If you don't object, let us walk. The weather is too fine to take a cab."

His friend answered: "I would like nothing better."

Jean replied: "It is hardly eleven o'clock. We shall arrive much before midnight, so let us go slowly."

A restless crowd was moving along the boulevard, that throng peculiar to summer nights, drinking, chatting, and flowing like a river, filled with a sense of comfort and joy. Here and there a *café* threw a flood of light upon a knot of patrons drinking at little tables on the sidewalk, which were covered with bottles and glasses, hindering the passing of the hurrying multitude. On the pavement the cabs with their red,

(3)

blue, or green lights dashed by, showing for a second, in the glimmer, the thin shadow of the horse, the raised profile of the coachman, and the dark box of the carriage. The cabs of the Urbaine Company made clear and rapid spots when their yellow panels were struck by the light.

The two friends walked with slow steps, cigars in their mouths, in evening dress and overcoats on their arms, with a flower in their buttonholes, and their hats a trifle on one side, as men will carelessly wear them sometimes, after they have dined well and the air is mild.

They had been linked together since their college days by a close, devoted, and firm affection. Jean de Servigny, small, slender, a trifle bald, rather frail, with elegance of mien, curled mustache, bright eyes, and fine lips, was a man who seemed born and bred upon the boulevard. He was tireless in spite of his languid air, strong in spite of his pallor, one of those slight Parisians to whom gymnastic exercise, fencing, cold shower and hot baths give a nervous, artificial strength. He was known by his marriage as well as by his wit, his fortune, his connections, and by that sociability, amiability, and fashionable gallantry peculiar to certain men.

A true Parisian, furthermore, light, sceptical, changeable, captivating, energetic, and irresolute, capable of everything and of nothing; selfish by principle and generous on occasion, he lived moderately upon his income, and amused himself with hygiene. Indifferent and passionate, he gave himself rein and drew back constantly, impelled by conflicting instincts, yielding to all, and then obeying, in the end, his own shrewd man-about-town judgment, whose weather-vane logic consisted in following the wind and drawing profit from circumstances without taking the trouble to originate them.

His companion, Léon Saval, rich also, was one of those superb and colossal figures who make women turn around in the streets to look at them. He gave the idea of a statue turned into a man, a type of a race, like those sculptured forms which are sent to the Salons. Too handsome, too tall, too big, too strong, he sinned a little from the excess of every-thing, the excess of his qualities. He had on hand countless affairs of passion.

As they reached the Vaudeville theater, he asked: "Have you warned that lady that you are going to take me to her house to see her?"

Servigny began to laugh: "Forewarn the Mar-quise Obardi! Do you warn an omnibus driver that you shall enter his stage at the corner of the boule-vard?"

Saval, a little perplexed, inquired: "What sort of person is this lady?"

His friend replied: "An upstart, a charming hussy, who came from no one knows where, who made her appearance one day, nobody knows how, among the adventuresses of Paris, knowing perfectly well how to take care of herself. Besides, what dif-ference does it make to us? They say that her real name, her maiden name — for she still has every claim to the title of maiden except that of innocence — is Octavia Bardin, from which she constructs the name Obardi by prefixing the first letter of her first name and dropping the last letter of the last name.

"Moreover, she is a lovable woman, and you, from your physique, are inevitably bound to become her lover. Hercules is not introduced into Messalina's home without making some disturbance. Nevertheless I make bold to add that if there is free entrance to this house, just as there is in bazaars, you are not exactly compelled to buy what is for sale. Love and cards are on the programme, but nobody compels you to take up with either. And the exit is as free as the entrance.

"She settled down in the Etoile district, a suspicious neighborhood, three years ago, and opened her drawing-room to that froth of the continents which comes to Paris to practice its various formidable and criminal talents.

"I don't remember just how I went to her house. I went as we all go, because there is card playing, because the women are compliant, and the men dishonest. I love that social mob of buccaneers with decorations of all sorts of orders, all titled, and all entirely unknown at their embassies, except to the spies. They are always dragging in the subject of honor, quoting the list of their ancestors on the slightest provocation, and telling the story of their life at every opportunity, braggarts, liars, sharpers, dangerous as their cards, false as their names, brave because they have to be, like the assassins who can not pluck their victims except by exposing their own lives. In a word, it is the aristocracy of the bagnio.

"I like them. They are interesting to fathom and to know, amusing to listen to, often witty, never commonplace as the ordinary French guests. Their

women are always pretty, with a little flavor of foreign knavery, with the mystery of their past existence, half of which, perhaps, spent in a House of
Correction. They generally have fine eyes and glo-
rious hair, the true physique of the profession, an
intoxicating grace, a seductiveness which drives men
to folly, an unwholesome, irresistible charm! They
conquer like the highwaymen of old. They are ra-
pacious creatures, true birds of prey. I like them,
too.

"The Marquise Obardi is one of the type of these
elegant good-for-nothings. Ripe and pretty, with a
feline charm, you can see that she is vicious to the
marrow. Everybody has a good time at her house,
with cards, dancing, and suppers; in fact there is
everything which goes to make up the pleasures of
fashionable society life."

"Have you ever been or are you now her lover?"
Léon Saval asked.

"I have not been her lover, I am not now, and I
never shall be. I only go to the house to see her
daughter."

"Ah! She has a daughter, then?"

"A daughter! A marvel, my dear man. She is
the principal attraction of the den to-day. Tall, magnificent, just ripe, eighteen years old, as fair as her
mother is dark, always merry, always ready for an
entertainment, always laughing, and ready to dance
like mad. Who will be the lucky man to capture
her, or who has already done so? Nobody can tell
that. She has ten of us in her train, all hoping.

"Such a daughter in the hands of a woman like
the Marquise is a fortune. And they play the game

together, the two charmers. No one knows just what they are planning. Perhaps they are waiting for a better bargain than I should prove. But I tell you that I shall close the bargain if I ever get a chance.

"That girl Yvette absolutely baffles me, moreover. She is a mystery. If she is not the most complete monster of astuteness and perversity that I have ever seen, she certainly is the most marvelous phenomenon of innocence that can be imagined. She lives in that atmosphere of infamy with a calm and triumphing ease which is either wonderfully profligate or entirely artless. Strange scion of an adventuress, cast upon the muck-heap of that set, like a magnificent plant nurtured upon corruption, or rather like the daughter of some noble race, of some great artist, or of some grand lord, of some prince or dethroned king, tossed some evening into her mother's arms, nobody can make out what she is nor what she thinks. But you are going to see her."

Saval began to laugh and said: "You are in love with her."

"No. I am on the list, which is not precisely the same thing. I will introduce you to my most serious rivals. But the chances are in my favor. I am in the lead, and some little distinction is shown to me."

"You are in love," Saval repeated.

"No. She disquiets me, seduces and disturbs me, attracts and frightens me away. I mistrust her as I would a trap, and I long for her as I long for a sherbet when I am thirsty. I yield to her charm, and I only approach her with the apprehension that I would feel concerning a man who was known to be a skillful thief. In her presence I have an irrational impulse

toward belief in her possible purity and a very reasonable mistrust of her not less probable trickery. I feel
myself in contact with an abnormal being, beyond
the pale of natural laws, an exquisite or detestable
creature — I don't know which."

For the third time Saval said: "I tell you that
you are in love. You speak of her with the mag-
niloquence of a poet and the feeling of a troubadour.
Come, search your heart, and confess."

Servigny walked a few steps without answering.
Then he replied:

"That is possible, after all. In any case, she fills
my mind almost continually. Yes, perhaps I am in
love. I dream about her too much. I think of her
when I am asleep and when I awake — that is surely
a grave indication. Her face follows me, accompanies
me ceaselessly, ever before me, around me, with me.
Is this love, this physical infatuation? Her features
are so stamped upon my vision that I see her the
moment I shut my eyes. My heart beats quickly
every time I look at her, I don't deny it.

"So I am in love with her, but in a queer fashion. I have the strongest desire for her, and yet the
idea of making her my wife would seem to me a
folly, a piece of stupidity, a monstrous thing. And I
have a little fear of her, as well, the fear which a
bird feels over which a hawk is hovering.

"And again I am jealous of her, jealous of all of
which I am ignorant in her incomprehensible heart.
I am always wondering: 'Is she a charming young-
ster or a wretched jade?' She says things that would
make an army shudder; but so does a parrot. She is
at times so indiscreet and yet modest that I am forced

to believe in her spotless purity, and again so in-
credibly artless that I must suspect that she has never
been chaste. She allures me, excites me, like a woman
of a certain category, and at the same time acts like
an impeccable virgin. She seems to love me and yet
makes fun of me; she deports herself in public as if
she were my mistress and treats me in private as if
I were her brother or footman.

"There are times when I fancy that she has as
many lovers as her mother. And at other times I
imagine that she suspects absolutely nothing of that
sort of life, you understand. Furthermore, she is a
great novel reader. I am at present, while awaiting
something better, her book purveyor. She calls me
her 'librarian.' Every week the New Book Store
sends her, on my orders, everything new that has
appeared, and I believe that she reads everything at
random. It must make a strange sort of mixture in
her head.

"That kind of literary hasty-pudding accounts
perhaps for some of the girl's peculiar ways. When
a young woman looks at existence through the medium of fifteen thousand novels, she must see it in a
strange light, and construct queer ideas about matters and things in general. As for me, I am waiting.
It is certain at any rate that I never have had for any
other woman the devotion which I have had for her.
And still it is quite certain that I shall never marry
her. So if she has had numbers, I shall swell the
number. And if she has not, I shall take the first
ticket, just as I would do for a street car.

"The case is very simple. Of course, she will
never marry. Who in the world would marry the

Marquise Obardi's daughter, the child of Octavia Bardin? Nobody, for a thousand reasons. Where would
they ever find a husband for her? In society?
Never. The mother's house is a sort of liberty-hall
whose patronage is attracted by the daughter. Girls
don't get married under those conditions.

"Would she find a husband among the trades-
people? Still less would that be possible. And besides the Marquise is not the woman to make a bad
bargain; she will give Yvette only to a man of high
position, and that man she will never discover.

"Then perhaps she will look among the common
people. Still less likely. There is no solution of the
problem, then. This young lady belongs neither to
society, nor to the tradesmen's class, nor to the common people, and she can never enter any of these
ranks by marriage.

"She belongs through her mother, her birth, her
education, her inheritance, her manners, and her customs, to the vortex of the most rapid life of Paris.
She can never escape it, save by becoming a nun,
which is not at all probable with her manners and
tastes. She has only one possible career, a life of
pleasure. She will come to it sooner or later, if indeed she has not already begun to tread its primrose
path. She cannot escape her fate. From being a
young girl she will take the inevitable step, quite
simply. And I would like to be the pivot of this
transformation.

"I am waiting. There are many lovers. You
will see among them a Frenchman, Monsieur de Belvigne; a Russian, called Prince Kravalow, and an
Italian, Chevalier Valreali, who have all announced

their candidacies and who are consequently maneuvering to the best of their ability. In addition to
these there are several freebooters of less importance.
The Marquise waits and watches. But I think that
she has views about me. She knows that I am very
rich, and she makes less of the others.

"Her drawing-room is, moreover, the most as-
tounding that I know of, in such exhibitions. You
even meet very decent men there, like ourselves. As
for the women, she has culled the best there is from
the basket of pickpockets. Nobody knows where
she found them. It is a set apart from Bohemia,
apart from everything. She has had one inspiration
showing genius, and that is the knack of selecting
especially those adventuresses who have children,
generally girls. So that a fool might believe that in
her house he was among respectable women!"

They had reached the avenue of the Champs-
Elysées. A gentle breeze softly stirred the leaves and
touched the faces of passers-by, like the breaths of a
giant fan, waving somewhere in the sky. Silent
shadows wandered beneath the trees; others, on
benches, made a dark spot. And these shadows
spoke very low, as if they were telling each other
important or shameful secrets.

"You can't imagine what a collection of fictitious
titles are met in this lair," said Servigny. "By the
way, I shall present you by the name of Count
Saval; plain Saval would not do at all."

"Oh, no, indeed!" cried his friend; "I would not
have anyone think me capable of borrowing a title,
even for an evening, even among those people.
Ah, no!"

Servigny began to laugh.

"How stupid you are! Why, in that set they call me the Duke de Servigny. I don't know how nor why. But at any rate the Duke de Servigny I am and shall remain, without complaining or protesting. It does not worry me. I should have no footing there whatever without a title."

But Saval would not be convinced.

"Well, you are of rank, and so you may remain. But, as for me, no. I shall be the only common person in the drawing-room. So much the worse, or, so much the better. It will be my mark of distinction and superiority."

Servigny was obstinate.

"I tell you that it is not possible. Why, it would almost seem monstrous. You would have the effect of a ragman at a meeting of emperors. Let me do as I like. I shall introduce you as the Vice-Roi du 'Haut-Mississippi,' and no one will be at all astonished. When a man takes on greatness, he can't take too much."

"Once more, no, I do not wish it."

"Very well, have your way. But, in fact, I am very foolish to try to convince you. I defy you to get in without some one giving you a title, just as they give a bunch of violets to the ladies at the entrance to certain stores."

They turned to the right in the Rue de Barrie, mounted one flight of stairs in a fine modern house, and gave their overcoats and canes into the hands of four servants in knee-breeches. A warm odor, as of a festival assembly, filled the air, an odor of flowers, perfumes, and women; and a composed and continuous murmur came from the adjoining rooms, which were filled with people.

A kind of master of ceremonies, tall, erect, wide of girth, serious, his face framed in white whiskers, approached the newcomers, asking with a short and haughty bow: "Whom shall I announce?"

"Monsieur Saval," Servigny replied.

Then with a loud voice, the man opening the door cried out to the crowd of guests:

"Monsieur the Duke de Servigny.

"Monsieur the Baron Saval."

The first drawing-room was filled with women. The first thing which attracted attention was the display of bare shoulders, above a flood of brilliant gowns.

The mistress of the house who stood talking with three friends, turned and came forward with a majestic step, with grace in her mien and a smile on her lips. Her forehead was narrow and very low, and was covered with a mass of glossy black hair, encroaching a little upon the temples.

She was tall, a trifle too large, a little too stout, over ripe, but very pretty, with a heavy, warm, potent beauty. Beneath that mass of hair, full of dreams and smiles, rendering her mysteriously captivating, were enormous black eyes. Her nose was a little narrow, her mouth large and infinitely seductive, made to speak and to conquer.

Her greatest charm was in her voice. It came from that mouth as water from a spring, so natural, so light, so well modulated, so clear, that there was a physical pleasure in listening to it. It was a joy for the ear to hear the flexible words flow with the

grace of a babbling brook, and it was a joy for the
eyes to see those pretty lips, a trifle too red, open as
the words rippled forth.

She gave one hand to Servigny, who kissed it,
and dropping her fan on its little gold chain, she gave
the other to Saval, saying to him: "You are welcome, Baron, all the Duke's friends are at home
here."

Then she fixed her brilliant eyes upon the Colossus
who had just been introduced to her. She had just
the slightest down on her upper lip, a suspicion of a
mustache, which seemed darker when she spoke.
There was a pleasant odor about her, pervading, intoxicating, some perfume of America or of the Indies.
Other people came in, marquesses, counts or princes.
She said to Servigny, with the graciousness of a
mother: "You will find my daughter in the other
parlor. Have a good time, gentlemen, the house is
yours."

And she left them to go to those who had come
later, throwing at Saval that smiling and fleeting
glance which women use to show that they are
pleased. Servigny grasped his friend's arm.

"I will pilot you," said he. "In this parlor
where we now are, women, the temples of the
fleshly, fresh or otherwise. Bargains as good as
new, even better, for sale or on lease. At the right,
gaming, the temple of money. You understand all
about that. At the lower end, dancing, the temple
of innocence, the sanctuary, the market for young
girls. They are shown off there in every light.
Even legitimate marriages are tolerated. It is the
future, the hope, of our evenings. And the most

curious part of this museum of moral diseases are these young girls whose souls are out of joint, just like the limbs of the little clowns born of mountebanks. Come and look at them."

He bowed, right and left, courteously, a compliment on his lips, sweeping each low-gowned woman whom he knew with the look of an expert.

The musicians, at the end of the second parlor, were playing a waltz; and the two friends stopped at the door to look at them. A score of couples were whirling — the men with a serious expression, and the women with a fixed smile on their lips. They displayed a good deal of shoulder, like their mothers; and the bodices of some were only held in place by a slender ribbon, disclosing at times more than is generally shown.

Suddenly from the end of the room a tall girl darted forward, gliding through the crowd, brushing against the dancers, and holding her long train in her left hand. She ran with quick little steps as women do in crowds, and called out: "Ah! How is Muscade? How do you do, Muscade?"

Her features wore an expression of the bloom of life, the illumination of happiness. Her white flesh seemed to shine, the golden-white flesh which goes with red hair. The mass of her tresses, twisted on her head, fiery, flaming locks, nestled against her supple neck, which was still a little thin.

She seemed to move just as her mother was made to speak, so natural, noble, and simple were her gestures. A person felt a moral joy and physical pleasure in seeing her walk, stir about, bend her head, or lift her arm.

"Ah! Muscade, how do you do, Muscade?" she repeated.

Servigny shook her hand violently, as he would a man's, and said: "Mademoiselle Yvette, my friend, Baron Saval."

"Good evening, Monsieur. Are you always as tall as that?"

Servigny replied in that bantering tone which he always used with her, in order to conceal his mistrust and his uncertainty:

"No, Mam'zelle. He has put on his greatest dimensions to please your mother, who loves a colossus."

And the young girl remarked with a comic seriousness: "Very well! But when you come to see me you must diminish a little if you please. I prefer the medium height. Now Muscade has just the proportions which I like."

And she gave her hand to the newcomer. Then she asked: "Do you dance, Muscade? Come, let us waltz." Without replying, with a quick movement, passionately, Servigny clasped her waist and they disappeared with the fury of a whirlwind.

They danced more rapidly than any of the others, whirled and whirled, and turned madly, so close together that they seemed but one, and with the form erect, the legs almost motionless, as if some invisible mechanism, concealed beneath their feet, caused them to twirl. They appeared tireless. The other dancers stopped from time to time. They still danced on, alone. They seemed not to know where they were nor what they were doing, as if they had gone far away from the ball, in an ecstasy. The musicians continued to play, with their looks fixed upon this mad couple; all the guests gazed at them, and when finally they did stop dancing, everyone applauded them.

She was a little flushed, with strange eyes, ardent and timid, less daring than a moment before, troubled eyes, blue, yet with a pupil so black that they seemed hardly natural. Servigny appeared giddy. He leaned against a door to regain his composure.

"You have no head, my poor Muscade, I am steadier than you," said Yvette to Servigny.

He smiled nervously, and devoured her with a look. His animal feelings revealed themselves in his eyes and in the curl of his lips. She stood beside him looking down, and her bosom rose and fell in short gasps as he looked at her.

Then she said softly: "Really, there are times when you are like a tiger about to spring upon his prey. Come, give me your arm, and let us find your friend."

Silently he offered her his arm and they went down the long drawing-room together.

Saval was not alone, for the Marquise Obardi had rejoined him. She conversed with him on ordinary and fashionable subjects with a seductiveness in her tones which intoxicated him. And, looking at her with his mental eye, it seemed to him that her lips uttered words far different from those which they formed. When she saw Servigny her face immediately lighted up, and turning toward him she said:

"You know, my dear Duke, that I have just leased a villa at Bougival for two months, and I count upon your coming to see me there, and upon

your friend also. Listen. We take possession next
Monday, and shall expect both of you to dinner the
following Saturday. We shall keep you over Sunday."

Perfectly serene and tranquil Yvette smiled, saying
with a decision which swept away hesitation on his
part:

"Of course Muscade will come to dinner on Saturday. We have only to ask him, for he and I intend to commit a lot of follies in the country."

He thought he divined the birth of a promise in
her smile, and in her voice he heard what he thought
was invitation.

Then the Marquise turned her big, black eyes
upon Saval: "And you will, of course, come, Baron?"

With a smile that forbade doubt, he bent toward
her, saying, "I shall be only too charmed, Madame."

Then Yvette murmured with malice that was either
naïve or traitorous: "We will set all the world by
the ears down there, won't we, Muscade, and make my
regiment of admirers fairly mad." And with a look,
she pointed out a group of men who were looking
at them from a little distance.

Said Servigny to her: "As many follies as *you*
may please, Mam'zelle."

In speaking to Yvette, Servigny never used the
word "Mademoiselle," by reason of his close and long
intimacy with her.

Then Saval asked: "Why does Mademoiselle always call my friend Servigny 'Muscade'?"

Yvette assumed a very frank air and said:

"I will tell you: It is because he always slips
through my hands. Now I think I have him, and
then I find I have not."

The Marquise, with her eyes upon Saval, and evidently preoccupied, said in a careless tone: "You children are very funny."

But Yvette bridled up: "I do not intend to be funny; I am simply frank. Muscade pleases me, and is always deserting me, and that is what annoys me."

Servigny bowed profoundly, saying: "I will never leave you any more, Mam'zelle, neither day nor night."

She made a gesture of horror:

"My goodness! no—what do you mean? You are all right during the day, but at night you might embarrass me."

With an air of impertinence he asked: "And why?"

Yvette responded calmly and audaciously, "Because you would not look well *en déshabillé.*"

The Marquise, without appearing at all disturbed, said: "What extraordinary subjects for conversation. One would think that you were not at all ignorant of such things."

And Servigny jokingly added: "That is also my opinion, Marquise."

Yvette turned her eyes upon him, and in a haughty, yet wounded, tone said: "You are becoming very vulgar—just as you have been several times lately." And turning quickly she appealed to an individual standing by:

"Chevalier, come and defend me from insult."

A thin, brown man, with an easy carriage, came forward.

"Who is the culprit?" said he, with a constrained smile.

Yvette pointed out Servigny with a nod of her head:

"There he is, but I like him better than I do you, because he is less of a bore."

The Chevalier Valreali bowed:

"I do what I can, Mademoiselle. I may have less ability, but not less devotion."

A gentleman came forward, tall and stout, with gray whiskers, saying in loud tones: "Mademoiselle Yvette, I am your most devoted slave."

Yvette cried: "Ah, Monsieur de Belvigne." Then turning toward Saval, she introduced him.

"My last adorer — big, fat, rich, and stupid. Those are the kind I like. A veritable drum-major — but of the *table d'hôte*. But see, you are still bigger than he. How shall I nickname you? Good! I have it. I shall call you 'M. Colossus of Rhodes, Junior,' from the Colossus who certainly was your father. But you two ought to have very interesting things to say to each other up there, above the heads of us all — so, by-bye."

And she left them quickly, going to the orchestra to make the musicians strike up a quadrille.

Madame Obardi seemed preoccupied. In a soft voice she said to Servigny:

"You are always teasing her. You will warp her character and bring out many bad traits."

Servigny replies: "Why, haven't you finished her education?"

She appeared not to understand, and continued talking in a friendly way. But she noticed a solemn looking man, wearing a perfect constellation of crosses and orders, standing near her, and she ran to him:

"Ah! Prince, Prince, what good fortune!"

Servigny took Saval's arm and drew him away:

"That is the latest serious suitor, Prince Krava-low. Isn't she superb?"

"To my mind they are both superb. The mother would suffice for me perfectly," answered Saval.

Servigny nodded and said: "At your disposal, my dear boy."

The dancers elbowed them aside, as they were forming for a quadrille.

"Now let us go and see the sharpers," said Servigny. And they entered the gambling-room.

Around each table stood a group of men, looking on. There was very little conversation. At times the clink of gold coins, tossed upon the green cloth or hastily seized, added its sound to the murmur of the players, just as if the money was putting in its word among the human voices.

All the men were decorated with various orders, and odd ribbons, and they all wore the same severe expression, with different countenances. The especially distinguishing feature was the beard.

The stiff American with his horseshoe, the haughty Englishman with his fan-beard open on his breast, the Spaniard with his black fleece reaching to the eyes, the Roman with that huge mustache which Italy copied from Victor Emmanuel, the Austrian with his whiskers and shaved chin, a Russian general, whose lip seemed armed with two twisted lances, and a Frenchman with a dainty mustache, displayed the fancies of all the barbers in the world.

"You won't join the game?" asked Servigny.

"No, shall you?"

"Not now. If you are ready to go, we will come back some quieter day. There are too many people here to-day, and we can't do anything."

"Well, let us go."

And they disappeared behind a door-curtain into the hall. As soon as they were in the street Servigny asked: "Well, what do you think of it?"

"It certainly is interesting, but I fancy the women's side of it more than the men's."

"Indeed! Those women are the best of the tribe for us. Don't you find that you breathe the odor of love among them, just as you scent the perfumes at a hairdresser's?"

"Really such houses are the place for one to go. And what experts, my dear fellow! What artists! Have you ever eaten bakers' cakes? They look well, but they amount to nothing. The man who bakes them only knows how to make bread. Well! the love of a woman in ordinary society always reminds me of these bake-shop trifles, while the love you find at houses like the Marquise Obardi's, don't you see, is the real sweetmeat. Oh! they know how to make cakes, these charming pastry-cooks. Only you pay five sous, at their shops, for what costs two sous elsewhere."

"Who is the master of the house just now?" asked Saval.

Servigny shrugged his shoulders, signifying his ignorance.

"I don't know, the latest one known was an English peer, but he left three months ago. At present she must live off the common herd, or the gambling, perhaps, and on the gamblers, for she has her caprices. But tell me, it is understood that we dine with her on Saturday at Bougival, is it not? People are more free in the country, and I shall succeed in finding out what ideas Yvette has in her head!"

"I should like nothing better," replied Saval. "I have nothing to do that day."

Passing down through the Champs-Elysées, under the steps they disturbed a couple making love on one of the benches, and Servigny muttered: "What foolishness and what a serious matter at the same time! How commonplace and amusing love is, always the same and always different! And the beggar who gives his sweetheart twenty sous gets as much return as I would for ten thousand francs from some Obardi, no younger and no less stupid perhaps than this nondescript. What nonsense!"

He said nothing for a few minutes; then he began again: "All the same, it would be good to become Yvette's first lover. Oh! for that I would give—"

He did not add what he would give, and Saval said good night to him as they reached the corner of the Rue Royale.

CHAPTER II.

Bougival and Love

THEY had set the table on the veranda which overlooked the river. The Printemps villa, leased by the Marquise Obardi, was halfway up this hill, just at the corner of the Seine, which turned before the garden wall, flowing toward Marly.

Opposite the residence, the island of Croissy formed a horizon of tall trees, a mass of verdure, and they could see a long stretch of the big river as far as the floating *café* of La Grenouillère hidden beneath the foliage.

The evening fell, one of those calm evenings at the waterside, full of color yet soft, one of those peaceful evenings which produces a sensation of pleasure. No breath of air stirred the branches, no shiver of wind ruffled the smooth clear surface of the Seine. It was not too warm, it was mild — good weather to live in. The grateful coolness of the banks of the Seine rose toward a serene sky.

The sun disappeared behind the trees to shine on

other lands, and one seemed to absorb the serenity of the already sleeping earth, to inhale, in the peace of space, the life of the infinite.

As they left the drawing-room to seat themselves at the table everyone was joyous. A softened gaiety filled their hearts, they felt that it would be so delightful to dine there in the country, with that great river and that twilight for a setting, breathing that pure and fragrant air.

The Marquise had taken Saval's arm, and Yvette, Servigny's. The four were alone by themselves. The two women seemed entirely different persons from what they were at Paris, especially Yvette. She talked but little, and seemed languid and grave.

Saval, hardly recognizing her in this frame of mind, asked her: "What is the matter, Mademoiselle? I find you changed since last week. You have become quite a serious person."

"It is the country that does that for me," she replied. "I am not the same, I feel queer; besides I am never two days alike. To-day I have the air of a mad woman, and to-morrow shall be as grave as an elegy. I change with the weather, I don't know why. You see, I am capable of anything, according to the moment. There are days when I would like to kill people,—not animals, I would never kill animals,—but people, yes, and other days when I weep at a mere thing. A lot of different ideas pass through my head. It depends, too, a good deal on how I get up. Every morning, on waking, I can tell just what I shall be in the evening. Perhaps it is our dreams that settle it for us, and it depends on the book I have just read."

She was clad in a white flannel suit which delicately enveloped her in the floating softness of the material. Her bodice, with full folds, suggested, without displaying and without restraining, her free chest, which was firm and already ripe. And her superb neck emerged from a froth of soft lace, bending with gentle movements, fairer than her gown, a pilaster of flesh, bearing the heavy mass of her golden hair.

Servigny looked at her for a long time: "You are adorable this evening, Mam'zelle," said he, "I wish I could always see you like this."

"Don't make a declaration, Muscade. I should take it seriously, and that might cost you dear."

The Marquise seemed happy, very happy. All in black, richly dressed in a plain gown which showed her strong, full lines, a bit of red at the bodice, a cincture of red carnations falling from her waist like a chain, and fastened at the hips, and a red rose in her dark hair, she carried in all her person something fervid,—in that simple costume, in those flowers which seemed to bleed, in her look, in her slow speech, in her peculiar gestures.

Saval, too, appeared serious and absorbed. From time to time he stroked his pointed beard, trimmed in the fashion of Henri III., and seemed to be meditating on the most profound subjects.

Nobody spoke for several minutes. Then as they were serving the trout, Servigny remarked:

"Silence is a good thing, at times. People are often nearer to each other when they are keeping still than when they are talking. Isn't that so, Marquise?"

She turned a little toward him and answered:

"It is quite true. It is so sweet to think together about agreeable things.

She raised her warm glance toward Saval, and they continued for some seconds looking into each other's eyes. A slight, almost inaudible movement took place beneath the table.

Servigny resumed: "Mam'zelle Yvette, you will make me believe that you are in love if you keep on being as good as that. Now, with whom could you be in love? Let us think together, if you will; I put aside the army of vulgar sighers. I'll only take the principal ones. Is it Prince Kravalow?"

At this name Yvette awoke: "My poor Muscade, can you think of such a thing? Why, the Prince has the air of a Russian in a wax-figure museum, who has won medals in a hairdressing competition."

"Good! We'll drop the Prince. But you have noticed the Viscount Pierre de Belvigne?"

This time she began to laugh, and asked: "Can you imagine me hanging to the neck of 'Raisiné'?" She nicknamed him according to the day, Raisiné, Malvoisie, * Argenteuil, for she gave everybody nicknames. And she would murmur to his face: "My dear little Pierre," or "My divine Pedro, darling Pierrot, give your bow-wow's head to your dear little girl, who wants to kiss it."

"Scratch out number two. There still remains the Chevalier Valreali whom the Marquise seems to favor," continued Servigny.

Yvette regained all her gaiety: "'Teardrop'?

---

* Preserved grapes and pears, malmsey, — a poor wine.

Why he weeps like a Magdalene. He goes to all the first-class funerals. I imagine myself dead every time he looks at me."

"That settles the third. So the lightning will strike Baron Saval, here."

"Monsieur the Colossus of Rhodes, Junior? No. He is too strong. It would seem to me as if I were in love with the triumphal arch of L'Etoile."

"Then Mam'zelle, it is beyond doubt that you are in love with me, for I am the only one of your adorers of whom we have not yet spoken. I left myself for the last through modesty and through discretion. It remains for me to thank you."

She replied with happy grace: "In love with you, Muscade? Ah! no. I like you, but I don't love you. Wait—I—I don't want to discourage you. I don't love you—yet. You have a chance—perhaps. Persevere, Muscade, be devoted, ardent, submissive, full of little attentions and considerations, docile to my slightest caprices, ready for anything to please me, and we shall see—later."

"But, Mam'zelle, I would rather furnish all you demand afterward than beforehand, if it be the same to you."

She asked with an artless air: "After what, Muscade?"

"After you have shown me that you love me, by Jove!"

"Well, act as if I loved you, and believe it, if you wish."

"But you—"

"Be quiet, Muscade; enough on the subject."

The sun had sunk behind the island, but the

7 G. de M.—16

whole sky still flamed like a fire, and the peaceful
water of the river seemed changed to blood. The
reflections from the horizon reddened houses, objects,
and persons. The scarlet rose in the Marquise's hair
had the appearance of a splash of purple fallen from
the clouds upon her head.

As Yvette looked on from her end, the Marquise
rested, as if by carelessness, her bare hand upon
Saval's hand; but the young girl made a motion and
the Marquise withdrew her hand with a quick gesture, pretending to readjust something in the folds
of her corsage.

Servigny, who was looking at them, said:

"If you like, Mam'zelle, we will take a walk on
the island after dinner."

"Oh, yes! That will be delightful. We will go
all alone, won't we, Muscade?"

"Yes, all alone, Mam'zelle!"

The vast silence of the horizon, the sleepy tranquillity of the evening captured heart, body, and voice.
There are peaceful, chosen hours when it becomes
almost impossible to talk.

The servants waited on them noiselessly. The
firmamental conflagration faded away, and the soft
night spread its shadows over the earth.

"Are you going to stay long in this place?"
asked Saval.

And the Marquise answered, dwelling on each
word: "Yes, as long as I am happy."

As it was too dark to see, lamps were brought.
They cast upon the table a strange, pale gleam beneath the great obscurity of space; and very soon a
shower of gnats fell upon the tablecloth—the tiny

gnats which immolate themselves by passing over the glass chimneys, and, with wings and legs scorched, powder the table-linen, dishes, and cups with a kind of gray and hopping dust.

They swallowed them in the wine, they ate them in the sauces, they saw them moving on the bread, and had their faces and hands tickled by the countless swarm of these tiny insects. They were continually compelled to throw away the beverages, to cover the plates, and while eating to shield the food with infinite precautions.

It amused Yvette. Servigny took care to shelter what she bore to her mouth, to guard her glass, to hold his handkerchief stretched out over her head like a roof. But the Marquise, disgusted, became nervous, and the end of the dinner came quickly. Yvette, who had not forgotten Servigny's proposition, said to him:

"Now we'll go to the island."

Her mother cautioned her in a languid tone: "Don't be late, above all things. We will escort you to the ferry."

And they started in couples, the young girl and her admirer walking in front, on the road to the shore. They heard, behind them, the Marquise and Saval speaking very rapidly in low tones. All was dark, with a thick, inky darkness. But the sky swarmed with grains of fire, and seemed to sow them in the river, for the black water was flecked with stars.

The frogs were croaking monotonously upon the bank, and numerous nightingales were uttering their low, sweet song in the calm and peaceful air.

Yvette suddenly said: "Gracious! They are not walking behind us any more, where are they?" And she called out: "Mamma!" No voice replied. The young girl resumed: "At any rate, they can't be far away, for I heard them just now."

Servigny murmured: "They must have gone back. Your mother was cold, perhaps." And he drew her along.

Before them a light gleamed. It was the tavern of Martinet, restaurant-keeper and fisherman. At their call a man came out of the house, and they got into a large boat which was moored among the weeds of the shore.

The ferryman took his oars, and the unwieldy barge, as it advanced, disturbed the sleeping stars upon the water and set them into a mad dance, which gradually calmed down after they had passed. They touched the other shore and disembarked beneath the great trees. A cool freshness of damp earth permeated the air under the lofty and clustered branches, where there seemed to be as many nightingales as there were leaves. A distant piano began to play a popular waltz.

Servigny took Yvette's arm and very gently slipped his hand around her waist and gave her a slight hug.

"What are you thinking about?" he said.

"I? About nothing at all. I am very happy!"

"Then you don't love me?"

"Oh, yes, Muscade, I love you, I love you a great deal; only leave me alone. It is too beautiful here to listen to your nonsense."

He drew her toward him, although she tried, by

little pushes, to extricate herself, and through her soft flannel gown he felt the warmth of her flesh. He stammered:

"Yvette!"

"Well, what?"

"I do love you!"

"But you are not in earnest, Muscade."

"Oh, yes I am. I have loved you for a long time."

She continually kept trying to separate herself from him, trying to release the arm crushed between their bodies. They walked with difficulty, trammeled by this bond and by these movements, and went zig-zagging along like drunken folk.

He knew not what to say to her, feeling that he could not talk to a young girl as he would to a woman. He was perplexed, thinking what he ought to do, wondering if she consented or did not understand, and curbing his spirit to find just the right, tender, and decisive words. He kept saying every second:

"Yvette! Speak! Yvette!"

Then, suddenly, risking all, he kissed her on the cheek. She gave a little start aside, and said with a vexed air:

"Oh! you are absurd. Are you going to let me alone?"

The tone of her voice did not at all reveal her thoughts nor her wishes; and, not seeing her too angry, he applied his lips to the beginning of her neck, just beneath the golden hair, that charming spot which he had so often coveted.

Then she made great efforts to free herself. But

he held her strongly, and placing his other hand on her shoulder, he compelled her to turn her head toward him and gave her a fond, passionate kiss, squarely on the mouth.

She slipped from his arms by a quick undulation of the body, and, free from his grasp, she disappeared into the darkness with a great swishing of skirts, like the whir of a bird as it flies away.

He stood motionless a moment, surprised by her suppleness and her disappearance, then hearing nothing, he called gently: "Yvette!"

She did not reply. He began to walk forward, peering through the shadows, looking in the underbrush for the white spot her dress should make. All was dark. He cried out more loudly:

"Mam'zelle Yvette! Mam'zelle Yvette!"

Nothing stirred. He stopped and listened. The whole island was still; there was scarcely a rustle of leaves over his head. The frogs alone continued their deep croakings on the shores. Then he wandered from thicket to thicket, going where the banks were steep and bushy and returning to places where they were flat and bare as a dead man's arm. He proceeded until he was opposite Bougival and reached the establishment of La Grenouillère, groping the clumps of trees, calling out continually:

"Mam'zelle Yvette, where are you? Answer. It is ridiculous! Come, answer! Don't keep me hunting like this."

A distant clock began to strike. He counted the hours: twelve. He had been searching through the island for two hours. Then he thought that perhaps she had gone home; and he went back very anxiously, this time by way of the bridge. A servant dozing on a chair was waiting in the hall.

Servigny awakened him and asked: "Is it long since Mademoiselle Yvette came home? I left her at the foot of the place because I had a call to make."

And the valet replied: "Oh! yes, Monsieur, Mademoiselle came in before ten o'clock."

He proceeded to his room and went to bed. But he could not close his eyes. That stolen kiss had stirred him to the soul. He kept wondering what she thought and what she knew. How pretty and attractive she was!

His desires, somewhat wearied by the life he led, by all his procession of sweethearts, by all his explorations in the kingdom of love, awoke before this singular child, so fresh, irritating, and inexplicable. He heard one o'clock strike, then two. He could not sleep at all. He was warm, he felt his heart beat and his temples throb, and he rose to open the window. A breath of fresh air came in, which he inhaled deeply. The thick darkness was silent, black, motionless. But suddenly he perceived before him, in the shadows of the garden, a shining point; it seemed a little red coal.

"Well, a cigar!" he said to himself. "It must be Saval," and he called softly: "Léon!"

"Is it you, Jean?"

"Yes. Wait. I'll come down." He dressed, went out, and rejoining his friend who was smoking astride an iron chair, inquired: "What are you doing here at this hour?"

"I am resting," Saval replied. And he began to laugh.

Servigny pressed his hand: "My compliments, my dear fellow. And as for me, I — am making a fool of myself."

"You mean —"

"I mean that — Yvette and her mother do not resemble each other."

"What has happened? Tell me."

Servigny recounted his attempts and their failure. Then he resumed:

"Decidedly, that little girl worries me. Fancy my not being able to sleep! What a queer thing a girl is! She appears to be as simple as anything, and yet you know nothing about her. A woman who has lived and loved, who knows life, can be quickly understood. But when it comes to a young virgin, on the contrary, no one can guess anything about her. At heart I begin to think that she is making sport of me."

Saval tilted his chair. He said, very slowly:

"Take care, my dear fellow, she will lead you to marriage. Remember those other illustrious examples. It was just by this same process that Mademoiselle de Montijo, who was at least of good family, became empress. Don't play Napoleon."

Servigny murmured: "As for that, fear nothing. I am neither a simpleton nor an emperor. A man must be either one or the other to make such a move as that. But tell me, are you sleepy?"

"Not a bit."

"Will you take a walk along the river?"

"Gladly."

They opened the iron gate and began to walk along the river bank toward Marly.

It was the quiet hour which precedes dawn, the hour of deep sleep, of complete rest, of profound peacefulness. Even the gentle sounds of the night were hushed. The nightingales sang no longer; the frogs had finished their hubbub; some kind of an animal only, probably a bird, was making somewhere a kind of sawing sound, feeble, monotonous, and regular as a machine. Servigny, who had moments of poetry and of philosophy too, suddenly remarked:

"Now this girl completely puzzles me. In arithmetic, one and one make two. In love one and one ought to make one but they make two just the same. Have you ever felt that? That need of absorbing a woman in yourself or disappearing in her? I am not speaking of the animal embrace, but of that moral and mental eagerness to be but one with a being, to open to her all one's heart and soul, and to fathom her thoughts to the depths.

"And yet you can never lay bare all the fluctuations of her wishes, desires, and opinions. You can never guess, even slightly, all the unknown currents, all the mystery of a soul that seems so near, a soul hidden behind two eyes that look at you, clear as water, transparent as if there were nothing beneath a soul which talks to you by a beloved mouth, which seems your very own, so greatly do you desire it; a soul which throws you by words its thoughts, one by one, and which, nevertheless, remains further away from you than those stars are from each other, and more impenetrable. Isn't it queer, all that?"

"I don't ask so much," Saval rejoined. "I don't look behind the eyes. I care little for the contents, but much for the vessel."

And Servigny replied: "What a singular person Yvette is! How will she receive me this morning?"

As they reached the works at Marly they perceived that the sky was brightening. The cocks began to crow in the poultry-yards. A bird twittered in a park at the left, ceaselessly reiterating a tender little theme.

"It is time to go back," said Saval.

They returned, and as Servigny entered his room, he saw the horizon all pink through his open windows.

Then he shut the blinds, drew the thick, heavy curtains, went back to bed and fell asleep. He dreamed of Yvette all through his slumber. An odd noise awoke him. He sat on the side of the bed and listened, but heard nothing further. Then suddenly there was a crackling against the blinds, like falling hail. He jumped from the bed, ran to the window, opened it, and saw Yvette standing in the path and throwing handfuls of gravel at his face. She was clad in pink, with a wide-brimmed straw hat ornamented with a mousquetaire plume, and was laughing mischievously.

"Well! Muscade, are you asleep? What could you have been doing all night to make you wake so late? Have you been seeking adventures, my poor Muscade?"

He was dazzled by the bright daylight striking him full in the eyes, still overwhelmed with fatigue, and surprised at the jesting tranquillity of the young girl.

"I'll be down in a second, Mam'zelle," he answered. "Just time to splash my face with water, and I will join you."

"Hurry," she cried, "it is ten o'clock, and besides I have a great plan to unfold to you, a plot we are going to concoct. You know that we breakfast at eleven."

He found her seated on a bench, with a book in her lap, some novel or other. She took his arm in a familiar and friendly way, with a frank and gay manner, as if nothing had happened the night before, and drew him toward the end of the garden.

"This is my plan," she said. "We will disobey mamma, and you shall take me presently to La Grenouillère restaurant. I want to see it. Mamma says that decent women cannot go to the place. Now it is all the same to me whether persons can go there or cannot. You'll take me, won't you, Muscade? And we will have a great time — with the boatmen."

She exhaled a delicious fragrance, although he could not exactly define just what light and vague odor enveloped her. It was not one of those heavy perfumes of her mother, but a discreet breath in which he fancied he could detect a suspicion of iris powder, and perhaps a suggestion of vervain.

Whence emanated that indiscernible perfume? From her dress, her hair, or her skin? He puzzled over this, and as he was speaking very close to her, he received full in the face her fresh breath, which seemed to him just as delicious to inhale.

Then he thought that this evasive perfume which he was trying to recognize was perhaps only evoked by her charming eyes, and was merely a sort of deceptive emanation of her young and alluring grace.

"That is agreed, isn't it, Muscade? As it will be very warm after breakfast, mamma will not go out.

She always feels the heat very much. We will leave her with your friend, and you shall take me. They will think that we have gone into the forest. If you knew how much it will amuse me to see La Grenouillère!

They reached the iron gate opposite the Seine. A flood of sunshine fell upon the slumberous, shining river. A slight heat-mist rose from it, a sort of haze of evaporated water, which spread over the surface of the stream a faint gleaming vapor.

From time to time, boats passed by, a quick yawl or a heavy passage boat, and short or long whistles could be heard, those of the trains which every Sunday poured the citizens of Paris into the suburbs, and those of the steamboats signaling their approach to pass the locks at Marly.

But a tiny bell sounded. Breakfast was announced, and they went back into the house. The repast was a silent one. A heavy July noon overwhelmed the earth, and oppressed humanity. The heat seemed thick, and paralyzed both mind and body. The sluggish words would not leave the lips, and all motion seemed laborious, as if the air had become a resisting medium, difficult to traverse. Only Yvette, although silent, seemed animated and nervous with impatience. As soon as they had finished the last course she said:

"If we were to go for a walk in the forest, it would be deliciously cool under the trees."

The Marquise murmured with a listless air: "Are you mad? Does anyone go out in such weather?"

And the young girl, delighted, rejoined: "Oh, well! We will leave the Baron to keep you com-

pany. Muscade and I will climb the hill and sit on
the grass and read."

And turning toward Servigny she asked: "That
is understood?"

"At your service, Mam'zelle," he replied.

Yvette ran to get her hat. The Marquise shrugged
her shoulders with a sigh. "She certainly is mad."
she said.

Then with an indolence in her amorous and lazy
gestures, she gave her pretty white hand to the Baron,
who kissed it softly. Yvette and Servigny started.
They went along the river, crossed the bridge and
went on to the island, and then seated themselves on
the bank, beneath the willows, for it was too soon to
go to La Grenouillére.

The young girl at once drew a book from her
pocket and smilingly said: "Muscade, you are going to read to me." And she handed him the vol-
ume.

He made a motion as if of fright. "I, Mam'zelle?
I don't know how to read!"

She replied with gravity: "Come, no excuses, no
objections; you are a fine suitor, you! All for nothing, is that it? Is that your motto?"

He took the book, opened it, and was astonished.
It was a treatise on entomology. A history of ants
by an English author. And as he remained inert,
believing that he was making sport of her, she said
with impatience: "Well, read!"

"Is it a wager, or just a simple fad?" he asked.

"No, my dear. I saw that book in a shop. They
told me that it was the best authority on ants and I
thought that it would be interesting to learn about

the life of these little insects while you see them running over the grass; so read, if you please."

She stretched herself flat upon the grass, her el-
bows resting upon the ground, her head between her
hands, her eyes fixed upon the ground. He began to
read as follows:

"The anthropoid apes are undoubtedly the animals which approach nearest to man by their anatomical structure, but if we consider the habits of the ants, their organization into societies, their vast
communities, the houses and roads that they construct, their custom
of domesticating animals, and sometimes even of making slaves of
them, we are compelled to admit that they have the right to claim a
place near to man in the scale of intelligence."

He continued in a monotonous voice, stopping
from time to time to ask: "Isn't that enough?"

She shook her head, and having caught an ant on
the end of a severed blade of grass, she amused herself by making it go from one end to the other of
the sprig, which she tipped up whenever the insect
reached one of the ends. She listened with mute and
contented attention to all the wonderful details of the
life of these frail creatures: their subterranean homes;
the manner in which they seize, shut up, and feed
plant-lice to drink the sweet milk which they secrete,
as we keep cows in our barns; their custom of domesticating little blind insects which clean the ant-
hills, and of going to war to capture slaves who will
take care of their victors with such tender solicitude
that the latter even lose the habit of feeding themselves.

And little by little, as if a maternal tenderness had
sprung up in her heart for the poor insect which was

so tiny and so intelligent, Yvette made it climb on her finger, looking at it with a moved expression, almost wanting to embrace it.

And as Servigny read of the way in which they live in communities, and play games of strength and skill among themselves, the young girl grew enthusiastic and sought to kiss the insect which escaped her and began to crawl over her face. Then she uttered a piercing cry, as if she had been threatened by a terrible danger, and with frantic gestures tried to brush it off her face. With a loud laugh Servigny caught it near her tresses and imprinted on the spot where he had seized it a long kiss without Yvette withdrawing her forehead.

Then she exclaimed as she rose: "That is better than a novel. Now let us go to La Grenouillère."

They reached that part of the island which is set out as a park and shaded with great trees. Couples were strolling beneath the lofty foliage along the Seine, where the boats were gliding by.

The boats were filled with young people, working-girls and their sweethearts, the latter in their shirt-sleeves, with coats on their arms, tall hats tipped back, and a jaded look. There were tradesmen with their families, the women dressed in their best and the children flocking like little chicks about their parents. A distant, continuous sound of voices, a heavy, scolding clamor announced the proximity of the establishment so dear to the boatmen.

Suddenly they saw it. It was a huge boat, roofed over, moored to the bank. On board were many men and women drinking at tables, or else standing up, shouting, singing, bandying words, dancing, capering, to the sound of a piano which was groaning —out of tune and rattling as an old kettle.

Two tall, russet-haired, half-tipsy girls, with red lips, were talking coarsely. Others were dancing madly with young fellows half clad, dressed like jockeys, in linen trousers and colored caps. The odors of a crowd and of rice-powder were noticeable.

The drinkers around the tables were swallowing white, red, yellow, and green liquids, and vociferating at the top of their lungs, feeling as it were, the necessity of making a noise, a brutal need of having their ears and brains filled with uproar. Now and then a swimmer, standing on the roof, dived into the water, splashing the nearest guests, who yelled like savages.

On the stream passed the flotillas of light craft, long, slender wherries, swiftly rowed by bare-armed oarsmen, whose muscles played beneath their bronzed skin. The women in the boats, in blue or red flannel skirts, with umbrellas, red or blue, opened over their heads and gleaming under the burning sun, leaned back in their chairs at the stern of the boats, and seemed almost to float upon the water, in motionless and slumberous pose.

The heavier boats proceeded slowly, crowded with people. A collegian, wanting to show off, rowed like a windmill against all the other boats, bringing the curses of their oarsmen down upon his head, and disappearing in dismay after almost drowning two swimmers, followed by the shouts of the crowd thronging in the great floating *café*.

Yvette, radiantly happy, taking Servigny's arm, went into the midst of this noisy mob. She seemed

to enjoy the crowding, and stared at the girls with a
calm and gracious glance.

"Look at that one, Muscade," she said. "What
pretty hair she has! They seem to be having such
fun!"

As the pianist, a boatman dressed in red with a
huge straw hat, began a waltz, Yvette grasped her
companion and they danced so long and madly that
everybody looked at them. The guests, standing on
the tables, kept time with their feet; others threw
glasses, and the musician, seeming to go mad, struck
the ivory keys with great bangs, swaying his whole
body and swinging his head covered with that immense hat. Suddenly he stopped and, slipping to
the deck, lay flat, beneath his head-gear, as if dead
with fatigue. A loud laugh arose and everybody applauded.

Four friends rushed forward, as they do in cases
of accident, and lifting up their comrade, they carried him by his four limbs, after carefully placing his
great hat on his stomach. A joker following them
intoned the "De Profundis," and a procession formed
and threaded the paths of the island, guests and
strollers and everyone they met falling into line.

Yvette darted forward, delighted, laughing with
her whole heart, chatting with everybody, stirred by
the movement and the noise. The young men gazed
at her, crowded against her, seeming to devour her
with their glances; and Servigny began to fear lest
the adventure should terminate badly.

The procession still kept on its way, hastening its
step; for the four bearers had taken a quick pace,
followed by the yelling crowd. But suddenly, they

turned toward the shore, stopped short as they reached the bank, swung their comrade for a moment, and then, all four acting together, flung him into the river.

A great shout of joy rang out from all mouths, while the poor pianist, bewildered, paddled, swore, coughed, and spluttered, and though sticking in the mud managed to get to the shore. His hat which floated down the stream was picked up by a boat.

Yvette danced with joy, clapping and repeating: "Oh! Muscade, what fun! what fun!"

Servigny looked on, having become serious, a little disturbed, a little chilled to see her so much at her ease in this common place. A sort of instinct revolted in him, that instinct of the proper, which a well-born man always preserves even when he casts himself loose, that instinct which avoids too common familiarities and too degrading contacts. Astonished, he muttered to himself:

"Egad! Then *you* are at home here, are you?" And he wanted to speak familiarly to her, as a man does to certain women the first time he meets them. He no longer distinguished her from the russet-haired, hoarse-voiced creatures who brushed against them. The language of the crowd was not at all choice, but nobody seemed shocked or surprised. Yvette did not even appear to notice it.

"Muscade, I want to go in bathing," she said. "We'll go into the river together."

"At your service," said he.

They went to the bath-office to get bathing-suits. She was ready the first, and stood on the bank waiting for him, smiling on everyone who looked at

her. Then side by side they went into the luke--
warm water.

She swam with pleasure, with intoxication, caressed by the wave, throbbing, with a sensual delight, raising herself at each stroke as if she were
going to spring from the water. He followed her
with difficulty, breathless, and vexed to feel himself
mediocre at the sport.

But she slackened her pace, and then, turning
over suddenly, she floated, with her arms folded and
her eyes wide open to the blue sky. He observed,
thus stretched out on the surface of the river, the
undulating lines of her form, her firm neck and
shoulders, her slightly submerged hips, and bare
ankles, gleaming in the water, and the tiny foot that
emerged.

He saw her thus exhibiting herself, as if she were
doing it on purpose, to lure him on, or again to
make sport of him. And he began to long for her
with a passionate ardor and an exasperating impatience. Suddenly she turned, looked at him, and burst
into laughter.

"You have a fine head," she said.

He was annoyed at this bantering, possessed with
the anger of a baffled lover. Then yielding brusquely
to a half felt desire for retaliation, a desire to avenge
himself, to wound her, he said:

"Well, does this sort of life suit you?"

She asked with an artless air: "What do you
mean?"

"Oh, come, don't make game of me. You know
well enough what I mean!"

"No, I don't, on my word of honor."

"Oh, let us stop this comedy! Will you or will you not?"

"I do not understand you."

"You are not as stupid as all that; besides I told you last night."

"Told me what? I have forgotten!"

"That I love you."

"You?"

"Yes."

"What nonsense!"

"I swear it."

"Then prove it."

"That is all I ask."

"What is?"

"To prove it."

"Well, do so."

"But you did not say so last night."

"You did not ask anything."

"What absurdity!"

"And besides it is not to me to whom you should make your proposition."

"To whom, then?"

"Why, to mamma, of course."

He burst into laughter. "To your mother. No, that is too much!"

She had suddenly become very grave, and looking him straight in the eyes, said:

"Listen, Muscade, if you really love me enough to marry me, speak to mamma first, and I will answer you afterward."

He thought she was still making sport of him, and angrily replied: "Mam'zelle, you must be taking me for somebody else."

She kept looking at him with her soft, clear eyes. She hesitated and then said:

"I don't understand you at all."

Then he answered quickly with somewhat of ill nature in his voice:

"Come now, Yvette, let us cease this absurd comedy, which has already lasted too long. You are playing the part of a simple little girl, and the rôle does not fit you at all, believe me. You know perfectly well that there can be no question of marriage between us, but merely of love. I have told you that I love you. It is the truth. I repeat, I love you. Don't pretend any longer not to understand me, and don't treat me as if I were a fool."

They were face to face, treading water, merely moving their hands a little, to steady themselves. She was still for a moment, as if she could not make out the meaning of his words, then she suddenly blushed up to the roots of her hair. Her whole face grew purple from her neck to her ears, which became almost violet, and without answering a word she fled toward the shore, swimming with all her strength with hasty strokes. He could not keep up with her and panted with fatigue as he followed. He saw her leave the water, pick up her cloak, and go to her dressing-room without looking back.

It took him a long time to dress, very much perplexed as to what he ought to do, puzzled over what he should say to her, and wondering whether he ought to excuse himself or persevere. When he was ready, she had gone away all alone. He went back slowly, anxious and disturbed.

The Marquise was strolling, on Saval's arm, in the circular path around the lawn. As she observed Servigny, she said, with that careless air which she had maintained since the night before:

"I told you not to go out in such hot weather. And now Yvette has come back almost with a sun stroke. She has gone to lie down. She was as red as a poppy, the poor child, and she has a frightful headache. You must have been walking in the full sunlight, or you must have done something foolish. You are as unreasonable as she."

The young girl did not come down to dinner. When they wanted to send her up something to eat she called through the door that she was not hungry, for she had shut herself in, and she begged that they would leave her undisturbed. The two young men left by the ten o'clock train, promising to return the following Thursday, and the Marquise seated herself at the open window to dream, hearing in the distance the orchestra of the boatmen's ball, with its sprightly music, in the deep and solemn silence of the night.

Swayed by love as a person is moved by a fondness for horses or boating, she was subject to sudden tendernesses which crept over her like a disease. These passions took possession of her suddenly, penetrated her entire being, maddened her, enervated or overwhelmed her, in measure as they were of an exalted, violent, dramatic, or sentimental character.

She was one of those women who are created to love and to be loved. Starting from a very low station in life, she had risen in her adventurous career, acting instinctively, with inborn cleverness, accept ing money and kisses, naturally, without distinguishing between them, employing her extraordinary ability in an unthinking and simple fashion. From all her experiences she had never known either a genuine tenderness or a great repulsion.

She had had various friends, for she had to live, as in traveling a person eats at many tables. But occasionally her heart took fire, and she really fell in love, which state lasted for some weeks or months, according to conditions. These were the delicious moments of her life, for she loved with all her soul. She cast herself upon love as a person throws himself into the river to drown himself, and let herself be carried away, ready to die, if need be, intoxicated, maddened, infinitely happy. She imagined each time that she never had experienced anything like such an attachment, and she would have been greatly astonished if some one had told her of how many men she had dreamed whole nights through, looking at the stars.

Saval had captivated her, body and soul. She dreamed of him, lulled by his face and his memory, in the calm exaltation of consummated love, of present and certain happiness.

A sound behind her made her turn around. Yvette had just entered, still in her daytime dress, but pale, with eyes glittering, as sometimes is the case after some great fatigue. She leaned on the sill of the open window, facing her mother.

"I want to speak to you," she said.

The Marquise looked at her in astonishment. She loved her like an egotistical mother, proud of her beauty, as a person is proud of a fortune, too pretty

still herself to become jealous, too indifferent to plan
the schemes with which they charged her, too clever,
nevertheless, not to have full consciousness of her
daughter's value.

"I am listening, my child," she said; "what is it?"

Yvette gave her a piercing look, as if to read the
depths of her soul and to seize all the sensations
which her words might awake.

"It is this. Something strange has just happened."

"What can it be?"

"Monsieur de Servigny has told me that he loves
me."

The Marquise, disturbed, waited a moment, and,
as Yvette said nothing more, she asked:

"How did he tell you that? Explain yourself!"

Then the young girl, sitting at her mother's feet,
in a coaxing attitude common with her, and clasping
her hands, added:

"He asked me to marry him."

Madame Obardi made a sudden gesture of stupe-
faction and cried:

"Servigny! Why! you are crazy!"

Yvette had not taken her eyes off her mother's
face, watching her thoughts and her surprise. She
asked with a serious voice:

"Why am I crazy? Why should not Monsieur
de Servigny marry me?"

The Marquise, embarrassed, stammered:

"You are mistaken, it is not possible. You either
did not hear or did not understand. Monsieur de
Servigny is too rich for you, and too much of a
Parisian to marry."

Yvette rose softly. She added: "But if he loves me as he says he does, mamma?"

Her mother replied, with some impatience: "I thought you big enough and wise enough not to have such ideas. Servigny is a man-about-town and an egotist. He will never marry anyone but a woman of his set and his fortune. If he asked you in marriage, it is only that he wants—"

The Marquise, incapable of expressing her meaning, was silent for a moment, then continued: "Come now, leave me alone and go to bed."

And the young girl, as if she had learned what she sought to find out, answered in a docile voice: "Yes, mamma!"

She kissed her mother on the forehead and withdrew with a calm step. As she reached the door, the Marquise called out: "And your sunstroke?" she said.

"I did not have one at all. It was that which caused everything."

The Marquise added: "We will not speak of it again. Only don't stay alone with him for some time from now, and be very sure that he will never marry you, do you understand, and that he merely means to—compromise you."

She could not find better words to express her thought. Yvette went to her room. Madame Obardi began to dream. Living for years in an opulent and loving repose, she had carefully put aside all reflections which might annoy or sadden her. Never had she been willing to ask herself the question—What would become of Yvette? It would be soon enough to think about the difficulties when they arrived. She well knew, from her experience, that her daughter could not marry a man who was rich and of good society, excepting by a totally improbable chance, by one of those surprises of love which place adventuresses on thrones.

She had not considered it, furthermore, being too much occupied with herself to make any plans which did not directly concern herself.

Yvette would do as her mother, undoubtedly. She would lead a gay life. Why not? But the Marquise had rever dared ask when, or how. That would all come about in time.

And now her daughter, all of a sudden, without warning, had asked one of those questions which could not be answered, forcing her to take an attitude in an affair, so delicate, so dangerous in every respect, and so disturbing to the conscience which a woman is expected to show in matters concerning her daughter.

Sometimes nodding but never asleep, she had too much natural astuteness to be deceived a minute about Servigny's intentions, for she knew men by experience, and especially men of that set. So at the first words uttered by Yvette, she had cried almost in spite of herself: "Servigny, marry you? You are crazy!"

How had he come to employ that old method, he, that sharp man of the world? What would he do now? And she, the young girl, how should she warn her more clearly and even forbid her, for she might make great mistakes. Would anyone have believed that this big girl had remained so artless, so ill informed, so guileless?

And the Marquise, greatly perplexed and already
wearied with her reflections, endeavored to make up
her mind what to do without finding a solution of
the problem, for the situation seemed to her very embarrassing. Worn out with this worry, she thought:
"I will watch them more clearly, I will act according to circumstances. If necessary, I will speak
to Servigny, who is sharp and will take a hint."

She did not think out what she should say to
him, nor what he would answer, nor what sort of an
understanding could be established between them,
but happy at being relieved of this care without having had to make a decision, she resumed her dreams
of the handsome Saval, and turning toward that misty
light which hovers over Paris, she threw kisses with
both hands toward the great city, rapid kisses which
she tossed into the darkness, one after the other,
without counting; and, very low, as if she were
talking to Saval still, she murmured:

"I love you, I love you!"

CHAPTER III.

ENLIGHTENMENT

YVETTE, also, could not sleep. Like her mother, she leaned upon the sill of the open window, and tears, her first bitter tears, filled her eyes. Up to this time she had lived, had grown up, in the heedless and serene confidence of happy youth. Why should she have dreamed, reflected, puzzled? Why should she not have been a young girl, like all other young girls? Why should a doubt, a fear, or painful suspicion have come to her?

She seemed posted on all topics because she had a way of talking on all subjects, because she had taken the tone, demeanor, and words of the people who lived around her. But she really knew no more than a little girl raised in a convent; her audacities of speech came from her memory, from that unconscious faculty of imitation and assimilation which women possess, and not from a mind instructed and emboldened.

She spoke of love as the son of a painter or a musician would, at the age of ten or twelve years,

speak of painting or music. She knew or rather
suspected very well what sort of mystery this word
concealed, — too many jokes had been whispered before her, for her innocence not to be a trifle enlight-
ened, — but how could she have drawn the conclusion
from all this, that all families did not resemble hers?

They kissed her mother's hand with the sem-
blance of respect; all their friends had titles; they all
were rich or seemed to be so; they all spoke familiarly of the princes of the royal line. Two sons of
kings had even come often, in the evening, to the
Marquise's house. How should she have known?

And, then, she was naturally artless. She did not
estimate or sum up people as her mother did. She
lived tranquilly, too joyous in her life to worry herself about what might appear suspicious to creatures
more calm, thoughtful, reserved, less cordial, and
sunny.

But now, all at once, Servigny, by a few words,
the brutality of which she felt without understanding
them, awakened in her a sudden disquietude, unrea-
soning at first, but which grew into a tormenting
apprehension. She had fled home, had escaped like a
wounded animal, wounded in fact most deeply by
those words which she ceaselessly repeated to get all
their sense and bearing: "You know very well that
there can be no question of marriage between us —
but only of love."

What did he mean? And why this insult? Was
she then in ignorance of something, some secret,
some shame? She was the only one ignorant of it,
no doubt. But what could she do? She was frightened, startled, as a person is when he discovers some

hidden infamy, some treason of a beloved friend, one of those heart-disasters which crush.

She dreamed, reflected, puzzled, wept, consumed by fears and suspicions. Then her joyous young soul reassuring itself, she began to plan an adventure, to imagine an abnormal and dramatic situation, founded on the recollections of all the poetical romances she had read. She recalled all the moving catastrophes, or sad and touching stories; she jumbled them together, and concocted a story of her own with which she interpreted the half-understood mystery which enveloped her life.

She was no longer cast down. She dreamed, she lifted veils, she imagined unlikely complications, a thousand singular, terrible things, seductive, nevertheless, by their very strangeness. Could she be, by chance, the natural daughter of a prince? Had her poor mother, betrayed and deserted, made Marquise by some king, perhaps King Victor Emmanuel, been obliged to take flight before the anger of the family? Was she not rather a child abandoned by its relations, who were noble and illustrious, the fruit of a clandestine love, taken in by the Marquise, who had adopted and brought her up?

Still other suppositions passed through her mind. She accepted or rejected them according to the dictates of her fancy. She was moved to pity over her own case, happy at the bottom of her heart, and sad also, taking a sort of satisfaction in becoming a sort of a heroine of a book who must assume a noble attitude, worthy of herself.

She laid out the part she must play, according to events at which she guessed. She vaguely outlined this rôle, like one of Scribe's or of George Sand's. It should be endued with devotion, self-abnegation, greatness of soul, tenderness, and fine words. Her pliant nature almost rejoiced in this new attitude. She pondered almost till evening what she should do, wondering how she should manage to wrest the truth from the Marquise.

And when night came, favorable to tragic situations, she had thought out a simple and subtile trick to obtain what she wanted: it was, brusquely, to say that Servigny had asked for her hand in marriage.

At this news, Madame Obardi, taken by surprise, would certainly let a word escape her lips, a cry which would throw light into the mind of her daughter. And Yvette had accomplished her plan.

She expected an explosion of astonishment, an expansion of love, a confidence full of gestures and tears. But, instead of this, her mother, without appearing stupefied or grieved, had only seemed bored; and from the constrained, discontented, and worried tone in which she had replied, the young girl, in whom there suddenly awaked all the astuteness, keenness, and sharpness of a woman, understanding that she must not insist, that the mystery was of another nature, that it would be painful to her to learn it, and that she must puzzle it out all alone, had gone back to her room, her heart oppressed, her soul in distress, possessed now with the apprehensions of a real misfortune, without knowing exactly either whence or why this emotion came to her. So she wept, leaning at the window.

She wept long, not dreaming of anything now, not seeking to discover anything more, and little by little, weariness overcoming her, she closed her eyes. She dozed for a few minutes, with that deep sleep of people who are tired out and have not the energy to undress and go to bed, that heavy sleep, broken by dreams, when the head nods upon the breast.

She did not go to bed until the first break of day, when the cold of the morning, chilling her, compelled her to leave the window.

The next day and the day after, she maintained a reserved and melancholy attitude. Her thoughts were busy; she was learning to spy out, to guess at conclusions, to reason. A light, still vague, seemed to illumine men and things around her in a new manner; she began to entertain suspicions against all, against everything that she had believed, against her mother. She imagined all sorts of things during these two days. She considered all the possibilities, taking the most extreme resolutions with the suddenness of her changeable and unrestrained nature. Wednesday she hit upon a plan, an entire schedule of conduct and a system of spying. She rose Thursday morning with the resolve to be very sharp and armed against everybody.

She determined even to take for her motto these two words: "Myself alone," and she pondered for more than an hour how she should arrange them to produce a good effect engraved about her crest, on her writing paper.

Saval and Servigny arrived at ten o'clock. The young girl gave her hand with reserve, without embarrassment, and in a tone, familiar though grave, she said:

"Good morning, Muscade, are you well?"

"Good morning, Mam'zelle, fairly, thanks, and you?" He was watching her. "What comedy will she play me," he said to himself.

The Marquise having taken Saval's arm, he took Yvette's, and they began to stroll about the lawn, appearing and disappearing every minute, behind the clumps of trees.

Yvette walked with a thoughtful air, looking at the gravel of the pathway, appearing hardly to hear what her companion said and scarcely answering him.

Suddenly she asked: "Are you truly my friend, Muscade?"

"Why, of course, Mam'zelle."

"But truly, truly, now?"

"Absolutely your friend, Mam'zelle, body and soul."

"Even enough of a friend not to lie to me once, just once?"

"Even twice, if necessary."

"Even enough to tell me the absolute, exact truth?"

"Yes, Mam'zelle."

"Well, what do you think, way down in your heart, of the Prince of Kravalow?"

"Ah, the devil!"

"You see that you are already preparing to lie."

"Not at all, but I am seeking the words, the proper words. Great Heavens, Prince Kravalow is a Russian, who speaks Russian, who was born in Russia, who has perhaps had a passport to come to France, and about whom there is nothing false but his name and title."

7 G. de M.—18

She looked him in the eyes: "You mean that he is — ?"

"An adventurer, Mam'zelle."

"Thank you, and Chevalier Valreali is no better?"

"You have hit it."

"And Monsieur de Belvigne?"

"With him it is a different thing. He is of provincial society, honorable up to a certain point, but only a little scorched from having lived too rapidly."

"And you?"

"I am what they call a butterfly, a man of good family, who had intelligence and who has squandered it in making phrases, who had good health and who has injured it by dissipation, who had some worth perhaps and who has scattered it by doing nothing. There is left to me a certain knowledge of life, a complete absence of prejudice, a large contempt for mankind, including women, a very deep sentiment of the uselessness of my acts and a vast tolerance for the mob.

"Nevertheless, at times, I can be frank, and I am even capable of affection, as you could see, if you would. With these defects and qualities I place myself at your orders, Mam'zelle, morally and physically, to do what you please with me."

She did not laugh; she listened, weighing his words and his intentions; then she resumed:

"What do you think of the Countess de Lammy?"

He replied, vivaciously: "You will permit me not to give my opinion about the women."

"About none of them?"

"About none of them."

"Then you must have a bad opinion of them all. Come, think; won't you make a single exception?"

He sneered with that insolent air which he generally wore; and with that brutal audacity which he used as a weapon, he said: "Present company is always excepted."

She blushed a little, but calmly asked: "Well, what do you think of me?"

"You want me to tell. Well, so be it. I think you are a young person of good sense, and practicalness, or if you prefer, of good practical sense, who knows very well how to arrange her pastime, to amuse people, to hide her views, to lay her snares, and who, without hurrying, awaits events."

"Is that all?" she asked.

"That's all."

Then she said with a serious earnestness: "I shall make you change that opinion, Muscade."

Then she joined her mother, who was proceeding with short steps, her head down, with that manner assumed in talking very low, while walking, of very intimate and very sweet things. As she advanced she drew shapes in the sand, letters perhaps, with the point of her sunshade, and she spoke, without looking at Saval, long, softly, leaning on his arm, pressed against him.

Yvette suddenly fixed her eyes upon her, and a suspicion, rather a feeling than a doubt, passed through her mind as a shadow of a cloud driven by the wind passes over the ground.

The bell rang for breakfast. It was silent and almost gloomy. There was a storm in the air. Great

solid clouds rested upon the horizon, mute and heavy,
but charged with a tempest. As soon as they had
taken their coffee on the terrace, the Marquise asked:

"Well, darling, are you going to take a walk to-
day with your friend Servigny? It is a good time to
enjoy the coolness under the trees."

Yvette gave her a quick glance.

"No, mamma, I am not going out to-day."

The Marquise appeared annoyed, and insisted.
"Oh, go and take a stroll, my child, it is excellent
for you."

Then Yvette distinctly said: "No, mamma, I shall
stay in the house to-day, and you know very well
why, because I told you the other evening."

Madame Obardi gave it no further thought, preoccupied with the thought of remaining alone with
Saval. She blushed and was annoyed, disturbed on
her own account, not knowing how she could find a
free hour or two. She stammered:

"It is true. I was not thinking of it. I don't
know where my head is."

And Yvette taking up some embroidery, which
she called "the public safety," and at which she
worked five or six times a year, on dull days, seated
herself on a low chair near her mother, while the
two young men, astride folding-chairs, smoked their
cigars.

The hours passed in a languid conversation. The
Marquise fidgety, cast longing glances at Saval, seeking some pretext, some means, of getting rid of her
daughter. She finally realized that she would not
succeed, and not knowing what ruse to employ, she
said to Servigny:

"You know, my dear Duke, that I am going to keep you both this evening. To-morrow we shall breakfast at the Fournaise restaurant, at Chaton."

He understood, smiled, and bowed: "I am at your orders, Marquise."

The day wore on slowly and painfully under the threatenings of the storm. The hour for dinner gradually approached. The heavy sky was filled with slow and heavy clouds. There was not a breath of air stirring. The evening meal was silent, too. An oppression, an embarrassment, a sort of vague fear, seemed to make the two men and the two women mute.

When the covers were removed, they sat long upon the terrace; only speaking at long intervals. Night fell, a sultry night. Suddenly the horizon was torn by an immense flash of lightning, which illumined with a dazzling and wan light the four faces shrouded in darkness. Then a far-off sound, heavy and feeble, like the rumbling of a carriage upon a bridge, passed over the earth; and it seemed that the heat of the atmosphere increased, that the air suddenly became more oppressive, and the silence of the evening deeper.

Yvette rose. "I am going to bed," she said, "the storm makes me ill."

And she offered her brow to the Marquise, gave her hand to the two young men, and withdrew.

As her room was just above the terrace, the leaves of a great chestnut-tree growing before the door soon gleamed with a green hue, and Servigny kept his eyes fixed on this pale light in the foliage, in which at times he thought he saw a shadow pass. But suddenly the light went out. Madame Obardi gave a great sigh.

"My daughter has gone to bed," she said.

Servigny rose, saying: "I am going to do as much, Marquise, if you will permit me." He kissed the hand she held out to him and disappeared in turn.

She was left alone with Saval, in the night. In a moment she was clasped in his arms. Then, although he tried to prevent her, she kneeled before him murmuring: "I want to see you by the lightning flashes."

But Yvette, her candle snuffed out, had returned to her balcony, barefoot, gliding like a shadow, and she listened, consumed by an unhappy and confused suspicion. She could not see, as she was above them, on the roof of the terrace.

She heard nothing but a murmur of voices, and her heart beat so fast that she could actually hear its throbbing. A window closed on the floor above her. Servigny, then, must have just gone up to his room. Her mother was alone with the other man.

A second flash of lightning, clearing the sky, lighted up for a second all the landscape she knew so well, with a startling and sinister gleam, and she saw the great river, with the color of melted lead, as a river appears in dreams in fantastic scenes.

Just then a voice below her uttered the words: "I love you!" And she heard nothing more. A strange shudder passed over her body, and her soul shivered in frightful distress. A heavy, infinite silence, which seemed eternal, hung over the world. She could no longer breathe, her breast oppressed by something unknown and horrible. Another flash of lightning illumined space, lighting up the horizon for an instant, then another almost immediately came, followed by still others. And the voice, which she had already heard, repeated more loudly: "Oh! how I love you! how I love you!" And Yvette recognized the voice; it was her mother's.

A large drop of warm rain fell upon her brow, and a slight and almost imperceptible motion ran through the leaves, the quivering of the rain which was now beginning. Then a noise came from afar, a confused sound, like that of the wind in the branches: it was the deluge descending in sheets on earth and river and trees. In a few minutes the water poured about her, covering her, drenching her like a shower-bath. She did not move, thinking only of what was happening on the terrace.

She heard them get up and go to their rooms. Doors were closed within the house; and the young girl, yielding to an irresistible desire to learn what was going on, a desire which maddened and tortured her, glided downstairs, softly opened the outer door, and, crossing the lawn under the furious downpour, ran and hid in a clump of trees, to look at the windows.

Only one window was lighted, her mother's. And suddenly two shadows appeared in the luminous square, two shadows, side by side. Then distracted, without reflection, without knowing what she was doing, she screamed with all her might, in a shrill voice: "Mamma!" as a person would cry out to warn people in danger of death.

Her desperate cry was lost in the noise of the rain, but the couple separated, disturbed. And one of the shadows disappeared, while the other tried to discover something, peering through the darkness of the garden.

Fearing to be surprised, or to meet her mother at that moment, Yvette rushed back to the house, ran upstairs, dripping wet, and shut herself in her room, resolved to open her door to no one.

Without taking off her streaming dress, which clung to her form, she fell on her knees, with clasped hands, in her distress imploring some superhuman protection, the mysterious aid of Heaven, the unknown support which a person seeks in hours of tears and despair.

The great lightning flashes threw for an instant their livid reflections into her room, and she saw herself in the mirror of her wardrobe, with her wet and disheveled hair, looking so strange that she did not recognize herself. She remained there so long that the storm abated without her perceiving it. The rain ceased, a light filled the sky, still obscured with clouds, and a mild, balmy, delicious freshness, a freshness of grass and wet leaves, came in through the open window.

Yvette rose, took off her wet, cold garments, without thinking what she was doing, and went to bed. She stared with fixed eyes at the dawning day. Then she wept again, and then she began to think.

Her mother! A lover! What a shame! She had read so many books in which women, even mothers, had overstepped the bounds of propriety, to regain their honor at the pages of the climax, that she was not astonished beyond measure at finding herself enveloped in a drama similar to all those of her reading. The violence of her first grief, the cruel shock of surprise, had already worn off a little, in the confused remembrance of analogous situations. Her mind had rambled among such tragic adventures, painted by the novel-writers, that the horrible discovery seemed, little by little, like the natural continuation of some serial story, begun the evening before.

She said to herself: "I will save my mother." And almost reassured by this heroic resolution, she felt herself strengthened, ready at once for the devotion and the struggle. She reflected on the means which must be employed. A single one seemed good, which was quite in keeping with her romantic nature. And she rehearsed the interview which she should have with the Marquise, as an actor rehearses the scene which he is going to play.

The sun had risen. The servants were stirring about the house. The chambermaid came with the chocolate. Yvette put the tray on the table and said:

"You will say to my mother that I am not well, that I am going to stay in bed until those gentlemen leave, that I could not sleep last night, and that I do not want to be disturbed because I am going to try to rest."

The servant, surprised, looked at the wet dress, which had fallen like a rag on the carpet.

"So Mademoiselle has been out?" she said.

"Yes, I went out for a walk in the rain to refresh myself."

The maid picked up the skirts, stockings, and wet shoes; then she went away carrying on her arm, with fastidious precautions, these garments, soaked

as the clothes of a drowned person. And Yvette
waited, well knowing that her mother would come
to her.

The Marquise entered, having jumped from her
bed at the first words of the chambermaid, for a
suspicion had possessed her heart since that cry:
"Mamma!" heard in the dark.

"What is the matter?" she said.

Yvette looked at her and stammered: "I—I—"
Then overpowered by a sudden and terrible emotion,
she began to choke.

The Marquise, astonished, again asked: "What
in the world is the matter with you?"

Then, forgetting all her plans and prepared phrases,
the young girl hid her face in both hands and stammered:

"Oh! mamma! Oh! mamma!"

Madame Obardi stood by the bed, too much affected thoroughly to understand, but guessing almost
everything, with that subtile instinct whence she de-
rived her strength. As Yvette could not speak, choked
with tears, her mother, worn out finally and feeling
some fearful explanation coming, brusquely asked:

"Come, will you tell me what the matter is?"

Yvette could hardly utter the words: "Oh! last
night—I saw—your window."

The Marquise, very pale, said: "Well? what
of it?"

Her daughter repeated, still sobbing: "Oh! mamma!
Oh! mamma!"

Madame Obardi, whose fear and embarrassment
turned to anger, shrugged her shoulders and turned
to go.

"I really believe that you are crazy. When this ends, you will let me know."

But the young girl, suddenly took her hands from her face, which was streaming with tears.

"No, listen, I must speak to you, listen. You must promise me — we must both go away, very far off, into the country, and we must live like the country people; and no one must know what has become of us. Say you will, mamma; I beg you, I implore you; will you?"

The Marquise, confused, stood in the middle of the room. She had in her veins the irascible blood of the common people. Then a sense of shame, a mother's modesty, mingled with a vague sentiment of fear and the exasperation of a passionate woman whose love is threatened, and she shuddered, ready to ask for pardon, or to yield to some violence.

"I don't understand you," she said.

Yvette replied:

"I saw you, mamma, last night. You cannot — if you knew — we will both go away. I will love you so much that you will forget —"

Madame Obardi said in a trembling voice: "Listen, my daughter, there are some things which you do not yet understand. Well, don't forget — don't forget — that I forbid you ever to speak to me about those things."

But the young girl, brusquely taking the rôle of savior which she had imposed upon herself, rejoined:

"No, mamma, I am no longer a child, and I have the right to know. I know that we receive persons of bad repute, adventurers, and I know that, on that account, people do not respect us. I know more. Well, it must not be, any longer, do you hear? I do not wish it. We will go away: you will sell your jewels; we will work, if need be, and we will live as honest women, somewhere very far away. And if I can marry, so much the better."

She answered: "You are crazy. You will do me the favor to rise and come down to breakfast with all the rest."

"No, mamma. There is some one whom I shall never see again, you understand me. I want him to leave, or I shall leave. You shall choose between him and me."

She was sitting up in bed, and she raised her voice, speaking as they do on the stage, playing, finally, the drama which she had dreamed, almost forgetting her grief in the effort to fulfill her mission.

The Marquise, stupefied, again repeated: "You are crazy—" not finding anything else to say.

Yvette replied with a theatrical energy: "No, mamma, that man shall leave the house, or I shall go myself, for I will not weaken."

"And where will you go? What will you do?"

"I do not know, it matters little—I want you to be an honest woman."

These words which recurred, aroused in the Marquise a perfect fury, and she cried:

"Be silent. I do not permit you to talk to me like that. I am as good as anybody else, do you understand? I lead a certain sort of life, it is true, and I am proud of it; the 'honest women' are not as good as I am."

Yvette, astonished, looked at her, and stammered: "Oh! mamma!"

But the Marquise, carried away with excitement, continued:

"Yes, I lead a certain life — what of it? Otherwise you would be a cook, as I was once, and earn thirty sous a day. You would be washing dishes, and your mistress would send you to market — do you understand — and she would turn you out if you loitered, just as you loiter now because I am — because I lead this life. Listen. When a person is only a nursemaid, a poor girl, with fifty francs saved up, she must know how to manage, if she does not want to starve to death; and there are not two ways for us, there are not two ways, do you understand, when we are servants. We cannot make our fortune with official positions, nor with stockjobbing tricks. We have only one way — only one way."

She struck her breast as a penitent at the confessional, and flushed and excited, coming toward the bed, she continued: "So much the worse. A pretty girl must live or suffer — she has no choice!" Then returning to her former idea: "Much they deny themselves, your 'honest women.' They are worse, because nothing compels them. They have money to live on and amuse themselves, and they choose vicious lives of their own accord. They are the bad ones in reality."

She was standing near the bed of the distracted Yvette, who wanted to cry out "Help," to escape. Yvette wept aloud, like children who are whipped. The Marquise was silent and looked at her daughter, and, seeing her overwhelmed with despair, felt, herself, the pangs of grief, remorse, tenderness, and pity, and throwing herself upon the bed with open arms, she also began to sob and stammered:

"My poor little girl, my poor little girl, if you knew how you were hurting me." And they wept together, a long while.

Then the Marquise, in whom grief could not long endure, softly rose, and gently said:

"Come, darling, it is unavoidable; what would you have? Nothing can be changed now. We must take life as it comes to us."

Yvette continued to weep. The blow had been too harsh and too unexpected to permit her to reflect and to recover at once.

Her mother resumed: "Now, get up and come down to breakfast, so that no one will notice anything."

The young girl shook her head as if to say, "No," without being able to speak. Then she said, with a slow voice full of sobs:

"No, mamma, you know what I said, I won't alter my determination. I shall not leave my room till they have gone. I never want to see one of those people again, never, never. If they come back, you will see no more of me."

The Marquise had dried her eyes, and wearied with emotion, she murmured:

"Come, reflect, be reasonable."

Then, after a moment's silence:

"Yes, you had better rest this morning. I will come up to see you this afternoon." And having kissed her daughter on the forehead, she went to dress herself, already calmed.

Yvette, as soon as her mother had disappeared, rose, and ran to bolt the door, to be alone, all alone; then she began to think. The chambermaid knocked about eleven o'clock, and asked through the door:

"Madame the Marquise wants to know if Mademoiselle wishes anything, and what she will take for her breakfast."

Yvette answered: "I am not hungry, I only ask not to be disturbed."

And she remained in bed, just as if she had been ill. Toward three o'clock, some one knocked again. She asked:

"Who is there?"

It was her mother's voice which replied: "It is I, darling, I have come to see how you are."

She hesitated what she should do. She opened the door, and then went back to bed. The Marquise approached, and, speaking in low tones, as people do to a convalescent, said:

"Well, are you better? Won't you eat an egg?"

"No, thanks, nothing at all."

Madame Obardi sat down near the bed. They remained without saying anything, then, finally, as her daughter stayed quiet, with her hands inert upon the bedclothes, she asked:

"Don't you intend to get up?"

Yvette answered: "Yes, pretty soon."

Then in a grave and slow tone she said: "I have thought a great deal, mamma, and this—this is my resolution. The past is the past, let us speak no more of it. But the future shall be different or I know what is left for me to do. Now, let us say no more about it."

The Marquise, who thought the explanation finished, felt her impatience gaining a little. It was too
much. This big goose of a girl ought to have known
about things long ago. But she did not say anything in reply, only repeating:

"You are going to get up?"

"Yes, I am ready."

Then her mother became maid for her, bringing
her stockings, her corset, and her skirts. Then she
kissed her.

"Will you take a walk before dinner?"

"Yes, mamma."

And they took a stroll along the water, speaking
only of commonplace things.

CHAPTER IV.

FROM EMOTION TO PHILOSOPHY

THE following day, early in the morning, Yvette went out alone to the place where Servigny had read her the history of the ants. She said to herself:

"I am not going away from this spot without having formed a resolution."

Before her, at her feet, the water flowed rapidly, filled with large bubbles which passed in silent flight with deep whirlings. She already had summed up the points of the situation and the means of extricating herself from it. What should she do if her mother would not accept the conditions which she had imposed, would not renounce her present way of living, her set of visitors—everything and go and hide with her in a distant land?

She might go alone, take flight, but where, and how? What would she live on? By working? At what? To whom should she apply to find work? And, then, the dull and humble life of working-women, daughters of the people, seemed a little disgraceful, unworthy of her. She thought of becoming a governess, like young girls in novels, and of becoming loved by the son of the house, and then marrying him. But to accomplish that she must have been of good birth, so that, when the exasperated father should approach her with having stolen his son's love, she might say in a proud voice:

"My name is Yvette Obardi."

She could not do this. And then, even that would have been a trite and threadbare method.

The convent was not worth much more. Besides, she felt no vocation for a religious life, having only an intermittent and fleeting piety. No one would save her by marrying her, being what she was! No aid was acceptable from a man, no possible issue, no definite resource.

And then she wished to do something energetic and really great and strong, which should serve as an example: so she resolved upon death.

She decided upon this step suddenly, but tranquilly, as if it were a journey, without reflecting, without looking at death, without understanding that it is the end without recommencement, the departure without return, the eternal farewell to earth and to this life.

She immediately settled on this extreme measure, with the lightness of young and excited souls, and she thought of the means which she would employ. But they all seemed to her painful and hazardous, and, furthermore, required a violence of action which repelled her.

She quickly abandoned the poniard and revolver, which might wound only, blind her or disfigure her, and which demanded a practiced and steady hand. She decided against the rope; it was so common, the poor man's way of suicide, ridiculous and ugly; and against water because she knew how to swim. So poison remained — but which kind? Almost all of them cause suffering and incite vomitings. She did not want either of these things.

Then she thought of chloroform, having read in a newspaper how a young woman had managed to asphyxiate herself by this process. And she felt at once a sort of joy in her resolution, an inner pride, a sensation of bravery. People should see what she was, and what she was worth.

She returned to Bougival and went to a druggist, from whom she asked a little chloroform for a tooth which was aching. The man, who knew her, gave her a tiny bottle of the narcotic.

Then she set out on foot for Croissy, where she procured a second phial of poison. She obtained a third at Chaton, a fourth at Ruril, and got home late for breakfast.

As she was very hungry after this long walk, she ate heartily with the pleasurable appetite of people who have taken exercise.

Her mother, happy to see her so hungry, and now feeling tranquil herself, said to her as they left the table:

"All our friends are coming to spend Sunday with us. I have invited the Prince, the Chevalier, and Monsieur de Belvigne."

Yvette turned a little pale, but did not reply. She went out almost immediately, reached the railway station, and took a ticket for Paris. And during all the afternoon, she went from druggist to druggist, buying from each one a few drops of chloroform. She came back in the evening with her pockets full of little bottles.

She began the same system on the following day, and by chance found a chemist who gave her, at one stroke, a quarter of a liter. She did not go out on Saturday; it was a lowering and sultry day; she passed it entirely on the terrace, stretched on a long wicker-chair.

She thought of almost nothing, very resolute and very calm. She put on the next morning, a blue costume which was very becoming to her, wishing to look well. Then looking at herself in the glass, she suddenly said:

"To-morrow, I shall be dead." And a peculiar shudder passed over her body. "Dead! I shall speak no more, think no more, no one will see me more, and I shall never see anything again."

And she gazed attentively at her countenance, as if she had never observed it, examining especially her eyes, discovering a thousand things in herself, a secret character in her physiognomy which she had not known before, astonished to see herself, as if she had opposite her a strange person, a new friend.

She said to herself: "It is I, in the mirror, there. How queer it is to look at oneself. But without the mirror we would never know ourselves. Everybody else would know how we look, and we ourselves would know nothing."

She placed the heavy braids of her thick hair over her breast, following with her glance all her gestures, all her poses, and all her movements.

"How pretty I am!" she thought. "To-morrow I shall be dead, there, upon my bed." She looked at her bed, and seemed to see herself stretched out, white as the sheets.

Dead! In a week she would be nothing but dust, to dust returned! A horrible anguish oppressed her heart. The bright sunlight fell in floods upon the fields, and the soft morning air came in at the window.

She sat down thinking of it. Death! It was as if the world was going to disappear from her; but no, since nothing would be changed in the world, not even her bedroom. Yes, her room would remain just the same, with the same bed, the same chairs, the same toilette articles, but she would be forever gone, and no one would be sorry, except her mother, perhaps.

People would say: "How pretty she was! that little Yvette," and nothing more. And as she looked at her arm leaning on the arm of her chair, she thought again, ashes to ashes, dust to dust. And again a great shudder of horror ran over her whole body, and she did not know how she could disappear without the whole earth being blotted out, so much it seemed to her that she was a part of everything, of the fields, of the air, of the sunshine, of life itself.

There were bursts of laughter in the garden, a great noise of voices and of calls, the bustling gaiety of country house parties, and she recognized the sonorous tones of M. de Belvigne, singing:

"I am underneath thy window,
Oh, deign to show thy face."

She rose, without reflecting, and looked out. They all applauded. They were all five there, with two gentlemen whom she did not know.

She brusquely withdrew, annoyed by the thought that these men had come to amuse themselves at her mother's house, as at a public place.

The bell sounded for breakfast. "I will show them how to die," she said.

She went downstairs with a firm step, with something of the resolution of the Christian martyrs going into the circus, where the lions awaited them.

She pressed their hands, smiling in an affable but rather haughty manner. Servigny asked her:

"Are you less cross to-day, Mam'zelle?"

She answered in a severe and peculiar tone: "To-day, I am going to commit follies. I am in my Paris mood, look out!"

Then turning toward Monsieur de Belvigne, she said:

"You shall be my escort, my little Malmsey. I will take you all after breakfast to the *fête* at Marly."

There was, in fact, a *fête* at Marly. They introduced the two newcomers to her, the Comte de Tamine and the Marquis de Briquetot.

During the meal, she said nothing further, strengthening herself to be gay in the afternoon, so that no one should guess anything,—so that they should be all the more astonished, and should say: "Who would have thought it? She seemed so happy, so contented! What does take place in those heads?"

She forced herself not to think of the evening, the chosen hour, when they should all be upon the terrace.

She drank as much wine as she could stand, to nerve herself, and two little glasses of brandy, and she was flushed as she left the table, a little bewildered, heated in body and mind. It seemed to her that she was strengthened now, and resolved for everything.

"Let us start!" she cried. She took Monsieur de Belvigne's arm and set the pace for the others. "Come, you shall form my battalion, Servigny. I choose you as sergeant; you will keep outside the ranks, on the right. You will make the foreign guard march in front—the two exotics, the Prince, and the Chevalier—and in the rear the two recruits who have enlisted to-day. Come!"

They started. And Servigny began to imitate the trumpet, while the two newcomers made believe to beat the drum. Monsieur de Belvigne, a little confused, said in a low tone:

"Mademoiselle Yvette, be reasonable, you will compromise yourself."

She answered: "It is you whom I am compromising, Raisiné. As for me, I don't care much about it. To-morrow it will not occur. So much the worse for you: you ought not to go out with girls like me."

They went through Bougival to the amazement of the passers-by. All turned to look at them; the citizens came to their doors; the travelers on the little railway which runs from Ruril to Marly jeered at them. The men on the platforms cried:

"To the water with them!"

Yvette marched with a military step, holding Belvigne by the arm, as a prisoner is led. She did not laugh; upon her features sat a pale seriousness, a sort of sinister calm. Servigny interrupted his trumpet blasts only to shout orders. The Prince and the Chevalier were greatly amused, finding all this very funny and in good taste. The two recruits drummed away continually.

When they arrived at the *fête*, they made a sensation. Girls applauded; young men jeered, and a stout gentleman with his wife on his arm said enviously: "There are some people who are full of fun."

Yvette saw the wooden horses and compelled Belvigne to mount at her right, while her squad scrambled upon the whirling beasts behind. When the time was up she refused to dismount, constraining her escort to take several more rides on the back of these children's animals, to the great delight of the public, who shouted jokes at them. Monsieur de Belvigne was livid and dizzy when he got off.

Then she began to wander among the booths. She forced all her men to get weighed among a crowd of spectators. She made them buy ridiculous toys which they had to carry in their hands. The Prince and the Chevalier began to think the joke was being carried too far. Servigny and the drummers, alone, did not seem to be discouraged.

They finally came to the end of the place. Then she gazed at her followers in a peculiar manner, with a shy and mischievous glance, and a strange fancy came to her mind. She drew them up on the bank of the river.

"Let the one who loves me the most jump into the water," she said.

Nobody leaped. A mob gathered behind them.

Women in white aprons looked on in stupor. Two troopers, in red breeches, laughed loudly.

She repeated: "Then there is not one of you capable of jumping into the water at my desire?"

Servigny murmured: "Oh, yes, there is," and leaped feet foremost into the river. His plunge cast a splash over as far as Yvette's feet. A murmur of astonishment and gaiety arose in the crowd.

Then the young girl picked up from the ground a little piece of wood, and throwing it into the stream: "Fetch it," she cried.

The young man began to swim, and seizing the floating stick in his mouth, like a dog, he brought it ashore, and then climbing the bank he kneeled on one knee to present it.

Yvette took it. "You are handsome," said she, and with a friendly stroke, she caressed his hair.

A stout woman indignantly exclaimed: "Are such things possible!"

Another woman said: "Can people amuse themselves like that!"

A man remarked: "I would not take a plunge for that sort of a girl."

She again took Belvigne's arm, exclaiming in his face: "You are a goose, my friend; you don't know what you missed."

They now returned. She cast vexed looks on the passers-by. "How stupid all these people seem," she said. Then raising her eyes to the countenance of her companion, she added: "You, too, like all the rest."

M. de Belvigne bowed. Turning around she saw that the Prince and the Chevalier had disappeared.

Servigny, dejected and dripping, ceased playing on the trumpet, and walked with a gloomy air at the side of the two wearied young men, who also had stopped the drum playing. She began to laugh dryly, saying:

"You seem to have had enough; nevertheless, that is what you call having a good time, isn't it? You came for that; I have given you your money's worth."

Then she walked on, saying nothing further; and suddenly Belvigne perceived that she was weeping. Astounded, he inquired:

"What is the matter?"

She murmured: "Let me alone, it does not concern you."

But he insisted, like a fool: "Oh, Mademoiselle, come, what is the matter, has anyone annoyed you?"

She repeated impatiently: "Will you keep still?"

Then suddenly, no longer able to resist the despairing sorrow which drowned her heart, she began to sob so violently, that she could no longer walk. She covered her face with her hands, panting for breath, choked by the violence of her despair.

Belvigne stood still at her side, quite bewildered, repeating: "I don't understand this at all."

But Servigny brusquely came forward: "Let us go home, Mam'zelle, so that people may not see you weeping in the street. Why do you perpetrate follies like that when they only make you sad?"

And taking her arm he drew her forward. But as soon as they reached the iron gate of the villa she began to run, crossed the garden, and went upstairs, and shut herself in her room.

She did not appear again until the dinner hour,
very pale and serious. Servigny had bought from a
country storekeeper a workingman's costume, with
velvet pantaloons, a flowered waistcoat and a blouse,
and he adopted the local dialect. Yvette was in a
hurry for them to finish, feeling her courage ebbing.
As soon as the coffee was served she went to her
room again.

She heard the merry voices beneath her window.
The Chevalier was making equivocal jokes, foreign
witticisms, vulgar and clumsy. She listened, in despair. Servigny, just a bit tipsy, was imitating
the common workingman, calling the Marquise "the
Missus." And all of a sudden he said to Saval:
"Well, Boss?" That caused a general laugh.

Then Yvette decided. She first took a sheet of
paper and wrote:

"BOUGIVAL, Sunday, nine o'clock in the evening.
"I die so that I may not become a kept woman.
"YVETTE."

Then in a postscript:

"Adieu, my dear mother, pardon."

She sealed the envelope, and addressed it to the
Marquise Obardi.

Then she rolled her long chair near the window,
drew a little table within reach of her hand, and
placed upon it the big bottle of chloroform beside a
handful of wadding.

A great rose-tree covered with flowers, climbing
as high as her window, exhaled in the night a soft

and gentle perfume, in light breaths; and she stood for a moment enjoying it. The moon, in its first quarter, was floating in the dark sky, a little ragged at the left, and veiled at times by slight mists.

Yvette thought: "I am going to die!" And her heart, swollen with sobs, nearly bursting, almost suffocated her. She felt in her a need of asking mercy from some one, of being saved, of being loved.

The voice of Servigny aroused her. He was telling an improper story, which was constantly interrupted by bursts of laughter. The Marquise herself laughed louder than the others.

"There is nobody like him for telling that sort of thing," she said, laughing.

Yvette took the bottle, uncorked it, and poured a little of the liquid on the cotton. A strong, sweet, strange odor arose; and as she brought the piece of cotton to her lips, the fumes entered her throat and made her cough.

Then shutting her mouth, she began to inhale it. She took in long breaths of this deadly vapor, closing her eyes, and forcing herself to stifle in her mind all thoughts, so that she might not reflect, that she might know nothing more.

It seemed to her at first that her chest was growing larger, was expanding, and that her soul, recently heavy and burdened with grief, was becoming light, light, as if the weight which overwhelmed her was lifted, wafted away. Something lively and agreeable penetrated even to the extremities of her limbs, even to the tips of her toes and fingers and entered her flesh, a sort of dreamy intoxication, of soft fever.

She saw that the cotton was dry, and she was astonished that she was not already dead. Her senses seemed more acute, more subtle, more alert. She heard the lowest whisper on the terrace. Prince Kravalow was telling how he had killed an Austrian general in a duel.

Then, further off, in the fields, she heard the noise of the night, the occasional barkings of a dog, the short cry of the frogs, the almost imperceptible rustling of the leaves.

She took the bottle again, and saturated once more the little piece of wadding; then she began to breathe in the fumes again. For a few moments she felt nothing; then that soft and soothing feeling of comfort which she had experienced before enveloped her.

Twice she poured more chloroform upon the cotton, eager now for that physical and mental sensation, that dreamy torpor, which bewildered her soul.

It seemed to her that she had no more bones, flesh, legs, or arms. The drug had gently taken all these away from her, without her perceiving it. The chloroform had drawn away her body, leaving her only her mind, more awakened, more active, larger, and more free than she had ever felt it.

She recalled a thousand forgotten things, little details of her childhood, trifles which had given her pleasure. Endowed suddenly with an awakened agility, her mind leaped to the most diverse ideas, ran through a thousand adventures, wandered in the past, and lost itself in the hoped-for events of the future. And her lively and careless thoughts had a sensuous charm: she experienced a divine pleasure in dreaming thus.

She still heard the voices, but she could no longer distinguish the words, which to her seemed to have a different meaning. She was in a kind of strange and changing fairyland.

She was on a great boat which floated through a beautiful country, all covered with flowers. She saw people on the shore, and these people spoke very loudly; then she was again on land, without asking how, and Servigny, clad as a prince, came to seek her, to take her to a bull-fight.

The streets were filled with passers-by, who were talking, and she heard conversations which did not astonish her, as if she had known the people, for through her dreamy intoxication, she still heard her mother's friends laughing and talking on the terrace.

Then everything became vague. Then she awakened, deliciously benumbed, and she could hardly remember what had happened.

So, she was not yet dead. But she felt so calm, in such a state of physical comfort, that she was not in haste to finish with it—she wanted to make this exquisite drowsiness last forever.

She breathed slowly and looked at the moon, opposite her, above the trees. Something had changed in her spirit. She no longer thought as she had done just now. The chloroform quieting her body and her soul had calmed her grief and lulled her desire to die.

Why should she not live? Why should she not be loved? Why should she not lead a happy life?

Everything appeared possible to her now, and easy and certain. Everything in life was sweet, everything was charming. But as she wished to dream on still, she poured more of the dream-water on the cotton and began to breathe it in again, stopping at times, so as not to absorb too much of it and die.

She looked at the moon and saw in it a face, a woman's face. She began to scorn the country in the fanciful intoxication of the drug. That face swung in the sky; then it sang, it sang with a well-known voice the alleluia of love.

It was the Marquise, who had come in and seated herself at the piano.

Yvette had wings now. She was flying through a clear night, above the wood and streams. She was flying with delight, opening and closing her wings, borne by the wind as by a caress. She moved in the air, which kissed her skin, and she went so fast, so fast, that she had no time to see anything beneath her, and she found herself seated on the bank of a pond with a line in her hand; she was fishing.

Something pulled on the cord, and when she drew it out of the water, it bore a magnificent pearl necklace, which she had longed for some time ago. She was not at all astonished at this deed, and she looked at Servigny, who had come to her side — she knew not how. He was fishing also, and drew out of the river a wooden horse.

Then she had anew the feeling of awaking, and she heard some one calling down stairs. Her mother had said:

"Put out the candle."

Then Servigny's voice rose, clear and jesting:
"Put out your candle, Mam'zelle Yvette."

And all took up the chorus: "Mam'zelle Yvette, put out your candle."

She again poured chloroform on the cotton, but, as she did not want to die, she placed it far enough from her face to breathe the fresh air, while nevertheless her room was filled with the asphyxiating odor of the narcotic, for she knew that some one was coming, and taking a suitable posture, a pose of the dead, she waited.

The Marquise said: "I am a little uneasy! That foolish child has gone to sleep leaving the light on her table. I will send Clemence to put it out, and to shut the balcony window, which is wide open."

And soon the maid rapped on the door calling: "Mademoiselle, Mademoiselle!" After a moment's silence, she repeated: "Mademoiselle, Madame the Marquise begs you to put out your candle and shut the window."

Clemence waited a little, then knocked louder, and cried:

"Mademoiselle, Mademoiselle!"

As Yvette did not reply, the servant went away and reported to the Marquise:

"Mademoiselle must have gone to sleep, her door is bolted, and I could not awaken her."

Madame Obardi murmured:

"But she must not stay like that."

Then, at the suggestion of Servigny, they all gathered under the window, shouting in chorus:

"Hip! hip! hurrah! Mam'zelle Yvette."

Their clamor rose in the calm night, through the

transparent air beneath the moon, over the sleeping country; and they heard it die away in the distance like the sound of a disappearing train.

As Yvette did not answer the Marquise said: "I only hope that nothing has happened. I am beginning to be afraid."

Then Servigny, plucking red roses from a big rose-bush trained along the wall and buds not yet opened, began to throw them into the room through the window.

At the first rose that fell at her side, Yvette started and almost cried out. Others fell upon her dress, others upon her hair, while others going over her head fell upon the bed, covering it with a rain of flowers.

The Marquise, in a choking voice, cried: "Come, Yvette, answer."

Then Servigny declared: "Truly this is not natural; I am going to climb up by the balcony."

But the Chevalier grew indignant.

"Now, let me do it," he said. "It is a great favor I ask; it is too good a means, and too good a time to obtain a rendezvous."

All the rest, who thought the young girl was joking, cried: "We protest! He shall not climb up."

But the Marquise, disturbed, repeated: "And yet some one must go and see."

The Prince exclaimed with a dramatic gesture:

"She favors the Duke, we are betrayed."

"Let us toss a coin to see who shall go up," said the Chevalier. He took a five-franc piece from his pocket, and began with the Prince.

"Tail," said he. It was head.

The Prince tossed the coin in his turn saying to Saval: "Call, Monsieur."

Saval called "Head." It was tail.

The Prince then gave all the others a chance, and they all lost.

Servigny, who was standing opposite him, exclaimed in his insolent way: "*Parbleu!* he is cheating!"

The Russian put his hand on his heart and held out the gold piece to his rival, saying: "Toss it yourself, my dear Duke."

Servigny took it and spinning it up, said: "Head." It was tail.

He bowed and pointing to the pillar of the balcony said: "Climb up, Prince." But the Prince looked about him with a disturbed air.

"What are you looking for?" asked the Chevalier.

"Well,—I—would—like—a ladder." A general laugh followed.

Saval, advancing, said: "We will help you."

He lifted him in his arms, as strong as those of Hercules, telling him:

"Now climb to that balcony."

The Prince immediately clung to it, and Saval letting him go, he swung there, suspended in the air, moving his legs in empty space.

Then Servigny, seeing his struggling legs which sought a resting place, pulled them downward with all his strength; the hands lost their grip and the Prince fell in a heap on Monsieur de Belvigne, who was coming to aid him.

"Whose turn next?" asked Servigny. No one claimed the privilege.

"Come, Belvigne, courage!"

"Thank you, my dear boy, I am thinking of my bones."

"Come, Chevalier, you must be used to scaling walls."

"I give my place to you, my dear Duke."

"Ha, ha, that is just what I expected."

Servigny, with a keen eye, turned to the pillar. Then with a leap, clinging to the balcony, he drew himself up like a gymnast and climbed over the balustrade.

All the spectators, gazing at him, applauded. But he immediately reappeared, calling:

"Come, quick! Come, quick! Yvette is unconscious." The Marquise uttered a loud cry, and rushed for the stairs.

The young girl, her eyes closed, pretended to be dead. Her mother entered distracted, and threw herself upon her.

"Tell me what is the matter with her, what is the matter with her?"

Servigny picked up the bottle of chloroform which had fallen upon the floor.

"She has drugged herself," said he.

He placed his ear to her heart; then he added:

"But she is not dead; we can resuscitate her. Have you any ammonia?"

The maid, bewildered, repeated: "Any what, Monsieur?"

"Any smelling-salts."

"Yes, Monsieur."

"Bring them at once, and leave the door open to make a draft of air."

The Marquise, on her knees, was sobbing: "Yvette! Yvette, my daughter, my daughter, listen, answer me, Yvette, my child. Oh, my God! my God! what has she done?"

The men, frightened, moved about without speaking, bringing water, towels, glasses, and vinegar. Some one said: "She ought to be undressed." And the Marquise, who had lost her head, tried to undress her daughter; but did not know what she was doing. Her hands trembled and faltered, and she groaned:

"I cannot,—I cannot—"

The maid had come back bringing a druggist's bottle which Servigny opened and from which he poured out half upon a handkerchief. Then he applied it to Yvette's nose, causing her to choke.

"Good, she breathes," said he. "It will be nothing."

And he bathed her temples, cheeks, and neck with the pungent liquid.

Then he made a sign to the maid to unlace the girl, and when she had nothing more on than a skirt over her chemise, he raised her in his arms and carried her to the bed, quivering, moved by the odor and contact of her flesh. Then she was placed in bed. He arose very pale.

"She will come to herself," he said, "it is nothing." For he had heard her breathe in a continuous and regular way. But seeing all the men with their eyes fixed on Yvette in bed, he was seized with a jealous irritation, and advanced toward them.

"Gentlemen," he said, "there are too many of us in this room; be kind enough to leave us alone,— Monsieur Saval and me — with the Marquise."

He spoke in a tone which was dry and full of authority.

Madame Obardi had grasped her lover, and with her head uplifted toward him she cried to him:

"Save her, oh, save her!"

But Servigny turning around saw a letter on the table. He seized it with a rapid movement, and read the address. He understood and thought: "Perhaps it would be better if the Marquise should not know of this," and tearing open the envelope, he devoured at a glance the two lines it contained:

"I die so that I may not become a kept woman.
"YVETTE.
"Adieu, my dear mother, pardon."

"The devil!" he thought, "this calls for reflection." And he hid the letter in his pocket.

Then he approached the bed, and immediately the thought came to him that the young girl had regained consciousness but that she dared not show it, from shame, from humiliation, and from fear of questioning. The Marquise had fallen on her knees now, and was weeping, her head on the foot of the bed. Suddenly she exclaimed:

"A doctor, we must have a doctor!"

But Servigny, who had just said something in a low tone to Saval, replied to her: "No, it is all over. Come, go out a minute, just a minute, and I promise you that she will kiss you when you come back."

And the Baron, taking Madame Obardi by the arm, led her from the room.

Then Servigny, sitting by the bed, took Yvette's hand and said: "Mam'zelle, listen to me."

She did not answer. She felt so well, so soft and warm in bed, that she would have liked never to move, never to speak, and to live like that forever. An infinite comfort had encompassed her, a comfort the like of which she had never experienced.

The mild night air coming in by velvety breaths touched her temples in an exquisite almost imperceptible way. It was a caress like a kiss of the wind, like the soft and refreshing breath of a fan made of all the leaves of the trees and of all the shadows of the night, of the mist of rivers, and of all the flowers too, for the roses tossed up from below into her room and upon her bed, and the roses climbing at her balcony, mingled their heavy perfume with the healthful savor of the evening breeze.

She drank in this air which was so good, her eyes closed, her heart reposing in the yet pervading intoxication of the drug, and she had no longer at all the desire to die, but a strong, imperious wish to live, to be happy—no matter how—to be loved, yes, to be loved.

Servigny repeated: "Mam'zelle Yvette, listen to me."

And she decided to open her eyes.

He continued, as he saw her reviving: "Come! Come! what does this nonsense mean?"

She murmured: "My poor Muscade, I was so unhappy."

He squeezed her hand: "And that led you into a pretty scrape! Come, you must promise me not to try it again."

She did not reply, but nodded her head slightly with an almost imperceptible smile. He drew from his pocket the letter which he had found on the table:

"Had I better show this to your mother?"

She shook her head, no. He knew not what more to say for the situation seemed to him without an outlet. So he murmured:

"My dear child, everyone has hard things to bear. I understand your sorrow and I promise you—"

She stammered: "You are good."

They were silent. He looked at her. She had in her glance something of tenderness, of weakness; and suddenly she raised both her arms, as if she would draw him to her; he bent over her, feeling that she called him, and their lips met.

For a long time they remained thus, their eyes closed.

But, knowing that he would lose his head, he drew away. She smiled at him now, most tenderly; and, with both her hands clinging to his shoulders, she held him.

"I am going to call your mother," he said.

She murmured: "Just a second more. I am so happy."

Then after a silence, she said in a tone so low that it could scarcely be heard: "Will you love me very much? Tell me!"

He kneeled beside her bed, and kissing the hand she had given him, said: "I adore you."

But some one was walking near the door. He arose with a bound, and called in his ordinary voice, which seemed nevertheless a little ironical: "You may come in. It is all right now."

The Marquise threw herself on her daughter, with both arms open, and clasped her frantically, covering her countenance with tears, while Servigny with radiant soul and quivering body went out upon the balcony to breathe the fresh air of the night, humming to himself the old couplet:

> "A woman changeth oft her mind:
> Yet fools still trust in womankind."

5323